Macon's
Heart

NICOLE PYLAND

Macon's Heart

San Francisco Series Book #2

Macon Greene is a reluctant, world-renowned violinist. She'd never had a problem playing for a crowd as long as she wasn't giving a solo. Her friends never seemed to notice her reluctance. In fact, her friends seemed to only really notice one thing about Macon – she always had a different woman around her. Sometimes, she'd flirt. Sometimes, they would. Rarely would it go anywhere. Unfortunately for Macon, she had a bit of a reputation.

Joanna Mason had a new profession and a new group of friends. Things were looking up in her life, with the exception of love. She'd never been able to find the right guy for her. Of course, she was spending a lot of time with a group of lesbians these days through her friendship with Emma Colton. That might have something to do with it. While Emma had found her soulmate in Keira Worthy, Joanna was starting to wonder if she'd ever find the person she wanted to spend the rest of her life with.

As Joanna and Macon's friendship becomes the most important relationship for both women, Macon wonders if she'll ever have the courage to tell Joanna how she feels or if she'll just have to find a way to get over it. Joanna hadn't ever thought of being with a woman until she started spending all her free time with the beautiful and remarkably talented Macon. Suddenly, both women have a lot to think about.

To contact the author or for any additional information visit: **https://nicolepyland.com**

BY THE AUTHOR

Stand-alone books:

All the Love Songs

The Fire

The Moments

The Disappeared

Chicago Series:

- Introduction – Fresh Start

- Book #1 – The Best Lines

- Book #2 – Just Tell Her

- Book #3 – Love Walked into The Lantern

- Series Finale – What Happened After

San Francisco Series:

- Book #1 – Checking the Right Box

- Book #2 – Macon's Heart

Tahoe Series:

- Book #1 – Keep Tahoe Blue

CONTENTS

CHAPTER 1

"SHE'S STRAIGHT, MACON." Joanna passed Macon an apple martini. "And yet, she still insisted I bring this over to you." She sat down next to Macon at the table. "How do you do that?"

"I didn't do anything," Macon insisted. "And why do you call me Macon?" she tossed back.

"That's your name: Macon Greene." Joanna took a sip of her own rum and Coke and waved over the two women she recognized as they walked into the bar.

"And everyone calls me *Greene* because *Macon* is my great-grandfather's name and my parents clearly wished for a boy," Greene retorted to her friend.

Greene was about 5'8" and had electric green eyes. Joanna knew many people just assumed *Greene* was her nickname due to that fact. She had near jet-black hair that went straight just down to her shoulders and golden skin that perfectly demonstrated the blend of her parents' Italian and Irish heritage.

"Well, I like to call you *Macon*," Joanna replied and turned to greet their friends. "Hey, guys."

"Ladies." Keira Worthy sat next to her girlfriend of the past year, Emma Colton, and across from them at their four-top table. "Who bought Greene the drink?" Keira pointed at the apple martini.

"Why do you assume someone bought it for me?" Greene asked one of her best friends.

"Because I don't think I've ever been in a lesbian bar with you where someone else *didn't* buy your drinks," Keira retorted with a playful glance in her direction.

"Speaking of drinks, what do you want?" Emma asked Keira and stood.

"Whatever you're having is fine," Keira told her.

"I'll be back." She squeezed Keira's shoulder and walked toward the bar.

"Please don't tell me you two are *that* couple now, where you just drink alike and eat off each other's plates. Are you going to start wearing matching outfits now that you've been together for over a year?" Macon sipped the sweet martini and grimaced. "I hate apple martinis."

"Why are you drinking it then?" Joanna laughed at her.

"Free booze," Greene sipped again.

"So, how was the anniversary dinner?" Joanna asked Keira.

"Amazing," she replied with a smile. "Emma got us reservations at Laughlin's, downtown, and they did this pre-set menu for us." She glanced over at her girlfriend who was leaning over the bar, ordering from Indy, one of their friends who bartended here some nights.

Joanna had now met Indy several times and had also been hit on by her several times. She'd explained to Indy that she was straight and not interested. Indy had continued to try, but always did so playfully and never made Joanna feel uncomfortable. It was kind of amazing to Joanna how much her life had changed over the past year or so. She'd directed a team for the Health Department in San Francisco alongside Emma for about six months before she made a major career change.

She'd made a lot of changes in her life recently. In her opinion, they were all for the better. Joanna was thirty-three, and she had been working in the Health Department since she graduated from college with a degree in Photography and a minor in Philosophy; possibly the two worst degrees one could earn and actually find a job later. Her parents had said as much when she went off to school in New York. She returned to California at age twenty-three, after having tried to make ends meet with freelance work and waiting tables. After getting the Health

Department gig, she'd followed her mother's advice and went to graduate school to earn her degree in Business. She'd hated nearly every moment of it.

Emma had been a big help to her after she moved to San Francisco. The two shared many projects together along with their assistant, Mason. They'd formed a friendship. Joanna had taken to spending more time with Emma and Keira as a result. Keira had friends like Macon Greene and Hillary that she'd also come to know. She saw Macon nearly every other day as they seemed to enjoy hanging out together. Joanna had come to realize – through this new group of friends – that she hated her job. When she'd helped Keira's event planning business by taking pictures for a wedding, she'd remembered how much she'd loved photography and decided to take her savings and quit her job, returning to freelance photography work.

It had been slow-going at first, but things picked up once she started partnering with Keira as her photographer of choice. Joanna often worked from home when she wasn't on site taking pictures, but Keira had given her a desk at the office downtown. She was also free to use the conference room for meetings with clients or potential clients even if they were her freelance clients and not clients of *Worthy Bash*, Keira's company.

Joanna had never had a consistent group of friends in San Francisco. In college, she'd hung with the photography majors, and they'd often modeled for one another to help fill out their portfolios. Joanna had been a favorite model thanks – in most part – to her long blonde hair and bright blue eyes along with her classic features. Her nose was small but went perfectly with her relatively thin lips and her upturned eyes that took the form of a classic almond shape, with a natural lift at the outer corners.

She'd enjoyed the career change as well as her move into a larger apartment down the street from the *Worthy*

Bash offices. Her career was going well; she had friends she loved spending time with and had a nice, new apartment she could've never afforded on a government salary. The only thing that was missing was a man in her life.

"What are we talking about?" Emma asked as she sat back down next to Keira, placing a white wine in front of her and then one in front of herself.

"Your super romantic dinner last night," Macon explained and finished the martini. "I need something stronger." She stood up. "And look at me: I'm going to the bar to buy my own drink." She moved toward the bar.

"She's going to flirt," Joanna said. "That girl – over there – is straight and here with her lesbian best friend. She was giving Greene the eyes earlier. I went to verify her status, and she told me she's entirely straight and here to support her friend who was just dumped. She then bought Macon an apple martini and asked me to bring it over."

"Greene has that effect on women," Keira said. "Straight or not."

"Think she's going to take her home?" Emma asked.

"Maybe." Keira shrugged and took a drink of her wine.

"Maybe?" Joanna asked. "Doesn't she always?"

"Not always," Keira replied. "She's not as bad as Indy." She nodded to their bartender friend who was hitting on yet another patron. "I asked her once how many women she'd slept with, and she told me she'd lost count."

"And does Greene remember her number?" Emma placed her arm over the back of Keira's chair.

"She said she did. She won't tell me what it is, but she says she knows how many women she's been with because she could never forget sharing something like that with someone."

"Romantic?" Emma asked.

"I guess." Keira laughed and placed her head on Emma's shoulder. "Jo, why do you keep coming to places like this with her? Make her go to a straight bar if you guys are going to hang out. You're not going to find your soulmate here." She motioned with her finger at the semi-crowded bar, filled only with females. "Hang out with a non-lesbian if she's unwilling. Or Emma and I can be your wing-women."

"I'm okay." Joanna laughed. "I've been focusing on work a lot. I haven't been paying a lot of attention to the whole dating thing."

"They say you find love when you least expect it," Emma said.

"But sitting in lesbian bars night after night isn't exactly going to help even if she's not expecting it."

"Honestly, I like it here," Joanna replied to Keira. "I don't have guys hitting on me all the time; and because I'm here with Macon or you guys, I don't get hit on by women unless I'm alone at the bar grabbing a drink."

"Did someone hit on you earlier?" Keira glanced toward the bar.

"The friend of the straight girl Macon is currently talking to. Just dumped and looking for a rebound, she told me. I politely declined."

"Well, I hate to tell you this, Jo, but you are hot, and you're pretty femme. You're going to get hit on a lot in places like this," Emma explained.

"It's not like I come here alone. I usually come in with Macon, just for a drink, and people leave us alone." She paused. "They mostly leave *me* alone. They still sometimes flirt with her. Should I take offense to that?"

"No. Greene just has that intense lesbian vibe to her that some gay women have even if they don't fit the stereotypes. You don't fit the stereotypes, but you don't have that *'come save me; I just need the right women to love me'* look about you either," Keira offered.

"And Macon does?" Joanna asked.

"Oh, yeah," Emma confirmed. "And I think a lot of women have tried to be that right woman and failed."

"She's a player, but not *really* a player; she never misleads a woman or anything. And she's nice to them while they're dating," Keira added.

"They just don't date very long," Emma said.

"I assume you're talking about me." Macon sat back down next to Joanna with a beer.

"It says a lot about you that you know that," Keira replied.

"Did you strike out?" Joanna asked and took a longer drink this time.

"I didn't even get into the batter's box," Macon replied. "I told you, I went to get a drink."

"And you two were talking," Joanna said.

"Yeah, her name is Heath. She's twenty-three. She's seen me in here before and just wanted to say hi."

"By buying you a martini and giving you flirty eyes?" Joanna asked.

"I guess so."

"But you're not going to do anything about it?" Keira checked.

"No. Did you miss the part where she's twenty-three and straight?" Macon took a drink of her beer.

"When has that ever stopped you?" Keira laughed.

"I'm thirty-four years old, Keira. I'm not interested in a twenty-three-year-old college student who doesn't know what she wants and would obviously just be using me as her one girl-on-girl experiment. I'm not into that."

"Since when?" Keira pressed.

"Babe, leave the woman alone." Emma smiled in Keira's direction.

"Yeah, leave the woman alone." Macon pointed her beer bottle in Emma's direction. "Act like I go home with a woman every time I go out. Jo can attest that I've been very good lately."

"I haven't seen her leave with anyone." Joanna thought to herself for a moment. "Actually, I don't think I've ever seen you leave with a woman. You've flirted for sure, but have you left?" she asked Macon.

"Probably just didn't want to leave you in a gay bar by yourself," Emma suggested. "She's a good friend like that."

"We don't just hang out at gay bars," Joanna said. "We go other places. I've seen her get hit on and hit on women, but she hasn't run off with any of them."

"See? New leaf," Macon reminded.

Joanna looked down at her phone, which lit up with a text message. She checked the time above it and downed her drink.

"I should go; it's getting late. I have an early morning shoot tomorrow."

"The newborn shoot?" Macon asked and took a long drink of her beer.

"They want a sunrise included since the baby was born around that time." Joanna stood.

"And who was that text from? A certain Russel, perhaps?" Keira lifted an eyebrow at her.

"Yes," Joanna confirmed and grabbed the sweater – she'd brought and hung off the back of the chair – to slide it over her shoulders.

"Booty call?" Emma questioned.

"No," Joanna replied. "I told you, I'm not interested in him."

"Then, why is he still texting you?" Macon asked.

"I guess he can't take a hint." Joanna grabbed her phone and placed it into her purse. "I'm going home. I'll be alone. So, end of that discussion."

"I can walk you," Macon offered.

"It's not that far. I'll be fine." Joanna squeezed Macon's shoulder before waving at Keira and Emma. "You guys have fun." She turned to Macon. "I'll call you later."

"Okay." Macon lifted her beer to her lips again. "Night."

CHAPTER 2

"GREENE, I THOUGHT you said you were done chasing straight girls," Keira said the moment Joanna was out the door.

"Yeah, so?" Greene glanced at her.

"Never mind." Keira laughed. "And how is it Jo gets to call you Macon, but the moment anyone else does, you get angry and throw things at us?"

"I do not throw things," Greene argued.

"Yes, you do."

"Whatever." Greene finished her beer. "I'm going to head out."

"I thought we were going to hang out," Keira replied.

"I'm kind of tired. I had a long rehearsal today and then three lessons after that." She stood.

"Are you leaving?" Heath – the twenty-three-year-old straight girl she'd already politely turned down – had approached just as she stood.

"Yeah." Greene turned to her and gave a smile to be polite.

"I was just about to head out myself. Maybe we can walk together?"

"Actually, my friend is waiting outside for me. We're heading out together. She just had to take a phone call."

"The one that got you the drink earlier."

"That's her. I should go. She's probably wondering where I am," Greene lied. "I'll talk to you guys later." She looked at Keira and Emma and then headed toward the door, leaving them and Heath behind.

Greene made her way outside, hastily walked to the intersection and turned the corner, going a block out of her way to get home just to make sure she wouldn't be seen by Heath. She'd had a long day. As a member of the San Francisco orchestra, she spent much of her morning in rehearsal for the upcoming series of performances. The orchestra did not pay well, though. So, she offered lessons on the side. She usually only had one lesson per day, but she'd taken on a few more students recently, hoping to make some extra cash.

Greene sent a quick text to Joanna asking her to let her know that she'd gotten home safely. A few minutes later, she got a response with a middle finger emoticon. She laughed as she made her way onto her own street. One of the first times they'd hung out after meeting each other, Greene had requested the same thing. Joanna had explained that she was perfectly capable of getting herself home safely. When Greene had insisted, Joanna had flipped her off as a joke and later sent that same emoticon. It had become their signal. When Greene arrived at her own apartment five minutes later, she returned the favor. She moved into the kitchen to grab a snack before she'd shower and head to bed.

Her apartment was a one-bedroom and on the third floor of a walk-up, which wasn't fun most of the time. She was grateful she'd chosen a violin as a child and not the cello. She grabbed the popcorn and pulled back at the plastic before shoving it into the microwave and pressing the popcorn button. She'd lived in the same apartment since she'd returned from Boston, after getting the job in the orchestra.

She sat on her sofa and flipped on the sixty-inch flat screen that had been an impulse buy a few months prior, changing the channel to some reality cooking show while she waited for her popcorn to finish. Her apartment was her domain. It was her fortress that kept all the crap away from the world outside. The building was pre-war and had great structure. It gave her great acoustics to play her instrument, which was secured on its stand on the shelf she'd built for that purpose. The sofa had been a hand-me-down from her parents when they'd upgraded their own furniture. Her bookshelf beside the TV, coffee table, dining room table, and chairs had all come from them. They weren't exactly Greene's style – being that they were light wood, and she preferred dark – but they'd been free. The dining room barely fit the four-seater table and was off the kitchen. The one bathroom was to the right of that table, and her bedroom was across the hall from the bathroom.

If she had one complaint about the apartment, it was that it didn't have a washer and dryer. She had to lug her laundry weekly to the laundromat down the street. That had annoyed her for several years until recently, when she and Joanna had become friends. Joanna lived only a couple of blocks away and had a washer and dryer. She'd let Greene borrow it every Sunday for the past few months. If Joanna wasn't out on a job, they'd eat lunch together or just hang out. Joanna had even given Greene a key to her place.

The microwave beeped five times in a row, indicating that her popcorn was done. She headed in that direction and pulled the hot bag out while grabbing a bowl from the cabinet above at the same time. After putting the popcorn in the glass bowl and adding salt, she moved back to her sofa and tried to feign interest in the show. She made it another ten minutes, finished half the popcorn, and returned the bowl to the kitchen to deal with tomorrow before heading to the bathroom, where she showered and readied for bed. When she got to her bedroom, she noted it was only just after ten. She rolled her eyes at herself and slid under the thick, comfortable blanket.

**

"Hey, it's me," Greene announced as she entered Joanna's apartment the following day.

"Hey, come on in," Joanna replied. "I just got back. I'm working on some stuff in the office."

Joanna's office was really just a section of her bedroom she separated with a large box-type shelf, enabling her to store her photography equipment in each of the slots along with other items, while her desk was on one side and her actual bedroom on the other.

"I brought tacos from the truck outside. Interested?" Greene held up a plastic bag in the doorway that read *Thank You, Thank You* on it.

"I'm starving." Joanna stood from her desk, where she'd been working on her Mac, and stretched as she walked toward Greene.

"You're still wearing your glasses," Greene said.

"Oh." Joanna turned back and set her reading glasses on the desk. "Let me change first. I need to get out of these clothes." She was wearing loose fitting jeans and a white button-down short-sleeved shirt.

"Living room? I'll start my first load." Greene said.

"Give me five," Joanna replied and headed toward her closet.

Greene made her way out to the living room where she placed the bag of food on the table, reached for her laundry basket that she'd already sorted, and headed back to the closet that held a small washer with a dryer on top. She placed her whites inside and started the wash before returning to the living room where she sat on the sofa and began pulling out the food. Joanna walked wordlessly into the kitchen, wearing a pair of black sweatpants and a light gray t-shirt. She moved to one of the cabinets where she pulled out plates, grabbed some paper towels, and placed them on the table for Greene.

"Do you still have—" Greene started.

"That pico from last time? Yeah," Joanna interrupted and headed back to the kitchen to pull a small, plastic container with pico de gallo. "Mexican Coke?" she asked.

"Yes, please. My weakness," Greene admitted.

Joanna laughed at her as she placed two bottles in front of the plates Greene had already organized, and offered Greene the pico.

"It's the actual sugar," Joanna reminded. "Better than the fake stuff."

"Absolutely," Greene agreed. "So, how was the job?"

"Fine. Adorable baby," Joanna replied and set about adding the salsa from another similar plastic container to her taco. "The name was a little weird."

"Yeah?" Greene took a bite.

"Margarine," Joanna stated.

"I'm sorry, what?" Greene added more pico to her taco. "Like butter?"

"Like butter." Joanna laughed lightly as she took a drink. "I guess they call her Margie, but still."

"What's her middle name? *Parkay, Country Crock, Blue Bonnet?*" she asked. "Those are the only brands I know."

Joanna laughed louder this time. Greene watched her as she tried to avoid choking on the taco she'd just taken a large bite out of.

"Stop," she insisted and gave Greene a soft shove.

"I thought my name was weird."

"Your name is nice. I hate my name."

"Why? It's nice."

"My parents named me after my grandmother. Well, technically, her name was Josephine, but my mom didn't like that. They compromised and went with Joanna and Jo for short."

"I like Jo." Greene took a drink.

"I would have preferred something else, I guess."

"Like Margarine?" Greene asked.

Joanna smirked at her and said, "Maybe like Macon."

"Please." Greene scoffed. "It's like my parents knew I'd be gay and gave me a guy's name or something to try to fit the stereotype. I didn't exactly turn out butch, though. I got my revenge."

"Macon is a nice name, and you should use it more often. What's your middle name though?"

"No." Greene sat her Coke back down.

"Come on. I'll tell you mine."

"I know your middle name," Greene said.

"What? How?"

"You told Keira. Keira told me."

"Well, that's not fair." Joanna laughed.

"No, it's not, Joanna Isabella Martin."

"Isabella was my other grandmother," she explained. "Your turn."

"Macon Sage Greene," she offered and cringed.

"Sage? Macon, that's so pretty. Why don't you go by that if you don't like Macon?"

"Sage was my great-great-grandmother's last name. It's a family thing. My mom's middle name is also Sage. My grandmother's middle name was Sage. My sister's middle name is Sage. She's older. And she decided she wanted to go by Sage instead of the plain name she'd been given. She's Sage. I'm Greene. Even my parents call me Greene."

"She wanted to go by Sage instead of Sarah? I guess I can get that."

"Most people just called me Make. But when I got to high school, I could kind of start over. I just asked the teachers to call me Greene, and it stuck."

"People think it's because of your eyes." Joanna finished her taco. "I did before I knew your last name."

"Why? A lot of people have green eyes," Greene replied.

"Not like those." Joanna pointed with one hand while her other picked up her bottle.

"What's that mean?" Greene asked and leaned back on the sofa.

"You have to know your eyes aren't like normal green eyes, right?"

"They're normal to me."

"They're the brightest green eyes I've ever seen. They're only green. Most people have green with brown or dark green, but your eyes are almost glowing sometimes."

"I have glowing eyes? Thanks, Jo. I sound like an alien."

Joanna laughed and sat down her bottle before turning to Greene.

"They're perfect on you. You have this dark complexion and these bright eyes with your black hair. I'm convinced it all makes you seem mysterious, which is why all the ladies want you." She turned back to her food. "Well, that, and I'm sure you're good in bed."

"Gee, thanks," the woman returned sarcastically but a little hurt.

Joanna turned to see her lower her head.

"Macon, I didn't mean it like that." She placed her hand on Greene's thigh. "It was a joke. I meant that you're gorgeous, and your particular brand of beauty evokes mystery that reels people in. But, once they're there–"

"They stay for the sex. Yeah, I got that part." Greene sat back up.

"Hey, you're awesome. I wouldn't be hanging out with you if you weren't. I've been spending a lot of time with you for months now, and there's been no sex."

"Like I'd want to have sex with you anyway," Greene teased.

"Like I'd let you," Joanna tossed back. "You okay?"

"Yeah. Why?"

"You seemed a little weird last night with that girl. You asked me to check her out, and then nothing."

"I thought she was cute."

"But when she said she was straight, that was a deal breaker?"

"Well, yeah," Greene said.

"But you've been with girls who said they were straight before."

"A couple." Greene took a drink.

"A couple a month? A year?" she asked.

"A couple total. I know my friends make me sound like I'm constantly having sex, but I think you would know by now that that's not the case. I mean, I see you practically every day and most nights. Like you said last night, you've never seen me go home with a woman."

"You could be arranging booty calls after hours." Joanna wiggled her eyebrows at her.

"I'm not." Greene polished off the rest of the taco.

"Because you don't want that all of a sudden?"

"Because I'm not really the person everyone seems to think I am." Greene stood. "I'm going to check on the laundry."

"Which is in the washer and has at least twenty more minutes. Sit." Joanna tugged on Greene's sweatshirt.

"What?" she asked softly and sat.

"You can't say something like that and then expect me to drop the conversation."

"I came over here for laundry and lunch, Jo. I didn't come here to have a debate about my persona versus my actual person."

"The Philosophy minor in me is going nuts right now." Joanna laughed.

"Who minors in Philosophy?" Macon laughed.

"A kid who didn't know what she wanted to do," Joanna returned. "What's this persona you're talking about?"

"When I was younger, I went out a lot. That part is true. I dated a lot. That part is also true. When my friends met me, I was in the date around stage. But dating doesn't mean I'm reckless with women's hearts or that I just use them for sex and move on. Women hit on me. I'm nice to them. I'm not a bitch. I don't just send them away. Because of that, people sometimes assume that I sleep with every woman that approaches me." She paused, realizing she'd never uttered this out loud. "I don't. When I meet a woman and I like her, I am genuinely interested in seeing what could be there."

"Yeah?" Joanna seemed to wonder if that was really true.

"Yes," Greene replied and turned her body into Joanna. "I don't just take a woman home and sleep with her. I've done that one time. It didn't end well. I try to get to know them. And yes, sometimes there's sex; less than what my friends think, though. It's just never worked out much beyond a few weeks. I have this thing where I think I'll know."

"Know?"

"Like I'll meet a woman, and I'll know. I've always believed that. It might happen the second I meet her or maybe after our first kiss or the first time we make love, but I'll know."

"Know that she's the one?"

"Yes." Macon nodded. "I know it's silly and sounds like a romantic comedy, which I hate. That's part of the reason I don't exactly blurt this out to people. I've never felt that thing. When it's been a couple of weeks with a woman, I start to wonder if I will. If it's not there, it's not there, and I end it."

"Make, why don't you tell your friends this? It's got to bother you that they think you're some kind of player, going around breaking hearts."

"It's not a big deal."

"Liar." Joanna chuckled at her. Then, her expression changed. "So, you've never felt it? Never been in love?"

"No, I guess not. You?"

"Once or twice, I think."

"You think?"

"It's hard to answer that question. It's like… you're in the relationship; you love them. You *know* it's love. Then, you break up; you're heartbroken, but you're still sure it's love. Later, you get time and space between you and the relationship and you start to wonder: was it really love? Was that it? If that was it, did I lose it? Will I ever get it back? So, I know when I was with a couple of my exes, I was in love. I was happy. But as I get older and get further away from those relationships, I start to become not so sure. Because, if that was love, then I don't really know what all the fuss is about."

Macon laughed and drank more of her Coke before placing it back down and running her finger along the condensation that had formed on the glass.

"The longest relationship I had was nine months. I was a junior in college. Her name was Daniella, and she was a senior at BU. She was a Drama major. We met when I played in the orchestra for one of her performances. I played in the pit. One night after the final show, we all went out for drinks. She was beautiful, talented, and funny."

"Was she the one you—"

"Yeah, we went back to her apartment since her roommate was out of town. That was my first time."

"Wait. What? First time or first time with a woman?" Joanna asked.

"Both," Greene revealed. "I was twenty-one, and she was my first. I'd known I was gay. I'd kissed a few girls, but that was the furthest it went until her. I had offers. Not to sound conceited about that, but I did. I just hadn't gone through with any of them for various reasons until Daniella. It was nice. It was sweet and slow. She made sure I was okay with everything. We started dating after that."

"And you dated for nine months?"

"Yes. We were together a few months after she graduated and started working at a costume shop in New York while she auditioned for Broadway shows. We'd take the train back and forth from there to Boston to see each other when we could. It seemed like it was going well."

"But you've never been in love before?"

"She'd said it, at first. We'd been together for about four months when she said it the first time. I didn't say it back. It took her another month to try again. I still couldn't say it. She'd tried one more time around month seven. And by month eight, she was cheating on me, and I had no idea," she explained with little emotion in her voice. "I went to New York to visit at least seven times. She'd had someone else the whole time. I guess once that girl said she'd loved her, Daniella realized it was confession time, told me the whole story, and ended things."

"Sorry, Make."

"I was too. I blamed myself for a while. If I would have just said '*I love you,*' maybe that would have been enough. But I don't think that now. I didn't love her. I would have been lying. That wasn't right either."

"Why did you stay with her?"

"Because I liked her. I thought I would love her one day. I kept waiting for that day to come. It never did. I never felt that thing with her. After a few months, I stayed because she was my first. Then, I stayed because I was scared of losing her. Then, I stayed because she loved *me*. I knew that. I at least needed someone to love me, I thought. It was wrong. I should have ended things, and I should have done it sooner. I was a kid; I didn't know any better."

"So, that's why now you end things before it gets that far."

Greene finished the Coke in front of her and said, "It's easier for everyone this way. If you don't feel it, what's the point?"

"Do your friends know this?"

"You're my friend, and you know."

"Greene, you know what I mean."

"They know about Daniella. They know that whole story. The only thing they don't really know is that she was my first, and that there have only been eight since." She let out a deep exhale and met Joanna's eyes.

"Nine?" she asked. "That can't be—"

"I've been with nine women total my whole life. I think my friends assume I'm with nine a month or, at a minimum, nine a year. And it's nine total for me. I'm a bit of a kissing slut; that's true. But I'm not the sex fiend that everyone assumes."

"I feel bad," Joanna replied.

"What did you think? What number?" Greene smiled and rested her head on her hand and her elbow on the back of the sofa.

"Oh, I'm not answering that. That is a trap." Joanna turned away.

"Fine. Tell me your number then." Greene laughed.

"What? No way!"

"I told you mine."

"I didn't ask you to," Joanna replied.

"Come on." She gave her shoulder a light shove. "Your number still probably makes me seem slutty."

"Why would you say that?"

"I've known you for, like, almost a year now, and I don't think I've seen you go on a date. The only guy you've mentioned is this Russell from that magazine you did work for, and you say you're not interested. So, I'm extrapolating."

"Extrapolating?" Joanna laughed. "So, it's not just your looks. It's the big words that get the girls."

"I'm just saying that you don't talk a lot about the guys you've dated. I haven't seen you actually date. I'm running off the data I have, Isabella."

"I've been with ten guys," she revealed.

"What? You've been with more guys than I've been with women?"

"Why do you think I was so shocked before?" Joanna ran her hand through her long blonde hair. "I started a little younger than you, though, to be fair."

"Oh yeah?" Greene smiled a sinister smile. "Let's hear that story."

"No." Joanna grabbed Greene's plate along with her own to carry them to the kitchen. "You'll get out of me that I was sixteen. That's all."

"Who was he? Come on." Greene followed her into the kitchen and leaned over the counter as Joanna worked on the dishes.

"We dated all through sophomore year. Then, we broke up. Junior year, I had a new boyfriend. He was my second. Senior year, there was no one. And in college, there were three."

"So, we're at five. Go on." Greene smiled.

"After college, I had two serious boyfriends. Those were the ones I mentioned before." She paused as she wiped off a plate. "I guess that takes us to about twenty-seven. I had a one-night stand in there, which was a mistake. I dated a guy for about six months after that. He left me for someone at work. Then, I dated my ex for about two years before that ended last year. It was right about when Emma moved here. She and I went out for drinks a few times. She let me sulk." She placed the plate into the cabinet and moved onto the next. "So, that's ten. I feel bad because I assumed you'd been with so many more than me, and also because I've been with a lot of guys, I think."

"You were in serious relationships with all of them except one, Jo. Think about Indy for a second: she doesn't even know her number. There have been that many. I know a woman who works in music. She plays bass on tours. She literally sleeps with someone after every show to help her wind down. She's on tour, like, half the year."

"Gross," Joanna commented.

"I know. Then, there are people like my friend Anna. I haven't seen her in years, but we went to college together. She married the only guy she's ever been with. I have a cousin that did the same thing. She met her husband in high school. It's just different for everyone. That's what I'm saying," Greene said.

"So, the term *'slut'* is relative? That's what you're saying?" Joanna lifted her eyebrow.

"I think everything's relative," she explained.

CHAPTER 3

JOANNA WENT INTO the office on Monday morning. She had a meeting with a potential client that Keira's company had acquired for their upcoming wedding. This would be the largest event Joanna had ever done and would require her to find a few assistants. She worked on her edits at the desk Keira had been kind enough to give her while the other employees milled about. By early afternoon, she was starving and didn't have time to run out for something. Just as she'd settled on ordering delivery, a bag of something was dropped on her desk. She looked up to see Macon standing there.

"I was in the neighborhood." Greene glanced down at the bag. "And I've been standing here for like two minutes. You're really into whatever you're working on, aren't you?"

"Sorry. Noise canceling," Joanna referenced the headphones she pulled off and then pointed at her screen. "And I'm editing the shoot from yesterday so I can get the package to the customer. What's this?"

"I brought you lunch. I just finished the rehearsal." Greene had her violin in its case over her shoulder. "I texted Keira, but she said she had lunch planned with a client. I texted you. You didn't reply. I guessed you were busy and had forgotten to eat, like every other day of the week."

"Macon, you didn't have to bring me lunch," she said but was silently praising God that she had. "Thank you."

"Sure." Macon shifted her violin to her other shoulder. "I should head out."

"What? Why? You're not eating with me?"

"No, you seem like you're going to be working through lunch. I don't want to distract you."

"Come on. Eat with me." She placed a hand on Macon's forearm, encouraging her to sit down, but then realized there was no chair next to her desk. "Hold on." She stood, walked to find one of the guest chairs, and pulled it over to her desk for Greene to sit beside it. "You can help me if you're interested."

"Help you?"

"Take a look at these for me. Pick which ones I should send. I took over a thousand pictures. I have to sift through all of them and edit the ones I know they'll want, and then send more for them to choose from. The bigger the photo package, the more money for me." She turned her MacBook Pro around toward Macon.

"I'm not a photographer." Macon sat. "Is this little Margarine?" she asked with a laugh.

"It is." Joanna laughed as well and pulled out a styrofoam container from the bag. "What did you bring me?"

"California club," Macon replied without taking her eyes off the computer. "And their homemade chips."

"You spoil me," Joanna replied.

She watched Macon's green eyes flit from one image to another with an unreadable expression on her face. She'd long ago given up on trying to read Macon. This woman was someone that had developed the ability to hide her true feelings from people long ago; it was fruitless to try to get her to reveal them until she wanted to do so. Joanna waited a long moment and bit into the sandwich with extra avocado, which Macon knew she loved.

"I don't know, Jo. I like them, but they all kind of look the same to me. There's a baby in a blanket in a basket, and a baby in a blanket in a basket with a slight change in expression," she said.

She pulled out the aioli dipping sauce that came with the chips, opened it, and placed it in front of the container before stealing a chip, dipping it, and crunching into it.

"You're no help." Joanna chuckled and snagged a chip for herself.

"I get that a lot." Macon offered a playful wink in her direction. "You're not wearing your glasses."

"I hate them, so I usually avoid wearing them when I can."

"Why? They look nice on you," Macon complimented and grabbed another chip.

"Ladies," Keira said.

"I thought you had a lunch." Macon turned her head back to Keira. "I would have brought you something."

"I did. I just got back." Keira grabbed a chip and bit into it. "You decided to stop by after all?" She looked down at Macon.

"You declined, but I have other friends," Macon explained. "And this one never remembers to eat when she's deep in project mode." She pointed at Joanna.

"I'm bad." Joanna shrugged her shoulders and bit into the sandwich. "How'd it go?" she asked Keira.

"Fine," Keira replied and finished off the chip. "Wendy and her mom will be in the conference room at two. I'm going to borrow Greene here for a second and then I have to make a few calls."

"You're borrowing me?" Macon asked her. "What for exactly?"

"Just come here." Keira laughed at her.

"I'll be right back." Macon stood. "I think."

Joanna dove into the second half of the sandwich and snacked on a few more chips while she picked more pictures to add to her list to edit after the meeting. She created a custom link to her site for the family and began adding the ones she'd already edited or some of the raw images she loved just to see if they'd agree. By the time she had about twenty-five images chosen and five more to edit later, Macon had exited Keira's office and was in an entirely different mood than when she'd entered. Joanna hadn't paid attention to the meeting between the two friends, so she had no idea what had occurred.

"Hey, what's wrong?" she asked when Macon picked up the violin case she'd left at her desk.

"Nothing. I'm going to head out." She slid it over her shoulder.

"Did Keira piss you off or something?"

"She's just getting into my business, which I am not a fan of." She paused and stared down at Joanna. "I'll see you later, okay?"

"Yeah, sure." Joanna tried again to read the woman but stopped when she realized she'd probably fail. "Hey, what's your schedule like tomorrow? I can buy you lunch since you got today's."

"I have rehearsal until two and then lessons from three to five. I'll just call you later, okay?"

"Okay." She wasn't sure what had happened. Macon had been in her usual mood before she went into Keira's office. "You sure you're okay?" She stood and offered a hand on Macon's forearm again.

Macon promptly pulled back. Then, she took a definitive step away from Joanna.

"I'm good. I'll see you later."

"*7Ups* tomorrow night?" Joanna suggested to try to get Macon to commit to something before she ran for the elevator.

"I'll let you know." Macon's lips formed a straight line. She backed away. "I should go." She motioned with her thumb toward the elevator.

"I still have our points saved up from last time, so if you don't want me to get lame prizes you wouldn't approve of, you'll meet me there at seven."

She referenced the adult arcade they'd been to a few times since becoming friends.

"Don't get a bunch of pencil erasers." Macon pointed out, and a bit of her light-heartedness returned. "Or the damn lava lamp." She pointed accusingly and turned to press the button on the elevator to head down.

"*I* like the lava lamp. No promises." Joanna laughed and sat back at her computer. "Seven," she repeated.

With Macon gone, she thought back to the last trip they'd made to the arcade, which had only opened in their neighborhood the year prior and boasted at least a hundred games and prizes for kids and adults alike for the points they earned on their card. The place was eighteen and older after 8 p.m. Mondays through Thursdays. They served light appetizers and alcohol as well in their bar next to the rows and rows of games. Patrons could even use the points they'd earned on the food, but Macon had made it clear that she wanted to save up their jointly earned points for a large prize.

Joanna had mentioned a desire for a green lava lamp that would fit so well in her office. Then, she'd joked about how they had pencil erasers shaped like unicorns, rainbows, and butterflies for three points each. They could get hundreds of them and build some sort of eraser collage. Macon had only glared at her suggestion and pointed at the iPad Pro that was available for only twenty thousand points. Between them, they had accumulated six thousand points. They hadn't yet discussed the custody situation for the iPad Pro, nor had she asked Macon if she intended for them to get to forty thousand so they could each get one. She could ask her tomorrow night, assuming Macon showed up.

"Hey, you ready?" Keira approached, carrying her laptop under her arm.

"Is it two already?" Joanna looked up.

"Almost."

"Then, let's do it." She stood and grabbed her own computer. "Hey, what happened with Macon earlier?"

"What do you mean?" Keira deflected.

"She went in your office joking about the baby named after fake butter and then walked out angry at the world."

"Greene isn't a fan of people's opinions sometimes."

"Opinions on what?" Joanna persisted.

"Doesn't matter. She'll be fine." Keira opened the conference room door. They entered to find the receptionist for the office helping the client get settled. "Wendy, nice to see you again. Mrs. Morgan, how are you?" she greeted the two women and approached to shake their hands.

The meeting began shortly after, tabling their conversation automatically. Joanna put on her best smile before presenting them with a few examples of her work.

***

"Hey, Jo."

Mason, Joanna's former assistant at the Health Department and the current employee at *Worthy Bash*, sat in the chair she'd pulled over earlier for Macon.

"Hey, Mason."

"Did I see Greene in here earlier when I got back from lunch?"

"She stopped by, yeah." She grabbed her phone off the desk and noticed she'd missed a text from Russell.

"To see you or Keira?"

"She brought me lunch. Why?"

He stood and started to walk toward the elevator with her.

"Nothing. It's just... you two have been hanging out a lot lately."

She pressed the button on the side of the elevator and replied, "What's really going on in that head, Mason? I'm not your boss anymore. Just spill."

"So, Maggie kind of asked me something the other day, after we all went for drinks at *Landry's*." He held the door open while Joanna climbed into the elevator. "I'll go down with you." He entered alongside her, and the door closed, leaving them alone as it went down.

"Mason, the elevator ride is all of thirty seconds," she said when he seemed to hesitate.

"Maggie asked me if you were dating Greene," he revealed just as the elevator made its way to the lobby and the door opened.

"What?"

They both exited the elevator.

"It's just that the last three times we've all hung out, Greene was there. You weren't with a guy; she wasn't with a woman. Maggie said you guys seemed extra close; her words." He held his hands up in defense. "Don't shoot the messenger."

"Maggie knows I'm straight, Mason," she replied, lowering her voice as the lobby was teeming with people moving in and out of the building.

"I reiterated that to her. I'm honestly just starting to wonder about it myself," he added with a look of worry. "Not about you. I guess maybe a little about you. You two do seem really close. You haven't known her as long as Keira has, but you seem closer to Greene now than Keira is. I'm more concerned that she might be into you."

Joanna laughed a deep laugh because the thought of Macon Greene – the near ethereal goddess of a woman that could have any other woman, including straight or confused girls at bars – would be into her was impossible to fathom.

"Mason, she isn't into me like that; trust me. Macon can have anyone she wants."

"And I think she wants you. Maggie does, too."

"We're just friends. Macon isn't exactly the settling down type. She talks about finding love sometimes, but it's like she doesn't think it's possible. I don't even think she'd like to be in a relationship."

"And you're only a relationship person?"

"Yes, and straight."

"Maybe talk to Keira about it then. I'll tell Maggie to give it up, since I told you. She's been bugging me about it. She really likes Greene. I don't think she wants her to end up hurt."

"I really like Macon. She's probably my closest friend these days. I would never hurt her, Mason."

"I know."

"But keep an eye on your girlfriend, though. Seems *she* might be interested," Joanna said with a smile and left the building.

Once she'd turned to start her walk home, her smile disappeared. Joanna hadn't had a lesbian best friend before Macon. Was she doing something wrong? Should she spend less time with her? She tended to touch Macon's arm sometimes or her shoulder. Maybe she should stop. She might be giving Macon signals. She shook her head as she walked on. Macon Greene liked her as a friend, and that was the end of it. Joanna loved the friendship they'd created seemingly out of nowhere last year. She didn't want it to change. She made it home just at the realization that she hadn't dated anyone since she'd met Macon. She'd just confirmed that Macon hadn't dated anyone in a while either. Maybe it was time she gave Russell a call back after all.

CHAPTER 4

GREENE WAS pissed. And when Greene was pissed, she went to the gym. After leaving *Worthy Bash* and trying to walk off how frustrated she was, she went through her lessons with the two students that struggled the most. She had little patience for that struggle today. She got home, changed into her workout clothes, and ran to the gym three blocks over, where she first went to the elliptical. She spent twenty minutes there before shifting gears to the treadmill and then headed to the weight room. She wrapped her hands and punched the bag while a trainer, Randy, helped by holding it.

As Greene punched away, feeling the tension in her body build while the tension in her mind released, she thought about maybe asking Randy to go home with her. They could have a nice time together. She watched as Randy watched her. She noted the flash of arousal in the woman's eyes at Greene's movements, which were hard and swift. Greene knew Randy was thinking about hard and swift movements in another way. It was that realization that made her stop mid-punch.

She'd had this strange feeling for a while now that she couldn't identify. She'd been able to deal with it and push it out of her mind, especially when she was playing in rehearsal. Her violin gave her the freedom that nothing else did. For a few hours each day, she could forget about whatever was going on with her. But after that, it would catch up to her, and she'd be left feeling out of sorts.

Earlier, she'd been enjoying hanging out with Joanna, when Keira had interrupted and pissed her off. Keira rarely made her angry. In fact, Greene prided herself on her ability to keep her cool, but Keira had pulled her into an office, like a principal would a student, and scolded her about her friendship with Joanna.

"Make, what the heck are you doing?" she'd asked and sat behind her desk.

"I *was* hanging out. Now, I'm in your office because you needed to borrow me." She'd sat in one of the chairs across from Keira's desk.

"She's straight, Greene."

"Who?"

"Joanna Martin."

"Jo?"

"Yes, Jo. Greene, I'm worried about you. In all the time I've known you, you've never been *actually* interested in a woman. You date them; you charm them; but I've never seen you act how you act around her. I'm just worried."

"You think I'm into Jo and that I'm going to try something with her and be disappointed or something?"

"Are you into her?"

"No, Keira. Contrary to popular belief, I am not interested in every single woman in this city. Or is it the whole country you guys seem to think I'm interested in? The world, maybe? Any woman of age, of course, or a certain level of attractiveness? Or is it just women that I'm able to charm?"

"Greene, that's not what I mean."

"Then, what do you mean, Keira? Jo is a friend. You are the reason she and I even met, remember? We helped you out on that party last year."

"Of course, I remember that." Keira had leaned forward and clasped her hands together on her desk, making her seem even more like a school principal than before. "You two have been spending more and more time together, Greene. I don't ever see you alone anymore. It's like you're with her all the time. It honestly feels like Emma and I are double dating when the four of us are out, but that's not the case. I just don't want you to get your heart broken."

"So, because I'm spending time with a straight woman, I'm going to get my heart broken?"

"Greene, stop. It's like you're trying to fight with me now, when all I'm trying to do is tell you that people are noticing; they're asking questions. People see how you are with her. I know how she is with you. She cares about you. She's told me you're her best friend. I'm scared because I've seen your reaction when she touches your arm or gets the hair out of your face, like she did at the wharf when we went to *Tarantino's* together. She had her arm through yours, Greene. You were smiling."

"I was smiling because I was having a good time, Keira. Jesus!" Greene had stood and run a hand through her hair. "I don't need a lecture from you. Jo and I are friends. I'm fine with that, and I am done with this conversation."

"Greene, come on. I'm sorry. Hillary and Emma both asked me to—"

"To talk to me? To offer a straight woman intervention?" She'd made her way to the door, gripped the handle, and turned back to her. "I don't need it, Keira. My life is my life; my friends are my friends; and if I'm enjoying spending time with one of them a little more than the others right now, that's my decision." She'd opened the door and walked through it to be met with Joanna's concerned expression.

After the gym and her walk home, Greene reached for her violin. The orchestra would be doing a *Schindler's List* piece to celebrate the *John Williams'* score, among other works of his from different films. She'd be featured in one of the pieces, which was violin-heavy, called *Remembrances.* She enjoyed the piece a lot and felt it evoked perfectly the emotions conveyed in the film.

Greene had never felt like much of a composer herself. Many musicians at her level often played as long as their bodies held up, then – moved onto composing or even conducting. Greene hadn't planned that far ahead. She could always teach, she thought as she rested her violin on her shoulder. She enjoyed teaching enough. She could teach ten students a day if it came to making ends meet, but she felt no pull toward that eventual career path either.

She began the slow piece with her eyes open, referencing her sheet music, before she gave into it. She closed her eyes, letting the music take over and the vibrations from the bow against her instrument reverberate through her body.

***

Greene woke to the sound of someone in her kitchen. There shouldn't be anyone in her kitchen. Greene didn't bring women back to her apartment; her sanctuary. She lifted herself slowly from her bed, deciding she'd take a peek while reaching for the baseball bat she kept in the corner by the bedroom door. Her friends all had keys to her place. Keira and Hillary both had one, and the person currently making the sounds in her kitchen had one too.

"Jo?"

"Put the bat down and get out here," Joanna replied.

"Did I know you were coming over? It's like eight in the morning."

"I know." She was working in the kitchen on the espresso machine. "I wanted to check on you. I was going to go for a walk around the city and take some shots. I thought I'd stop by here first and make sure you were okay." She placed a cup of coffee in front of Greene, who was now sitting on her sofa. "Also, you're in your underwear." Joanna pointed and then turned away with a slight red creeping onto her cheeks.

"You're in my house at eight in the morning. You get what you get." Greene laughed as she looked down, noticing she was in a pair of navy boy shorts and a matching tank top. "I sleep in this."

"Well, I'm going to give you this," she tossed the throw blanket from the sofa onto Greene's lap with a laugh and sat down, "and ask again."

"I'm fine." Greene knew the question. She stared at the coffee cup, which was full to the brim and had a leaf pattern in the frothy milk on top. "How did you do that?"

"Do what?" Joanna asked.

"That?" Greene pointed.

"Oh, I was a barista for a while in college; a pretty good one, actually. I went to a competition one year and took the fourth place. I can do leaves like that and other stuff, too. It's called *free pouring*. It sometimes involves wiggling the cup a lot. The best baristas with latte art can make things like tulips, swans, or birds. I saw a scorpion once that was pretty cool, and an angel, too. The angel was surfing. The guy that made it won that year."

Greene sat mesmerized with her speech. She hadn't heard about Joanna's past career as latte artist or barista and wondered at how she even discovered she had that talent and that there were competitions for people who did.

"You said *wiggling*," Greene replied, laughed, and leaned back against the sofa.

"It's an important part of the process."

"The wiggling?"

"Yes. Do you want me to show you?"

"Wiggling?" Greene's eyes went wide.

"Why do you keep saying that?" Joanna's laugh continued. "You have to wiggle the–" She leaned forward again and went to demonstrate by miming holding the stainless steel container she'd just used in Greene's kitchen to froth and pour the milk.

"No, stop!" Greene laughed. "You can't keep saying *wiggle*." She laughed more and rested her head back on the sofa, with Joanna following and doing the same.

"What's so funny about that word? Do you have a

problem with it like some people have a problem with the word *moist*?"

"What? No?" Greene laughed again. "*Moist* is a gross word, though."

"Yes, it is," she agreed. "So, why is *wiggle* so funny?"

Greene met Joanna's eyes, and they were so blue. They were like endless oceans she wanted to stare at all day, but she averted her glance almost as soon as it had started.

"It's just that *wiggle* is a funny word." She downplayed her very visceral reaction to the word *wiggle*, which was one that always made her stomach flip, her body tense and then release, because it evoked memories of fingers wiggling inside a woman's body, bringing her slowly or quickly to orgasm by applying just enough pressure and varying the contact with a wiggle of two or three fingers inside the pliant body of an attractive woman.

"No, you're lying. What is it really?" Joanna chuckled and turned her head to Greene.

Greene moved to reach for the coffee Joanna had made for her. She took a long sip of the burning liquid as her cheeks matched the heat and turned crimson before she placed it down.

"Lesbian sex," she stated.

"I'm sorry?" Joanna guffawed in surprise.

"It's one of my moves," she continued and tried her best to rid her skin of the redness in mild embarrassment.

"Oh?" Joanna asked and seemed to move away from her slightly.

"I guess it's not a move. It's not a big deal. The word makes me think of it sometimes." Greene picked up the coffee again and took another drink. "I almost hate to drink this because of how good it looks."

"So, you *wiggle*?"

Greene lowered the cup and turned to see Joanna staring back at her with a confused expression and a lifted eyebrow. Greene wasn't sure what to do. Normally, if a woman was curious like this – even if she was straight prior to the conversation, Greene would lean in. Her voice would lower to her sultrier bedroom voice, and she'd explain exactly what she'd do to a woman. She'd usually end up with a nice, long make-out session out of that. In the past couple of years especially, it would end there. She'd go home and take care of herself, if she felt the need. But more often than not, the woman's reaction was enough to sate her.

"Do you really want to know this?" Greene tried to play it off with a laugh. "And this is really good," she said about the coffee.

"I guess not." Joanna stood abruptly. "I just kind of showed up on you. I'm sorry. I'll–"

"Jo, you don't have to leave," she interrupted and wanted to reach for Joanna's hand.

She decided against it for two reasons. One, they were talking about sex right now. She could feel her body reacting to just the thought of touching another woman again. And two, because she was still dressed only in her underwear. If she moved too much, the blanket would fall, and Joanna might be able to tell just how much she'd been recalling those touches or thinking about future ones.

"No, it's fine. I have some stuff to work on at home anyway." Joanna reached for the purse she'd brought with her.

"You're lying." Greene laughed lightly. "Just sit down. I'll go put on real clothes. You want breakfast? I can make us eggs or something. I think I have bacon."

"I guess I could stand your cooking." The woman sat back down.

"You love my cooking." Greene slid over to turn her legs away from Joanna and stood, leaving the blanket behind. "You're over here like twice a week."

"Is it my fault you make my eggs just the way I like them or that you know how to marinate steak?" she asked.

Greene walked around the table in front of the sofa

and noticed Joanna's eyes out of the corner of her own now dark green ones. Joanna was watching her walk. Her eyes weren't on any particular area of Greene's body, but they were on her. She turned her own head away to make sure Joanna couldn't see the look of desire in her eyes or the blush that was still present on her cheeks.

"Is it my fault I am an awesome cook?" Greene went into her bedroom.

"You probably win all the ladies over by cooking them dinner here and then playing your violin until they swoon. What's your go-to dish? Your go-to performance piece?"

She was smiling. Greene couldn't see her face, but she could tell Joanna was smiling. Greene reached for the pair of shorts on the floor she'd discarded the day before and slid them up her legs. She smiled at Joanna's comment and returned to the living room.

"I don't let women into my apartment." She moved into the kitchen.

"Never?" Joanna asked and turned on the sofa, hanging her legs over its arm so she could watch Greene in the kitchen.

"Never."

"You let me in. I have a key. I'm a woman."

Greene nearly made a comment about having *more* than noticed that Joanna was all woman, but she resisted and moved her lips into a straight line to prevent the words from escaping on their own.

"You are? I hadn't noticed," Greene said sarcastically.

"How did I gain entry into this inner sanctum then, asshole?"

"I don't bring women I sleep with back here," she clarified. "Not that I've done that a lot recently, because I haven't. I've been in this apartment for almost a decade. I've never had a sleepover, if you know what I mean."

"Why not?"

"I never wanted any of them to see this place." She

bent over to pull out the carton of eggs and a package of half-eaten bacon from the fridge. "Scrambled, with cheese today?"

"Yes. Can you add that stuff to it?"

"I don't have chives, but I can do a regular onion, or I have onion powder. I have red peppers. I'm out of the yellow ones."

"What are you making for yourself? Just make me that," Joanna replied and rested her hand on her head and her elbow on her leg as her legs still hung over the arm of the sofa.

That posture had become her typical posture when Greene cooked due to the size of the kitchen and the fact that the spot was the only one she could sit in and watch and talk at the same time.

"I'm going with an omelet with red and green peppers, cheese, and ham. No bacon for me today."

"That's tough, because you know how I love bacon."

"I do. That's why I got it out. I'll do the omelet for you, with no ham, and make the bacon on the side."

Joanna didn't say anything, which caused Greene to turn around after pulling out a bowl to mix the ingredients in.

"Sorry, that sounds perfect." Joanna smiled. "Thank you."

"Where'd you go just then?" Greene waved the fork in her direction accusingly.

"Nowhere. I'm here." Joanna smiled wider.

"Okay." Greene chuckled to herself as she started mixing.

"Can I help with anything?" Joanna asked after a moment of shared silence.

"No, I'm good. It's not exactly built for two cooks."

"I like your apartment," Joanna returned. "It's you."

"What's that mean?" Greene asked after breaking the last of the eggs and getting the stove turned on.

"I don't know. It just suits you." Joanna's voice

sounded much closer than before.

Greene turned to find her leaning against the open entry of the kitchen with outstretched hands.

"Come on. I can do something. I'm not a terrible cook."

"That's not…" Greene wanted to say that wasn't why she didn't want her in the kitchen. She didn't want her in the kitchen because it was small and harder to work around another person, but also because the closer she got to Joanna physically, the more she started to consider that maybe Keira had been right. "Never mind; you can be in charge of the stove. Grab the pans. That kind of a thing."

Joanna walked past her spot at the counter to the cabinet next to the stove where she knew Greene stored the pans. Greene watched as she moved to pull out the skillet needed for the eggs and then a smaller one for the bacon. She placed them on the burners and made sure they were turned to the appropriate level of heat while Greene worked in silence, slicing the peppers and onions, and adding them to the mix along with the cheese and other ingredients. By the time Greene was done, the stove was ready. She brought the bowl with her and stood next to Joanna. The stove butted up against the wall at the end of the kitchen tunnel. There was nowhere for her to go except next to her.

"I'm in charge of the stove. Hand it over." Joanna held out her hands to take the bowl from Greene.

"You're cooking now? Good. I can go sit."

"Walk me through it. You make this stuff so much better than I do." Joanna took the bowl from her and met her eyes.

"Bacon literally requires no work. Place it in the pan." She laughed. "And these are mixed. Just add half of that to the pan. We'll do the other one after."

"You say it like it's so easy." Joanna moved over to be in front of the skillet, forcing Greene to take a couple of steps back behind her. "If I dump this, it's all going in."

Greene shook her head in silent laughter and moved a step into her. She felt it then: the pull she'd possibly experienced all along to this woman. She recalled the day they'd met. It had been in Keira's old apartment. They'd been drafted to help her with a last-minute wedding before *Worthy Bash* had really taken off. Greene and Joanna had ended up next to one another on the sofa while Keira went over every detail. At that time, Greene only knew that Joanna worked in Emma's office.

She'd never been one to conform to those lesbian stereotypes, but even using them in her initial impression of Joanna, Greene hadn't been able to tell if she was straight or not. Joanna had caused her to take a step back that day, because she was gorgeous. That was easy to see instantly, but the woman was also funny and smart. She was someone Greene liked talking to that day. The next day, at the wedding, they'd spent more time together. Once Keira had moved into her new office, they'd cemented their friendship by helping her move in. Greene loved spending time with Joanna. Joanna, though, was straight as she later discovered and had been reminded by Keira the day before.

"Have you ever made an omelet before?"

Greene wrapped her arms around Joanna to grip the bowl with her and encourage her to tip it forward slightly. She allowed enough of their omelet mixture to sizzle into the pan before lifting the bowl back up, leaving enough for a second omelet.

"No," Joanna replied.

Greene gulped at Joanna's perfume. She'd put perfume on to come to Greene's apartment? It was maybe something like sandalwood, and it didn't seem like lotion or shampoo to her. It seemed like perfume. The scent was more distinct behind the woman's ears and at the base of her neck. It smelled like Joanna to her. She wanted to stand there longer, breathing it in, but she let go of the bowl and took a step back.

"No?" she asked.

"I've never made an omelet for two people before. It's different. The quantities are different. Then, there's the pouring you just demonstrated. I have a problem where I drop things. You know that."

"You've never made an omelet for a guy you dated?"

"No. With some of them I was in high school. Then, in college, my boyfriends seemed to live off Red Bull, booze, and pizza. After that, I had one that was allergic to eggs, one that just didn't like them, and the rest liked them differently, I guess: over easy or hard-boiled or something."

"Bacon time."

"Oh, right." Joanna turned back to the stove, placed the bowl on the counter, and began removing strips of bacon, adding them to the pan. "Are you planning on telling me about what happened with Keira yesterday?"

"No plans to, no."

Greene stood back further, needing to be as far away as she could from Joanna as the woman stood in her kitchen, in front of her stove, wearing jeans that were capris and tight to her body along with a light knit sweater in a shade of pink that looked so good against her much paler skin.

"You can tell me anything. You know that, right?" She turned her head back to Greene. "And get back here, to tell me when to flip this in that half-moon thing you do." She motioned with one hand folding onto the other as she turned around to face her.

Greene couldn't resist smiling at that movement and at how Joanna's eyes looked with the fluorescent light in the middle of the kitchen ceiling, creating a glow in their blue depths. She swallowed and inhaled deeply before moving toward Joanna. She gripped the woman's hips and hesitated only an instant before she moved her to the right and let go. She picked up the spatula and began inspecting the omelet.

CHAPTER 5

JOANNA STOOD next to Macon, who was flipping the omelet. She faced away from the stove because Macon's hands had just been on her hips and she'd moved her over. That was it. She'd moved her to the side in order to get to work. But that touch, and the look in Macon's eyes as she'd made it, had Joanna warm and wondering. They'd touched one another before; hands and arms mostly, along with the occasional pat to the thigh. But it had always been brief and innocent. This wasn't that. Joanna could feel Macon's grip through her sweater. She could sense more, too. She wasn't sure what it was, but as she heard crackling behind her, she turned to discover she'd nearly burned the bacon.

"Shit!" She grabbed Macon's spatula to flip the strips over and turn off the stove.

"You're an amazing cook. Don't let anyone ever tell you any different." Macon offered her a cocky smile and stole the spatula back.

That was it, what she was sensing. It was raw sexuality. It was the look she'd observed Macon give women when they went out. She'd talk to some of them briefly, but the ones she was more interested in, she'd look at them like that. She oozed sex. Those eyes and lips only made it even more obvious what she was doing with them. But she'd just done that to Joanna. Joanna moved back to grab the plates, deciding she'd seen that wrong. Macon began the other omelet as she slid the first onto the plate Joanna had provided. Joanna stood back and watched her work from behind. Macon was beautiful; Joanna had always known that. She had no problem saying when a woman was attractive.

She started to think about Macon and herself. Macon was more than attractive. She was stunning. The dark skin she'd inherited due to her part Italian ancestry mixed so well with that dark hair and those bright eyes. It was easy to see why women fawned over her. On top of that, the woman was toned everywhere, if Joanna had to guess. She knew Macon worked out often and that walking around a lot in the city made her calves strong and toned. Joanna stared at them for a moment as they were visible because Macon was wearing short sleep shorts. Her eyes moved up to the back of Macon's toned thighs and then higher to where the shorts covered her ass. Why was she staring at Macon's ass? Her eyes lifted but only ended up on Macon's lower back, because the woman had her hand under her shirt, scratching a spot there. She then removed it, straightening her shirt as she did, and returned to the cooking.

Joanna moved beside her again to get the bacon out of the pan and onto a paper towel. Her shoulder bumped gently into Macon's, who ignored the touch. Joanna felt the toned muscles in her arms maybe for the first time. She managed to get the bacon from the towel to her plate and slid two strips onto Macon's with a hopeful expression. Macon just shook her head but didn't turn down the offered bacon.

"What are you up to today?" Joanna asked as she bit into an extra crunchy piece.

"Rehearse here on my own. I have a meeting with the conductor. I'll head over there at around 10:30. Lessons after that until 5."

"What's the meeting with the conductor about?" she asked and finished the bacon as the omelet slid from pan to plate.

"I don't know. He just set it up through his assistant. I guess I could be fired. Or, it could just be that he wants to talk to me about my playing."

"You think you could get fired?" Joanna asked with

instant concern.

"No." Macon laughed and carried both plates to the coffee table. "You should make yourself some of that fancy coffee."

"I'm good with water."

"Grab one."

Joanna moved to the fridge where she removed a bottle of water and grabbed silverware and paper towels for their impromptu breakfast.

"And why are you so confident about not getting fired?" She passed Macon her fork and knife, placing the roll of paper towels between them and sitting down.

"Because I'm good." Macon sliced at her omelet.

"Cocky, aren't you?" Joanna laughed.

"No, I'm not." Macon turned to her. "I'm very good."

"I don't think I've ever heard you play. I was supposed to go to that performance, but my mom went to the hospital, remember?"

"Yeah."

"I need to see you play."

"Okay."

"We hang out all the time. How have you never played for me before?"

"I don't play for people." Macon took a large bite of her omelet.

"So, I shouldn't be offended?"

Macon placed her fork and knife on the table next to her plate. She turned her entire body to Joanna, who felt suddenly nervous at the focused attention.

"You know how some violinists have solo careers? There's Nicola Benedetti, Joshua Bell, and, of course, Itzhak Perlman. There are more. They're known worldwide and are amazing violinists."

"I haven't heard of the other two, but I've heard of Itzhak Perlman," Joanna replied.

"I picked up the violin when I was two. My uncle

played. When he ran to stop me from dropping the thing, he didn't make it in time. And I'd seen him play, so I put it to my shoulder. Everyone else just sat there and waited to see what I'd do. I ran the bow along the strings, and I was hooked. I started lessons at three and picked it up very quickly. I was reading music before I was reading words. It took off from there." She paused for a moment. "I am very good," she said. "I've chosen to stay in the orchestra and not to pursue the solo tour thing. If I wanted it, I could have it. At Berklee, all the teachers wanted me to perform on my own or take on more solos than I wanted. I wasn't interested."

"Why not?"

"I like the orchestra. I love how it all sounds when we're playing together. I like the people I play with. When you're on tour, it gets lonely. There's this pressure that I've never wanted. People want you to record albums or do special performances. Then, they start wondering about when you'll transition."

"Transition?" Joanna still hadn't touched her breakfast.

"Into composing or conducting. I don't know about either of those things yet, but I knew in school like I know now: I don't want the soloist life. I'm content doing what I'm doing."

"When can I hear you play?" she asked.

"Come to a performance." Macon turned back to the table and her plate.

"Your violin is three feet away." Joanna laughed.

"I'm eating breakfast."

Joanna stared at her with that obvious deflection and considered what to say next.

"Have you played in front of Keira or Hillary before?"

"No," she answered immediately. "Well, they've been to performances, so… yes, I guess."

"Never just here?"

"No."

"Hey, Make?"

"Huh?" Macon turned and slid another bite into her mouth.

"Why don't you play in front of people?"

"I play in front of people every day, Jo." She bit into the bacon. "This is terrible." She laughed and put it back on the plate.

"But alone?"

"Alone?"

"Macon, do you ever just play for someone when it's you and them, and that's it?"

"No, I guess not. Sometimes, I had to play with just me and a teacher or just me and the conductor."

"But not a spectator? Only in front of the orchestra?"

"No, and yes."

"So, you're a violin prodigy that could have an amazing solo career and have worldwide fame, but you don't play for anyone and avoid some of the solos you're offered in the orchestra?"

"Yes. Why is this a thing we're talking about?" She laughed and turned to the coffee. "This is getting cold. Any chance I can convince you to make me another one and do that scorpion this time?" Macon smiled at her.

"I'd have to wiggle the milk," she replied and wiggled her eyebrows with her smile.

Macon laughed hard and nearly spilled her coffee over the gray carpet. Joanna just watched her gracefully recover and put it down before shaking her head in disbelief.

***

Joanna went to Clarion Alley, one of her favorite parts of the city, because it changed often. Clarion Alley was a set of streets that allowed graffiti artist to tag the buildings. The work was always colorful and, sometimes, remarkable. She enjoyed all of it and loved photographing the work. There were different sections painted nearly every time she stopped by. After spending a couple of hours walking and taking pictures, she decided to have lunch and go home to edit what she'd taken. As she sat on her sofa and ate, she stared blankly at the television she had connected to the Wi-Fi. She'd loaded the pictures onto her computer as soon as she got home. The TV was currently running a slideshow for her, which allowed her to see the images much larger and decide which were worth keeping to work on and which weren't. She was staring blankly, though, because she couldn't stop thinking about two things.

Mason had thrown her a curveball by suggesting that Macon liked her as more than a friend. She hadn't thought it possible. This morning, she'd stopped by to be a good friend and try to uncover what had made Macon so upset the day before. She'd ended up staring into Macon's sexy gaze. She'd gotten grabbed at the hips and moved out of the way. She'd never been touched that way by a woman. *She* hadn't actually been touched. Macon, technically, had only touched her sweater and her jeans. But there was something about that moment that made Joanna return to it constantly throughout her entire day. Her phone rang as she forced herself not to think about Macon's hands on her. She grabbed at it quickly, nearly knocking over her plate in the process.

"Hey, Emma," she greeted.

"Hi. Key and I are going to catch a movie tonight. I thought I'd invite you and Macon."

"So, you're calling to invite both of us?"

"Yeah, is that okay?"

"I don't know what her plans are. I think she mentioned something about wanting to be alone tonight."

"No worries. What about you?" Emma asked.

"Third wheel your date with Keira?" Joanna laughed. "No thanks. You two have fun."

"We're not going to be making out in the theater, Jo. We're grabbing dinner after, if you're interested."

"I think I'll hang out on my own tonight, too. I'm kind of tired, honestly. I have some more editing to do."

"Sure. Some other time," Emma offered.

"Yeah."

Joanna hung up the phone and stared down at it. She and Macon hadn't discussed the night during their breakfast. Macon had expressed yesterday that she would think about joining her at *7Ups*, but Joanna hadn't brought it back up while they ate before she had to leave. She'd meant to ask her, but then she'd gotten sidetracked with breakfast and cleaning up next to Macon in that tiny kitchen. They'd washed and dried in silence, and it felt different today. They'd done dishes together after a meal once or twice, but the activity had never felt like this. Joanna unlocked her phone and entered the message app. She typed out her question to Macon and then moved into her bedroom to change into more comfortable clothes and get to work in her office. About thirty minutes later, she had a response from Macon.

***

"You are a sore loser," Macon said after Joanna's second loss to her at Skee-Ball.

"I am not." She rolled her eyes. "You cheat."

"How can I cheat at this?" Macon laughed and handed her the card they shared. "You want to throw the balls at the scary clown faces?"

"You're resourceful. I bet you found a way to cheat," Joanna replied. "And you love that damn game."

"I do. I'm good at it." Macon smiled at her as they headed toward two games, side-by-side, where there were three rows of clown heads and baseball-size rubber balls. They'd be throwing at those heads to knock them down. The more they knocked down, the higher their score would be. "And I'm unsure how I'd use any kind of resourcefulness to cheat at Skee-Ball. You roll the ball and either score high or score low. "

"I'm sure you charmed one of the female employees to weight the balls differently or something."

Macon stopped moving just as they arrived at the game. Joanna was starting to recognize something in her that she wasn't sure others did.

"Put it in." Macon motioned to the card reader, deflecting Joanna's comment.

"Hey, I'm glad you decided to come out tonight." She changed the subject. "We're a few points closer to that iPad Pro."

"Yeah," Macon agreed.

Joanna swiped the card for Macon's game. Then, she did the same for herself. She wasn't great at this one and would just throw alongside Macon because it was fun. While she tossed and hoped it hit a clown, Macon's arm speed was off the charts. Her expression was focused, possibly angry, and her aim was spot on. She knocked down the entire top row of clowns before Joanna had even thrown her first ball. Joanna was sure she hit at least a few, but when the time was up, she'd scored only fifty points, while Macon's score was over four hundred. She was winded and looking off toward the bar. Joanna wondered if she was the cause in her change in mood.

"Maybe we should choose a game that doesn't involve rolling or throwing for you," Macon remarked.

"Maybe we should get you a beer. You seem like you need one," Joanna said. "Here, use this. I'll go get us some drinks."

She ordered from the bartender and waited while he popped the top off the one she'd ordered for Macon. Then, he poured the draft she'd order for herself while she watched Macon play a game. By the time she returned with their drinks, Macon's mood had changed back to playful.

"I got the jackpot, and then I got a bonus spin," she

announced as she took her beer.

"Yeah? How many?"

"It was a three-thousand jackpot, and with the bonus, I doubled it." She smiled before taking a sip of her beer.

"So, in two spins, you doubled our entire ticket total?" Joanna asked.

"I am lucky tonight, I guess."

"Hey, two people who said they were each spending the night alone," Keira's voice rang out from behind them.

"Keira?" Joanna turned around to see Keira holding hands with Emma.

"We were on our way to our movie and saw the two of you in here from the street," Keira said. "Emma was told you needed a night in, Joanna Martin."

"I was planning on staying in, but–"

"Little Miss Macon convinced you to go out?"

"What? No," Macon replied and took another drink of her beer while turning her head back toward the game. "I'm going to grab some nachos or something. Do you want the potato skins?" she asked Joanna and then looked directly at Keira. "Because I am going to the bar to order my own food and I am a nice person."

Keira gave her a glance that Joanna wasn't certain she understood. Then, she turned to Macon, who was once again in that same mood from earlier and the day before as well.

"No, I'm good. But can you–"

"No jalapenos. I know," Macon interrupted and headed toward the bar.

"Okay, what is going on with you two?" Emma turned to her girlfriend and asked.

"Nothing," Keira replied and turned to Joanna. "Our movie starts in thirty. We should head out."

"You two want to come since you're already out?" Emma asked Joanna.

"She's getting food, so I don't know."

"I'll go talk to her," Keira suggested.

"Actually, let me," Joanna insisted. She placed a hand on Keira's forearm, knowing something was wrong between her and Macon but not knowing what. She walked past them toward the bar where she stood next to Macon, who leaned over it. "Penny for your thoughts," she said and received no response. "Or maybe a nickel? Are your thoughts pricier than the average thoughts?"

"I have high-priced thoughts, yes," Macon finally replied and turned her head to Joanna. "Did you change your mind about the potato skins?"

"No. Emma and Keira invited us to join them at the movie."

"Oh."

"But you don't want to go?"

"Not really." Macon turned her eyes to the bartender, who noticed them, smiled, and nodded that he'd be right over. "You can go, though. I don't mind. I'll just get something to-go and head home."

"I don't want to go without you," Joanna said before she could stop herself and stood back from the bar. "I'll tell them no. We can play some more."

"I think I'll just get the nachos to-go. I'm kind of done. I was tired before I got here. You can come to my place, though. I'll share."

Joanna glanced over at Emma and Keira, who appeared to be in conversation, and turned back to Macon.

"Let me get them on their way. I'll come back, and we can decide, okay?"

"Fine," she agreed as the bartender approached to take the order. "Can I get an order of nachos with no jalapenos, and an order of potato skins with extra bacon to-go?"

Joanna smiled at the order she heard as she walked away back toward Keira and Emma.

"We're going to pass," she explained. "She's tired. And, honestly, she *was* going to stay at home tonight. I convinced her to come out with me. I think I'm going to walk her home and head home myself. I have an early shoot tomorrow."

"I can sense the lies falling from your lips, but I'll allow it," Keira offered with a smile. "Tell her I'm sorry, okay?" she said in a lower voice.

"For what? She hasn't exactly filled me in on what happened between you two."

"And she won't. I know her. She won't want to tell you, but it'll be okay. She just needs to cool down and let me apologize, but she's not there yet. Maybe you can help grease the wheels, so to speak?"

"I guess," Joanna offered back and noticed Macon finishing off her beer and setting the bottle on the bar.

"Thanks," Keira said and tugged on Emma's hand before looking back at Joanna. "You two are good, right? Your friendship is good?"

"As far as I know. Why? Do you know something I don't?"

"No, I just wanted to check." Keira looked past her and toward the bar where Macon was still standing. "I've been spending a lot of time with this one here and at work." She referenced Emma. "Hillary's been busy herself. Kellan and Macon started to have a good friendship before she left for Tahoe. But, outside of that group, she doesn't really have a lot of close friends. I want to make sure she's taken care of, you know?"

"Oh. I spend most of my free time with her. I think things are good between us. She's probably my closest friend. I think she's comfortable enough with me to tell me if things are bothering her. I'm not sure why she can't tell me whatever you said to piss her off."

Keira's eyes hadn't left the spot at the bar Joanna didn't need to turn around to see Macon occupying.

"She will, someday," Keira said after a moment. "We'll leave you guys alone. Sorry to have bothered you and ruin the night."

"You didn't ruin the night, Keira. It's not a big deal."

"See you later?" Emma asked as Keira pulled her toward the door.

"Enjoy the movie."

"We will. I'm planning on making out with her during." Emma winked as Keira rolled her eyes at her playfully.

Joanna waited for them to go, took a big gulp of her beer, and headed back toward Macon, who was now sitting at one of the free stools.

"So, they're on their way out. What did you decide you want to do?"

"My place, food, and maybe a movie," she replied directly. "Unless you want to just go back to your place."

"Alone or with you?"

"Whatever you want."

"I'm asking you what *you* want, Macon. Obviously, Keira did something to tick you off. If you want to just go home and–"

"I told you what I want, Jo." She turned her head to reveal her still somewhat angry, though not as intensely, expression. "You, me, food, and a movie."

"Okay." Joanna nodded. "I'm picking the movie, though."

"Fine. But nothing sappy," Macon argued.

"Action or horror?"

"Action. Let's pick up that wine I like from the store downstairs."

"Sounds good. But can we get the wine I like, too, since the wine you like is terrible?" Joanna teased and gave Macon's shoulder a light bump with her own.

"Fine. But I get one of your potato skins."

"You can have two." Joanna slid her beer on the bar toward Macon, who took a drink.

CHAPTER 6

"SO, HOW'D THE MEETING with your conductor go?" Joanna asked while Greene sifted through the myriad of movie options available to stream.

"It was good," Greene replied. "Action, right?"

"So, you're not fired?" Joanna snagged a nacho and bit into it while Greene continued to sort.

"No." Greene laughed. "He offered me a job opportunity, actually."

"You already have a job." Joanna leaned back against the sofa after biting into her first potato skin.

"New action or old action?"

"Don't change the subject." Joanna pushed at her shoulder, and Greene leaned back to match her posture.

"I'm not. I'm trying to pick a movie."

"Then, pick one. I honestly don't care what we watch." Joanna motioned to the TV screen. "Seriously."

Greene hovered over a category on the screen and turned her head to Joanna. Joanna had all but finished the potato skin she'd grabbed and was sitting so close, the sides of their bodies were touching.

"Oh yeah?"

"Yeah. Answer my question." She smiled at her and finished the last bite.

"There's a new romance I've wanted to check out but haven't."

"I'm sorry." Joanna laughed and turned her head to

Greene. "Did Macon Greene just say she wanted to check out a romantic movie?"

"It's not the kind of romance you're probably used to." Greene turned back to the TV and scrolled over to the movie.

"How so?"

"It's a lesbian romance." She clicked on the film to reveal the title and details to allow Joanna to read. "I usually don't watch them, because ninety-five percent of them have sad endings, but I read some spoilers. This one is supposed to have a happy one."

"Why sad endings all the time?"

"Couldn't tell you." Greene shrugged and clicked on the purchase button to buy the movie for ten bucks. "It's a trend that's been around forever. I used to watch them when I first started to think I might like girls and then when I knew I did. They just depressed me, though. It felt like people were saying if you fell in love with a woman, you'd just end up losing her." She waited before pressing the start button to begin the film. "Either she died of some illness, or she was straight and returned to the husband. It took me years to find one with a happy ending where they ended up together."

Joanna stared at her as she spoke. She seemed to be interested in what Greene was saying. She turned back to the TV, because the intensity of Joanna's eyes was too much for her to handle these days.

"That's kind of depressing," she finally said. "So, you want to watch it?"

"If you're up for it, yeah. If not, I'm sure there's some other movie with car crashes and bombs blowing up buildings we can watch."

"It's fine. Put it on." Joanna laughed at her, leaned forward, and grabbed two potato skins. She passed both to Greene, who took them. "As promised." She stood then. "I'll grab my good wine and your terrible wine."

Greene laughed to herself as Joanna made her way

into her kitchen to open both bottles. Greene started the movie. She watched Joanna open her cutlery drawer, grab the corkscrew, and then open bottle number one followed by the second. The woman put the corkscrew back and opened a cabinet next to the sink to pull out two wine glasses. She poured a glass from one bottle and then the other before carrying the glasses into the living room, placing them on the table, and moving back to grab the bottles, bringing them with her, and setting them on the table as well. She was one of the few people Greene let into her apartment. She was the only one who knew it so well.

It hadn't felt strange to Greene. But she was starting to wonder if the reason it hadn't felt strange to her was because she secretly wanted to be in a relationship with the woman currently shoving a messy nacho in her mouth, trying to make room for the cheese that was congealed on top of it by moving her head to line up with it. Greene couldn't help but find it adorable. That was scary. She'd never been in this situation before. She'd had relationships, and she'd dated women, but she'd never felt something like this for any of them. Joanna wasn't an option. And Greene resigned herself in that moment to just being miserable until she could find a way to move past these feelings. She'd surely meet someone that made her feel the same. Joanna would start dating a guy. Seeing them together would set Greene's mind and heart right.

"Thanks," Greene said.

Joanna passed her the glass. She took a sip and placed it back, sinking into the sofa to watch the movie that had just started.

"So, what's this movie about exactly?" Joanna did the same.

"Girl meets girl. Girl loses girl. Girl gets girl back. It's just like every other movie, but it won a few festival awards. I thought it had to be decent enough," Greene told her.

"Well, I hope so," Joanna replied.

"If not, we can turn it off."

A few minutes later, the first female lead had met the second female lead. The movie had a high-quality feel to it, with a decent score. Greene always noticed the music in movies, even more sometimes than the plot. If it was terrible, she'd cringe and turn it off. If it was great, she had respect for the people who had put it all together. Ten minutes later, Joanna's head was on her shoulder. The two women on screen had shared a fun, awkward moment where it was clear they were progressing toward something more. Greene couldn't hear the music or the dialogue anymore because Joanna's head was on her shoulder. They'd stopped eating and had only snuck a few sips of their wine. Joanna had snuggled into her side, apparently, for the long haul, because at the thirty-minute mark, when the characters shared their first kiss, she was still there.

Greene's heart was racing. She'd been able to keep herself together as the characters moved into their first fight. Joanna stirred for a moment before getting up to use the bathroom. Greene missed the press of her body next to her immediately. When Joanna returned, though, she was torn. She wanted Joanna to move back into position. She also didn't want that, because it felt too good. Joanna finished her glass of wine and poured herself another. She topped off Greene's and settled back into her.

"What did I miss?" she asked.

"They made up," Greene replied. "Actually, they're still making up," she added and pointed at the screen.

"Oh."

The two very attractive women were nearly naked. One was on top of the other. Greene felt herself grow uncomfortable, which surprised her because she had no problem watching two women have fake sex in a movie. That was especially true because most of the lesbian sex in movies was pretty terrible or shot through a filter that made it nearly impossible to see anything worthwhile.

Having Joanna next to her, touching her skin, was enough to light her on fire. Once the women were both completely nude, and the camera was not shying away from particular areas of their bodies, Greene tensed. She felt Joanna also tense beside her. The scene continued. Greene's face grew red. She hadn't known the sex scene in this movie would be so graphic. The two actresses were clearly giving the scene their all. Greene's cheeks reddened further as one slid down between the other woman's legs and began a very specific activity she had not prepared herself to see with Joanna tucked into her body.

After a few more seconds, Joanna moved to sit up straight next to her. Greene didn't chance a look over at her face to check her reaction but noted that Joanna's hands were clasped tightly in her lap for the duration of that part of the scene. As the actress continued making sounds indicative of her impending fake orgasm, Joanna's hands tensed further. When the orgasm came, her hands released. Greene watched the remainder of the scene while Joanna sipped on her second glass of wine and seemed to be looking around the room at anywhere other than the TV.

Greene didn't know what that meant. Was Joanna turned on by the scene and needed to look away? Was she grossed out by the scene but didn't want to make Greene uncomfortable, so she looked elsewhere to save herself from having to watch two women have sex and then exchange their first *'I love you'* at the end of the scene?

"Sorry, I didn't know it was this graphic," Greene said.

"No, it's fine. It's a good movie so far."

Joanna downed the rest of her wine. She picked up the bottle to refill her glass. Greene hadn't seen her drink this much this quickly possibly ever.

"I can turn it off. We can just–"

"No, it's okay, Macon. Really; it's a good movie. They're…" Joanna seemed to stumble as she stared at the screen and at the two women who were now spooning and enjoying their shared afterglow. "Cute together." She drank half the glass she'd just poured.

"I was going to say *hot together*, but… sure." Greene tried to laugh it off and took a gulp of her own wine.

"That too." Joanna leaned back again but held onto her wine glass this time.

Another forty minutes went by. The characters had a few nice make-out sessions and a shorter sex scene, where they were still half-clothed and up against a wall. By then, Greene sensed Joanna was more than comfortable with what they were showing. That could've been due to the amount of alcohol she'd consumed more than the movie itself. She'd finished her beer at *7Ups* earlier. Then, she finished the entire bottle of wine she'd bought and even had half a glass of Greene's, despite telling her it was terrible more than once. When the movie ended, Joanna's legs were in Greene's lap. Her head was against the arm of the sofa and the small square pillow there. Her eyes were glassy. She was seemingly both tired and drunk.

"How about we call it a night?" Greene suggested and patted Joanna's legs, which she'd been innocently touching, thinking about what it might be like to slide her hands up the jeans and touch her bare calves.

"Huh?" Joanna turned her eyes from where they'd been entranced on the rolling credits.

"You're totally drunk." Greene laughed at her. "I don't think I've ever seen you drunk before."

"I'm not drunk. I'm tipsy. There's a difference." Joanna moved her legs and sat herself up. She was a little wobbly. Greene's hand went to the small of her back to try to settle her. "Okay, I might be a little drunk." She placed her hand on her forehead. "I'm calling an Uber to drive me home."

Greene watched her attempt to stand and stood with her, holding onto her waist to prevent her from falling over.

"Just stay here," Greene offered. "I'll get you something to wear. Come on." She motioned for Joanna to walk with her toward the bedroom.

"No way. That's your sanctuary," she argued without moving.

"You've been in my sanctuary for the past several hours and many more before that. It's not a big deal," Greene insisted. "It's better than you taking an Uber home. I'm too tired to get in the Uber with you to make sure you get home safely and then take the car back here. So, just borrow some clothes and go to sleep."

Joanna didn't respond but followed Greene as she pulled her by the hand into her bedroom. Greene pulled out a t-shirt and a pair of sweatpants for her to put on, and then left her there to go to the bedroom and change clothes herself. She brushed her teeth and then returned to the bedroom to find Joanna sitting on the edge of the bed, changed but looking groggy. Greene pulled her up by her hands and took her to the bathroom, where she pulled out the toothbrush she'd bought to replace her current one, put toothpaste on it, and handed it to Joanna before closing the door to give her privacy. A few minutes later, she heard the bathroom door open and turned to see the woman walking almost zombie-like toward the living room. Greene finished pulling the blankets back on the bed and followed her out there. She found Joanna lying on the sofa, pulling the throw blanket over her body.

"Goodnight," Joanna said when she realized Greene was in the room with her.

"What are you doing?" Greene laughed at her.

"Going to sleep."

"Why are you doing that out here?"

"Because you have one bed," Joanna argued and rolled onto her side to face Greene.

"Yeah, and it's a queen. There's plenty of room for both of us." Greene moved toward her. "Come on."

She moved them back into the bedroom and walked

Joanna around to the other side, pulling the blanket back a little more so the woman could slide in. She tucked her in and went back to the living room, where she moved the dishes and trash into the kitchen, turned off the lights, and made sure to lock up before returning to the bedroom. When she got to the doorway, she saw a gorgeous, blonde woman already asleep in her bed.

No woman had ever slept in that bed. As she stared at Joanna lying there, sleeping peacefully, she wondered if maybe this was a bad idea. Maybe she should have gone in the Uber with her and then come home and fallen asleep in her bed solo, as she'd done every other night, but she shook her head sideways and approached her own side of the bed. She slid under the blankets and flipped off the bedside lamp, leaving her in near complete darkness, save the light coming from the street lamps outside.

"Macon?" Joanna whispered.

Greene turned her head to see that she'd rolled on her side to face her.

"Yeah?"

"Am I the only woman that's been in this bed?" she asked a little louder.

"Yeah," Macon admitted.

"That's kind of nice," she replied and drifted back to sleep.

"Yeah, it kind of is." Greene slid in more comfortably, watching Joanna sleep.

CHAPTER 7

JOANNA WOKE to the alarm she had set to go off every morning on her phone. It sounded different this morning though; like it wasn't in its usual place: plugged in to charge for the night and next to the bottle of water she always kept there. She opened her eyes slowly at first, but then they shot open on their own when she didn't recognize where she was. It definitely wasn't her bedroom.

"Can you shut that off?" She heard a voice she recognized coming from behind her. Her eyes went wider while her eyebrows nearly shot off her forehead entirely. "Jo?" Macon's hand went to her shoulder and shook it.

"Sorry." Joanna reached for the phone she didn't remember placing there and stopped the incessant ringing. "I don't remember getting here. I mean, I don't remember getting into this bed."

"You drank a lot." Macon laughed a little. It was a rough, sleepy laugh that Joanna found she enjoyed. It was different from Macon's usual laugh, but pleasantly so. "I brought your phone in."

"Thank you."

"Don't. I regret my decision. Why is your alarm set for 6 a.m.?" she asked.

Joanna turned to see Macon lying on her back, rubbing her eyes with both hands.

"I always have it set for six," she replied and smiled at the look Macon gave her. "What?" She laughed.

"Why? You don't have to go into an office every day anymore." Macon rolled on her side to face her.

"Habit, I guess." Joanna rested her head on her arm, facing Macon. "I do have a nine o'clock shoot, though."

"I have rehearsal at nine too," Macon told her.

"Thanks for letting me stay over. Sorry I got drunk on you." Joanna tried not to be embarrassed, but it was hard. She'd rarely got drunk and definitely hadn't been drunk in front of Macon before. "I didn't mean to make you have to take care of me."

"I didn't mind." Macon tossed the blanket off her body.

Joanna's eyes flitted to the now bare legs and the shorts that hardly covered them, along with the white t-shirt that had gotten bunched up under her breasts and revealed that incredibly well-toned stomach.

"You do snore, though." Macon straightened her shirt and stood.

"I do not!" Joanna sat up.

Macon laughed as she stretched her limbs next to the bed.

"You don't." She smiled. "I was kidding. I'm going to hop in the shower, since I'm up at six when I could have slept in for another two hours." She glared playfully at Joanna.

"Sorry." Joanna wrinkled her eyebrows together. "I should have turned it off."

"Make it up to me by mixing up one of those fancy espresso drinks?" she asked with a hopeful expression.

Joanna nodded and watched as Macon headed toward the bathroom to take her shower. Joanna stretched her own body and then climbed out of bed just in time to hear the shower start. She made her way to where Macon had laid her clothes out for her on the dresser, changed, and placed Macon's clothes on the bed, folded nicely, before heading into the kitchen to make the coffee. As she ground the beans, she considered what was going on in the other room. Macon was naked in the shower. She was under hot, running water, rubbing soap over her skin. Maybe she used a shower gel instead. Joanna wondered what scent while she started to steam the milk, and decided the next time she was in the bathroom, she'd move the curtain aside to check.

She waited while the espresso poured and then made her latte art without thinking. When she looked down at her design, her eyes went big for the second time that morning. She considered covering up what she'd done but heard the shower stop running and sat the cup down quickly, left the milk container in the sink, and practically ran to her purse to toss her phone inside, slid on her shoes, and headed out of the apartment. Once she hit the street, she sent Macon a text, apologizing that she had to run, and made it to her own apartment about fifteen minutes later.

She showered herself and tried not to think about waking up next to Macon. She had a distinct memory of Macon pulling her up off the sofa and sliding her into bed, tucking her in for the night. She also had a memory of rolling over and staring at her sleeping form for several minutes before falling back to sleep and later waking again at six.

She'd woken in the middle of the night, wondering where she was for the first time, realizing she was in Macon's bed, having a momentary freak-out, and then rolling over to see her sleeping. She'd woken up because she was hot. Her skin was hot. She was sweating for some reason, despite the room being perfectly comfortable. It took her a second to recall the reason she'd woken up in sweat, and when she did, she'd rolled away from Macon. Macon was the reason she'd woken in that sweat.

The movie the night before hadn't exactly been what Joanna had expected. Truthfully, she hadn't known what to expect. She'd never seen a lesbian film. She'd seen movies with lesbians in them, or TV shows with gay characters, but she'd never watched a movie geared toward lesbians, with two female leads that fell in love and expressed that love very graphically on a giant flat screen a few feet away from her face while she happened to have her head on the shoulder of one of her best friends, who was also a lesbian and quite possibly had a crush on her, if the rumors were to be believed.

She'd tried to keep things light between the two of them by taking Macon to *7Ups* and playing silly games, but even that had gotten serious when Keira had arrived. She thought food and an action film would return them to their fun mood, but then action had turned to romance, and she'd watched two women going to town on each other while she felt Macon pressed into her side. She'd considered moving away at first but thought that would be obvious and make Macon uncomfortable or make her think Joanna had a problem with what the women were doing, which she didn't. She had no problem with what two women did to one another. She'd never put all that much thought into it, but then she met Emma, and later Macon, and she became close.

As she started hanging out with Macon, Emma, Keira, Hillary, and more lesbians, she heard a little more about things from them. She'd heard a woman whisper loudly into Macon's ear what she wanted to do to her later as they stood at the bar, waiting for the bartender to deliver their drinks. The woman mentioned her fingers thrusting deep inside and her tongue pressing hard. Joanna had pretended she hadn't heard any of that, while her skin turned a deep shade of red that was thankfully unseen due to the dim lighting of the club.

When she saw the expression on the woman's face in the movie – how much she was enjoying the other between her legs doing something Joanna couldn't exactly see clearly, while playing with one of her nipples with her fingers – Joanna grew hot then, too. Her body registered that it was probably normal for her to have that kind of reaction. She was a sexual being. She had urges, and those urges hadn't been fulfilled in a long time. She thought about that as she changed into her clothes for the day. The last time she'd had sex, had she felt like that woman in the movie? Had she made those sounds, those moans and gasps in surprise? Had she been driven to an explosion so intense, her hips had lifted off the mattress and then stayed there until guided back down by an arm over her hips? No, none of that had happened.

Macon had been the reason she'd woken in a sweat in the middle of the night. But she considered, it wasn't really Macon. It was the movie. The movie had caused the dream she'd experienced that rocketed her awake around three in the morning. That dream had been so real. It was one of the most visceral dreams she'd ever experienced. And at first, when she'd woken, she thought the dream was just a replay of the film: one actress was between the other actress's legs. But the sounds seemed familiar. They seemed that way because they were her sounds. Well, they were her sounds, but they were louder and more expressive than she remembered. She'd thought back to the dream while staring at Macon. She recalled that Macon had been the woman between her legs. It was Joanna's body, with Macon doing things to her. She knew this to be the case because in the dream, Macon had paused to look up at her, and Joanna would know those eyes anywhere.

She grabbed her gear and met her Uber driver outside at eight, since the drive at that time would take a little longer due to morning rush hour. As she settled into the backseat, arranging her camera bag next to her, her phone buzzed. It was a text from Macon, thanking her for the coffee and asking her to After Dark the following night. She thought back to the vision of Macon between her legs and shook her head. She replied and stared back out the window toward the traffic ahead.

***

Greene frowned at Joanna's text. She'd turned her down, claiming she had to work, but she hadn't mentioned a Thursday night shoot to her. Greene stood in her living room with her violin case over her shoulder, considering the night they'd shared and the morning they'd woken up, too. She hadn't expected eighty percent of what had happened in the previous fifteen or so hours. She should have just put on an action movie like they'd planned. She should have tried to stop Joanna from drinking that much, so she would have been able to go home. She'd fallen asleep next to the woman, and it was right before that she'd had to admit something to herself. She had feelings for Joanna Martin. She did. She had feelings for her. If she'd spent more time thinking about it, though, she would have admitted to herself that she didn't merely have feelings for Jo. She was falling for her. Hell, she'd *been* falling for her probably since the beginning.

She stared down at the response on her phone and tried to think about what to message back. She could reply with an understanding message and leave it at that, but that wasn't Greene's style. Whenever Jo turned her down for something or was equivocating, Greene gave her a hard time. She was often rewarded with Jo's attendance. That was what she'd normally do in this case. She'd already gotten their tickets. Since she'd finally gotten real with herself about her feelings for the straight woman in her bed, she wasn't sure what *normal* was for her anymore.

She found the whole thing confusing. She knew Jo was off limits. She was straight and attracted to men. Greene wasn't a man. It should have been that simple, but Greene's heart and mind wouldn't let it go as she made her way to rehearsal. There were moments where Greene wondered, and she hated herself because of it. That previous night, for example, she'd woken around one with Joanna's body pressed to her side. Jo's arm was over her stomach. And even though the woman's head wasn't on her shoulder but next to it, Joanna's lips were pressed to it. She could feel Joanna's breath against her arm, and she kept herself very still. She didn't want the contact to end.

In the morning, she'd woken up with her body

pressed to Joanna's back and with her arm slung over her body. She must have done it instinctively, feeling the presence of another body in her bed. And, as soon as she'd realized it, she'd slowly extracted herself. Five minutes later, the alarm had sounded. Fifteen minutes after that, she'd made her way out of the bathroom, expecting to find Joanna on her sofa. But instead, she had a text message and a coffee cup with a heart etched into the foam.

***

Joanna wrapped her shoot around eleven and headed home. She arrived at 11:30, downloaded her photos, and made herself some lunch. She headed into the *Worthy Bash* office and met with two potential clients before sitting at her borrowed desk for a couple of hours, editing and working on her website. By 6:30, she felt off, and it took her only about ten seconds to figure out why. She picked up her phone and noticed the lack of messages from Macon. These days, they rarely went more than a few hours between messages. She clicked on Macon's name and scrolled up to reveal their most recent exchange. She continued scrolling as she smiled at some of the things they'd sent back and forth.

"Hey, you want to grab some dinner?" Keira asked.

"Huh?" Joanna looked up with what was undoubtedly a goofy smile on her face.

"What's got you all smiley?" Keira pointed at her.

"What?"

"Can you no longer speak in complete sentences?" Keira laughed. "Wait! Are you perhaps texting back and forth with Russell, the one you're just *not* attracted to?"

"What? No."

"Then, who? Who's the new mystery man that's got you smiling?"

"Why does it have to be a mystery man?" She stuck her phone in her purse and stood.

"I guess it doesn't." Keira seemed to be taking the hint. "Anyway, dinner? Emma's got a work thing tonight, and I'm starving."

"Oh, sure," she agreed.

"I'd say call Greene, but she probably won't want to come if I'm there."

"What is going on with you two?" Joanna shouldered her bag, and they headed toward the elevator.

"It'll blow over." Keira gave a non-answer and pressed the elevator button.

"She's been acting strangely ever since," Joanna said. "Call me crazy, but I liked the old Macon. I'd like her back. So, can you fix it?" she asked as they walked into the elevator.

"She's acting strangely? How so?"

"I don't know," Joanna replied. "She just sees you, and her good mood turns bad."

"Oh, that's all?" Keira looked at the shiny floor of the elevator as they descended.

"Sorry."

"No, it's my fault." Keira looked back up at her. "I was honestly trying to help, but I overstepped. Did you tell her I apologize?"

"I tried; she changed the subject to the movie we were going to watch."

"Movie?" Keira stepped off once the doors opened.

"Yeah, I went to her place, and we watched a movie," Joanna explained and followed her out. "I dropped it, because I didn't want to put her in that mood again. I like when she's in a good mood."

Keira gave her a sideways glance as they made their way outside.

"She's pretty great, huh?"

"Yeah, she is," Joanna affirmed. "She's like an iceberg in human form."

"How so?" Keira laughed. "And want to hit up *Max's?*"

"Sure," she said about the restaurant down the block. "And, I don't know... I feel like there's this surface Macon, and then there's still seventy-five percent of her she doesn't let anyone see."

"But she lets you see it?" Keira asked.

"I'm chipping away little by little." Joanna smiled at the thought.

"And you like that? Chipping?"

"I do, yeah." Joanna shrugged her shoulders. "I like getting to know her more. I feel like there's even more to it than that, though. It's like she lets people believe things about her even if they're not true."

"Like what?" Keira turned and stopped walking.

"I don't think it's my place to tell." Joanna stopped beside her.

"I guess not." Keira began walking again. Joanna joined her. "But is there anything I should worry about?"

"No, I don't think so."

"Outside of our little spat we're currently in, she's never said anything to me about people believing things that aren't true. Am I... Have I said something or–"

"Maybe, when the two of you make up, you can ask her," she interrupted. "If it's important to her, I'm sure she'll talk to you."

"She talks to you now," Keira replied a little wistfully.

"What?"

"She doesn't talk to me how she used to. She talks to you now. I guess I've done the same with Emma, though. You meet someone, and then–" She stopped herself and turned her head toward the street, as if trying to avoid Joanna's gaze. "Anyway, it's a part of growing up, I guess."

"Aren't we kind of already grown?" Joanna suggested.

"You'd think that, wouldn't you?" Keira laughed. "Come on. I'm buying."

CHAPTER 8

GREENE MADE herself dinner and ate it at the dining room table, desiring a change from eating in front of the TV. When she finished, she took her time doing the dishes and then took that nice, long bath she'd been craving. She dressed for bed and reached for her violin. She played for an hour, focusing on the pieces for the orchestra's performances, and then she played something that had no sheet music. It had no rhyme or reason to it either. She just played. She never just played. She liked her sheet music. She liked the organized nature of the music and rarely deviated from the structure, thoughtfully and carefully crafted. She felt like there was a reason this music was played often years after the composer's death.

However, tonight was different. She felt like she might be able to coax something out of her instrument without the structure and without the knowledge of the notes that came next. She played and played. The music she created turned from happy and fast to somber and slow before she forced it back into the fast pace with the intention of changing her own mood. When it didn't work like it normally did, she lowered the violin and looked at the clock under the TV. It was past eleven.

She checked her phone once before she closed her eyes and found she had three texts from Joanna checking on her. She replied that she'd been rehearsing, so she hadn't heard the phone – which was true. Then, she followed that one up with one about being tired and going to sleep.

When Greene woke the next morning, she had two messages from her in reply. The first one told her she should talk to Keira. The second message asked if she wanted to come with her later to her shoot. Joanna was going to head out into the woods and take some nature shots. Greene had gone with her a few times. They'd hiked and talked while Jo had snapped some shots along the way. Greene wasn't sure she was up for a hike when she also had After Dark with Keira, Emma, and Hillary. It was their monthly ritual, and she'd always loved it in the past. There was a part of her that just didn't want to go tonight. She'd been particularly excited about it given the theme, but she'd also wanted Joanna there, and Joanna wasn't going to be in attendance. Greene texted back that she didn't feel like a hike today and readied for work.

"Miss Greene, have you given any thought to what we discussed the other day? They need an answer soon," the board president for the orchestra, Rose Brown, asked her after they'd finished rehearsal.

"I have, but I don't know yet," she replied as she walked down the stairs that led to the back door of the performance hall and to the street. "It's a lot to consider."

"It's a great opportunity for you. It will open up some doors." Rose walked behind her, and briskly at that, in an attempt to catch Greene before she could escape.

"I didn't even put myself up for it. How–"

"Miss Greene, people ask about you all the time." She held the door open as Greene made her way through it. Then, she followed her out to the street. "You are one of the finest violinists in a generation; no one understands why you're not on your own tours or soloing in every performance."

"I don't want to," she said directly as they stood on

the sidewalk and people walked around them.

"But, the way you play – it's inspiring. It's so technical and yet so fluid. You're like a ballet dancer with your instrument. It's graceful and wonderful, and more people should hear you play and not just as a part of an orchestra."

"It's a month," Greene said of the job offer she'd received the other day.

"Exactly. It's only one month. Is that really all that long in the grand scheme of things?" Rose asked. "You'd be the featured soloist. People around the world would get to hear you play. You've not done that in your career, Miss Greene."

"Greene."

"That's what I said."

"No, just Greene. You can drop the Miss part."

"Oh. Sure."

"It's only the one month? It won't lead to another month or three more months?" Greene asked after a minute.

"There are no plans for that at this time."

Greene squinted at her and replied, "And my contract with the orchestra remains intact?"

"Of course."

"I'll think about it."

"Oh, I thought you–"

"I have until next week to decide, right?"

"Technically, yes. They would like to know earlier to get the preparations started."

"I'll let you know as soon as I decide then."

"Can I ask what has you holding back?" Rose asked.

***

When she got home, Greene changed into her After Dark clothes: a V-neck shirt in a dark gray, a pair of jeans, and white tennis shoes. She grabbed her wallet, her phone, and some chapstick along with her keys, and shoved one thing in each of her four pockets. She made it to her front door and yanked it open, worrying about being late and getting chastised by Hillary for it. She saw Joanna standing there, just about to knock.

"Hey," Greene greeted her in surprise.

"Hi." Joanna dropped the hand that had been about to knock.

"Did I know you were coming over?" she asked and continued to stand in her own doorway.

"You invited me to After Dark," Joanna stated.

She looked great. She was wearing a sleeveless silk blouse in a royal blue, with a light black jacket over it that looked like leather but might have been fake. She hadn't seen Joanna wear it before. She had on black slacks and black flats with gold buckles on top of them. She looked like a woman who was going out on the town.

"I'm still invited, right?" she asked when Greene didn't respond and stood staring.

"Actually, I gave your ticket away," she said.

"Oh, do you have…" she faded out and turned her head to look down the hall, as if checking for someone who wasn't there, "… a date?"

Greene laughed at her and closed the door behind herself, locking it before she said anything.

"I'm kidding." She turned back to Joanna, who was glaring at her.

"Very funny. You're an ass."

"Sometimes," Greene agreed. "You weren't coming. What changed?" she asked, suddenly feeling much better than she had all day and much of last night.

"I didn't want to miss out after all. I'd have to wait until next month," Joanna said. Greene made her way down the stairs rapidly, forcing Joanna to keep up with her. "Are we racing there?"

"No, I just don't want to be late. Hill always gives me such a hard time when I'm late. It used to be Keira, but

Keira went and turned into an adult who met a girlfriend that always makes sure she shows up on time. Now, I'm the late one of the group."

"You're never late," Joanna replied as they made it to the door, and she moved past Greene to open it for her.

"I'm sometimes late," she said, and they made their way out to the street.

"I've known you for a year now. I don't think I've ever seen you be late for anything."

"Okay, so I'm not late."

"But you let them give you a hard time for it? So, when you're hanging out with just them, do you show up five minutes late on purpose or something?"

"What? No."

"Then, how are you the late person Hillary makes fun of?"

"Why are we talking about this? You're uninvited. I'm giving your ticket to the next person I see." Greene smiled at her as they walked.

"Don't do that." Joanna stopped walking.

"Do what?" Greene stopped, too, and turned back to her.

"What you always do: you deflect, you change the subject."

"I don't understand why we're talking about that subject," Greene stated.

"Why do you let your best friends think things about you that aren't true?"

"What are you talking about, Jo?" Greene's voice was louder than she'd intended, and a few people walking past them stared.

"You let Keira and Hillary, and now Emma, think you're this person that you're not."

"So?"

"I want to know why."

"Now? You have to know this now?"

"No, but I want to." Joanna ran her hand along

Greene's forearm. "Macon, you're not someone that shows up late. You're not the girl that sleeps around, but your closest friends think–"

"You're my closest friend," she interjected. "Jo, you're my closest friend. Don't you get that?" she asked and started walking again. "I love Keira and Hill, and I love Emma now, too. We're all friends, but I don't tell them stuff sometimes. I let them think things sometimes, too, because – I don't know – I guess because I think it doesn't really matter. I know who I am. I know who I am, Jo, and now you do, too. You know who I am." She'd been staring at the sidewalk as they walked but turned her head to Joanna at that last part. "You're the only person I care about knowing those things about me."

"Okay."

"Just okay?" Greene asked.

"Yeah, just okay."

Joanna smiled at her, and they walked on. Twenty minutes later, they arrived at the Exploratorium entrance to a waiting Keira, Hillary, and Emma.

"Greene, showing up late again?" Hillary teased.

"Actually, she's right on time; as always," Joanna tossed back.

She held out her phone, which she'd apparently prepared in advance for this moment. It showed seven on the dot.

"Oh, sorry," Hillary returned, a little surprised.

"We ready?" Emma asked.

"Let's go," Keira replied and nodded in Greene's direction.

Greene nodded back. Things weren't exactly okay between them, but she'd gotten some distance on the fight and could at least smile and nod tonight until they had a real chance to talk.

"What's the theme tonight?" Joanna asked.

"You didn't tell her?" Hillary looked at Greene.

"Didn't tell me what?"

Greene held open the door for Joanna and followed her inside.

"It's music," Greene returned.

***

After Dark had different themes each month. Joanna had seen the hot sauce theme, where there were different types of hot sauces people could taste and understand the composition of. She'd been when they'd done the theme of light and the absence of. And she'd been twice, accidentally, when they'd had the same theme, since they reoccurred sometimes. Fireworks was worth seeing twice, though. She'd been to that one on a date the first time with a guy named Keith. It had been a first and final date with Keith.

The second time, though, had been with Macon and the gang. Emma and Keira had been dating for several months. Hillary had been there with a date that later went nowhere. Those two couples went off on their own for a part of the night, leaving her alone with Macon. They'd been hanging out fairly regularly by then, but there had been something about that night that had always stood out to Joanna. As they made their way around the exhibits tonight, she recalled it, and it suddenly made sense.

That night had felt very much like a triple date. It might have just been the first of many of those nights, now that she thought about it. Nearly every night after that – when they'd gone out with Keira and Emma, or when Hillary had a date and they tagged along to a movie – it had felt oddly like a double date. That was weird, right? They weren't dating. She dated men. Macon dated women.

Macon was actually talking to one now. She shook herself out of her thoughts and realized that Macon wasn't next to her. She was standing about ten feet away, talking to a woman that looked to be in her mid-thirties. The woman was leaning in, sharing a headphone Macon was listening to as a part of an exhibit. The woman couldn't just wait her damn turn? Joanna felt her heart start to race, and she took a deep breath before approaching.

"Hey, where'd you go?" she asked Macon with a hand on the small of her back.

Macon turned around, removing the headphones and handing them to the woman.

"Just listening to the exhibit."

"Who's your friend?" the woman asked of Joanna.

"Joanna," she introduced herself and put out her hand for the woman to shake.

"Brit."

"Brit?" Joanna checked.

"We were just listening to the music in this one."

Macon sensed something, apparently, because she placed her hand on Joanna's back and gave her a slight nudge toward a box that was playing a video of a baby laughing.

"This is music?" Joanna questioned and looked at Macon.

"This is a regular exhibit. It's not a part of the music one," Macon corrected. "It was nice to meet you, Brit. We're going to go meet up with our friends though," she said politely.

"I didn't realize..." Brit pointed back and forth between the two of them.

Joanna knew what that meant. Macon had to have known what that meant. Neither of them bothered to correct her.

"Nice to meet you." Joanna gave her a nod and turned around.

Macon turned around, too. Her hand moved from Joanna's back to take Joanna's hand instead. Joanna couldn't breathe: Macon was holding her hand. Their fingers were intertwined as they walked away from Brit, and it felt different than the other times they'd held hands like this in passing.

"Might as well sell it." Macon leaned in. "Thanks for the save, by the way."

"What?" Joanna turned to her.

"She just came out of nowhere, asked my name, and started flirting with me. I wanted to get rid of her–"

"But you didn't." Joanna dropped Macon's hand.

"I'm sure she's nice, but she goes by *Brit*. She's at least thirty-six, thirty-seven." Macon laughed and rubbed her hands together in front of her.

"Right."

Joanna shouldn't have been surprised that Macon didn't send the woman away. She'd admitted to being polite to women when they hit on her. Joanna had no right to interrupt their exchange. She couldn't tell that Macon needed a save by the way she was interacting with Brit. She'd gone over there strictly out of her own selfish need.

"Come on." Macon smiled at her. "I want to show you something."

"Okay." Joanna followed.

Macon led her to an octagonal room, where there was an electronic drum set. Three people were leaving the room when they arrived. Macon held open the door for her to walk in first.

"What?" Joanna laughed. "You play the drums, too?"

"Once you learn one instrument, the rest aren't that hard," Macon answered modestly. "Sit." She motioned for Joanna to sit on the round stool in front of the drum set.

"Why?"

"Just do it, come on." Macon laughed.

"Okay, but I don't have rhythm. I can't even play the tambourine." She sat, and Macon placed headphones over her ears.

"It's going to guide you through it." She pointed to a screen about the size of a laptop that had music options. "Pick one."

"What's the easiest?" Joanna asked.

"Try blues." Macon's smirk indicated that none of

them were easy but that she might have a shot with blues.

Joanna pressed the icon on the screen indicating blues music. The screen changed to show an identical drum set to the one she was sitting in front of. Macon handed her white c she had no idea how to hold. The music started in her headphones. It was slow, like most blues songs, and the lyrics along with musical notes scrawled along the bottom as the drums on the screen lit up in different colors. She guessed that she was supposed to hit each drum at the same time, almost like a video game. She struck one drum that sounded low and reverberated inside her headphones.

"Oh," she exclaimed.

"Fun, huh?" Macon asked.

"I don't even know how to hold these." She referenced the drumsticks she held for a second like oversized chopsticks and then quickly used both of them to hit the drum that lit up in red because she'd already missed so many beats.

"Here." Macon moved behind her, and her arms appeared on either side of Joanna. "Your thumb should be opposite your index finger on the stick with about two inches of the butt-end extending from the back. Pinching like this is called a *fulcrum*. Now, turn your hands to a forty-five-degree angle: you can use both of your wrists more freely and still have power and control," she said all of this as she formed Joanna's hands in the path she'd described. "Try now." She was leaning down right behind her; her breasts were actually touching Joanna's back, and Joanna felt them there. She realized how close they were in that moment; that Macon's hands were on top of her hands. She was demonstrating how to use the drumsticks properly. "There. Cool, huh?" she asked and stood up, leaving Joanna to try to play on her own.

Joanna gave it the old college try for another few beats before she stood and relinquished the sticks to Macon.

"You show me how it's done." She pulled off the headphones and held them out.

"That's it?" Macon asked.

"I'm no musician, and I am in the company of a good one. So, teach me."

"Okay." Macon sat on the stool, selected a rock song, left off the headphones, and played the song perfectly.

Joanna's jaw nearly dropped at the freedom expressed in Macon's face as she hit the black drum pads sometimes gently and, more times, with the force appropriate for a rock song. Macon's hair shook as she gave in and played, and played, until the last note reverberated.

"Jesus," Joanna said, and Macon turned to face her, setting the drumsticks into their holder. "How many instruments can you play?" Joanna asked.

"What?" She laughed. "There's a line. We–"

"You're not getting out of this room until you answer my question." Joanna stood back in front of the door.

"Oh, really?" Macon laughed and took a step toward her, testing her.

"Yes, really."

"I moved you the other day. I can move you again." Macon laughed more.

"Try me." Joanna lifted an eyebrow in challenging response.

Macon took the two more steps until she was standing right in front of her. Joanna could feel her breath. She could smell her scent, and she could sense something palpable she couldn't define. Macon stared at her before placing her hands on Joanna's hips as she'd done the other day in her kitchen. Joanna prepared for her to slide her over in the same manner, and she smiled at Macon to indicate that it would be okay. But Macon turned her head to look through the clear plastic wall. Joanna's eyes followed and noticed Keira and Emma standing just outside the room. Keira's eyes were on Macon's, and then on Joanna's. They seemed to say two things at once: this was interesting and, also, this shouldn't be happening. Macon took a step back and looked at Joanna. Her hands were no longer on her hips, and her mood had instantly changed.

"A lot."

"What?" Joanna asked, trying to figure out again what had just happened.

"I can play a lot of instruments, like a lot of professional musicians. I can leave the room now, right?"

"Oh, sure." Joanna took a step sideways and allowed her to pass.

Macon pulled open the door to the room, allowing four twenty-somethings to have their turn on the skins. Joanna followed her out, turning in time to see Keira's eyes on her and scowling at the woman while following Macon, who seemed to be on a mission.

CHAPTER 9

GREENE MOVED briskly through the crowd without caring if anyone followed or even knew where she was. She ended up in the bathroom, where she leaned over the sink, gripping the countertop. She thought about splashing cold water over her face, but she knew that wouldn't help her calm down. She had two very specific emotions, and both needed to lower in intensity before she could go back out to the museum. She was angry. That one was clear and definable. She was angry at Keira for that face she'd just made, and for making her realize her feelings for Joanna. She was also angry with herself for having those feelings. She should know better.

Her other emotion wasn't so much an actual emotion; she would call it a physical reaction. She hadn't intended on teaching Joanna how to hold drumsticks or challenging her at the door like that, but she had. Her body had reacted in a normally welcomed way. But, in Joanna's case, she wanted the pulsing between her legs to cease and the pounding in her chest to stop. She stared at herself in the mirror, straightened her already straightened shirt, and headed back out to the museum.

"Hey," Keira greeted her the second she appeared.

"What, Keira?" she asked and put her head on a swivel to look for Joanna.

"I asked her if I could talk to you." Keira obviously knew what she was doing. "Greene, I'm sorry. It's your life. You can do what you want with it. I didn't want to see you get hurt. I've never seen you like this with anyone you've been with, and those women were gay. Joanna—"

"Yeah, I know," she interrupted. "I get it, Keira. I don't need a reminder from you about how she likes guys. I am fully aware of the fact that I have feelings for a straight woman, and that I'm going to have to get over them. I get it," she repeated. "What I don't need, though, is my friend constantly reminding me of that, or staring at me like I'm on exhibit at this place every time I'm around her."

"No, Greene, that wasn't what–"

"You okay?" Joanna had walked up behind Keira and held out a bottle of water to Greene.

"I'm good." She took it from her. "Thanks."

"Sure. So, I actually found something I want to show you," Joanna replied. "And I have about a million questions about it."

"What?" Greene asked.

Joanna moved up next to Keira.

"Can I borrow her?" she asked of Greene.

"Sure," Keira said, turning without another word; probably going off to find her girlfriend.

"What's up?" Greene turned to Joanna.

"Question one," she began. "Why the hell didn't you tell me?"

"I'm sorry?" Greene shook her head, attempting to keep her reaction tampered, in fear she'd reveal her real worry that Joanna had figured out how she felt about her.

"You planned this exhibit," Joanna exclaimed and motioned around the hall with her hand.

"Oh, not really," Greene replied. "Wait, how did–"

"There's a sign thanking the people who were involved in developing these exhibits. It thanks the orchestra and, in particular, a few key members of it, including one Macon Greene."

"I told them I didn't–"

"Macon, stop." Joanna approached her. "Stop hiding, please." She took both of Greene's hands and held onto them, forcing Greene to move the bottle of water to under her arm. "You helped them put this together, didn't you?"

Greene swallowed. Once again, Joanna was so close; their hands were linked. And even though Keira appearing right outside the bathroom had turned Greene completely off, she was now, unfortunately, turned completely back on.

"I helped with some of the music. That's all. They have scientists that put together the actual exhibits."

"Show me," she implored with a squeeze of Greene's hands.

"They just asked a few of us to play something or tell them about how the instruments work. They recorded some stuff and incorporated it into the exhibits. I didn't even know what they used."

"Can I ask you a question?"

"You told me you had a million," Greene reminded and dropped Joanna's hands.

"You might not like it."

"Jo, what?" She pulled the bottle out from under her arm, opened it, and took a drink before offering it to Joanna, who declined.

"What made you hide yourself like this?"

"What?"

"Macon, you invited me here tonight but didn't tell me you were an actual part of the exhibit. Your friends have no idea. You don't want to solo, or tour, or-"

"So, because I don't like showing off, something must be wrong with me?"

"I didn't say that," she returned. "Macon, I-"

"I'm probably going on tour soon anyway, since you're so curious about me playing violin on my own in front of a crowd."

"What? You're going on tour?"

"Maybe." She looked away from Joanna's concerned eyes and toward the rest of the exhibit. "Do you want to see the part I worked on?"

"No, I want you to tell me about this tour," Joanna replied.

"I might not do it."

"Why not?"

"Because I don't know if I want to."

"Why not?" Joanna persisted.

"Why do you care so much? God, Jo," she exclaimed and started to walk off, then stopped and turned back around. "It's my damn life. If I want to be a touring violinist, then I will. If I don't, I won't. Either way, these are my choices to make. If I don't want people knowing about things I do or how well I might do them, that's up to me." She turned back and didn't wait for a response.

***

Joanna was pissed. She rarely got pissed. She stood in that museum, after getting yelled at, for five full minutes before Emma approached her to check that she was okay. Macon had, apparently, fled the museum, leaving her there. Joanna refused to go after her. She hadn't deserved that kind of reaction from Macon. More importantly, she'd been hurt by it, and that was the worst part. She'd never been hurt by Macon before, and she did not like how it felt. She walked with Emma, Keira, and Hillary for about another thirty minutes, taking in the exhibits and wondering how they had no idea Macon had been a part of this.

There were listening stations around where people could listen to a tune and then attempt to play it back on a rudimentary form of the same instrument used. There were examples of instruments from all over the world, and the science behind how they were made was provided. But Joanna hadn't been distracted enough by any of it to forget how it felt to be there without Macon sharing it with her, or how it had felt being hurt by her words earlier. She made her way to the last of the exhibits and noticed the violin on a stand, with headphones in front of it. There was also a small video screen beside the violin. When she picked up the headphones to put them on, she pressed the play button and was immediately surrounded by the sound.

The video showed someone playing the instrument. It was a close-up shot of the hand on the bow, but Joanna recognized that hand: she'd been holding it an hour ago. She watched and listened as it played the slow song, sliding the bow back and forth over the strings. Her anger subsided with every movement. She discovered she couldn't be upset with Macon anymore if the woman could do *that* with the most beautiful instrument she'd ever seen.

***

"Jo?" Macon greeted when Joanna entered her apartment with her key.

"Yeah, it's me." Joanna closed the door behind her and made her way into the living room, where she found Macon applying rosin to her bow. She'd just learned at the museum that players of bowed string instruments rubbed blocks of rosin on their bow hair so it could grip the strings and make them vibrate clearly. She focused on watching Macon's hand rubbing the block of yellow rosin over the part of the bow that touched the instrument. "Sorry, did I interrupt you rehearsing?"

"No, I was just about to play," Macon replied and lowered the rosin to the table.

"Can I hear you?" Joanna sat down next to her on the sofa.

"You still want to hear me play even after I treated you like that?"

"You can make it up to me by playing me something." She smiled at her.

"You're trying to bribe me because I feel bad," Macon replied.

"Yes," she stated confidently.

"What do you want to hear?" Macon asked and lifted her violin while standing.

"Whatever you want to play."

"No, if I pick something, you'll just pick something else and make me play that after. I know how your mind works there, Jo-Jo."

"God, don't call me that." Joanna laughed. "And honestly, I don't even know where to start. I know nothing of violin. That's your fault, by the way," she pointed. "I've known you for this long, and you've taught me nothing."

Macon laughed and put the violin to her shoulder, pressing down on the chinrest. She moved the bow to hover over the strings.

"I teach lessons, if you're interested, but you will have to put in the time. At least an hour a day of practice is required. Since you'd be playing catch up, you'd owe me three." She paused, and her green eyes lit up. "I'll play you something you'll recognize then."

Joanna nodded and waited for the song to begin. A few moments later, she saw Macon's eyes close, and she began to play. Within a few slides of the bow to the strings, Joanna knew what she was playing. They'd gone to see *West Side Story* as a group last year. Keira had gotten the tickets through a friend, and they'd had great seats. She'd seen the movie as a kid but hadn't ever seen the live production. She'd loved it. And later, on her way out, she'd bought the soundtrack of the performance. She'd uploaded the music to her computer, and then phone, and listened to it repeatedly. Macon knew this. She was playing her favorite song from the performance that night. She was playing *Somewhere*. That particular song was the quintessential song for star-crossed lovers like Tony and Maria. The lyrics were heartbreaking and hopeful at the same time.

Joanna listened as Macon played, and she sang along in her head, hearing the voice of the performer that night. Macon's eyes remained closed during the entire song. She held onto the last, perfect note before she lowered the bow and the violin, opening her eyes.

"That was the most beautiful thing I've ever seen,"

Joanna whispered after a long moment.

"You mean heard," Macon stated and bent down to place her violin on its stand.

"No, I don't," Joanna corrected.

Macon's eyes met hers; they were intensely green. They maintained their usual brightness but also included a darkness to them she hadn't noticed before this moment. Macon stood upright. Her hands went into the pockets of her jeans. Joanna stood and slowly approached her; her heart was beating wildly in her chest. Macon cleared her throat.

Joanna detected a bit of nerves from her. She couldn't understand why, but she smiled shyly at her as she leaned in and kissed Macon on the cheek. Macon turned her head a little so that her ear was now next to Joanna's still present lips. It felt like she wanted to pull away more but was trying to be polite. Joanna pulled back a little and tried to gauge her expression, but Macon's face was turned entirely to the side now. She reached her hand up to Macon's chin and turned it back to her. It was then that she knew for sure.

Macon's eyes showed desire. They showed a fire Joanna hadn't seen in them before – she'd born witness to the myriad of women that had hit on Macon in the bars, the clubs, the stores, the museums, on the streets – and damn it was hot. Macon was hot. Her olive skin, with those green eyes, was a dangerous combination. And when those eyes were dark like they were now, it was even more dangerous.

Joanna's hand moved to Macon's neck and stayed there for a second as her eyes followed the thumb she used to glide across Macon's soft skin. She could feel the pulse beneath. It was running almost as quickly as her own heart. She leaned forward again and pressed her lips to the corner of Macon's mouth. She pulled back slowly, not wanting to disconnect but needing to meet Macon's eyes again.

"Jo?"

It was a question, and Joanna wasn't sure how to answer it with words, so she didn't. She leaned forward again and pressed her lips entirely to Macon's for only a few seconds before she pulled her mouth away. She watched Macon's eyes open; her face registered something Joanna hadn't seen in it before. It was something like contentment. She leaned forward again to test not only her own reaction but Macon's as well. Her lips held onto Macon's for a second longer this time before pulling back again. To most, it was a simple, chaste kiss. But, to Joanna, it was more. She guessed by Macon's reaction that the woman felt the same. She wasn't sure if she should lean back in again, since Macon hadn't exactly responded to her kisses physically. Macon's hands were on her hips, and she pulled. Joanna wasn't ready. Macon's thumbs were under her shirt, on her stomach, while she leaned forward and captured Joanna's lips with her own.

Joanna couldn't breathe. Her lips were still; her hands were at her sides; she was completely frozen. Macon's lips were pressed hard to hers. They were attempting to move against Joanna's, but Joanna was still frozen. She was kissing Macon. Their lips were attached. She was kissing her. No, she wasn't. She wasn't technically doing the kissing; she was standing still. Macon was pulling away.

Macon's stare was worried. Joanna knew she was afraid she'd done something Joanna hadn't wanted. Her hands started to slide off, but Joanna took Macon's hands and held them in place before she leaned forward and captured Macon's lips this time. Macon responded instantly; her lips were soft but insistent; her hands were wrapping around Joanna and pulling her in closer. Joanna's went around Macon's neck and did the same. She'd never kissed a woman before. She hadn't even thought about kissing a woman before this moment; before Macon Greene.

Macon's hands were sliding up and down her back;

but over her shirt, not under it. While her hands innocently explored, her mouth was hot, open, and her tongue sought more. Joanna opened her mouth to allow her inside. As she did, she pulled them backward toward the sofa, because it suddenly felt hard to stand. Her legs were jelly as she bumped them into the table before recovering enough to move around it. Macon wasn't stopping. Her tongue was toying with Joanna's, and Joanna heard her moan a low throaty and, damn it, sexy moan.

Joanna relinquished the contact for a moment while she flopped back onto the sofa into a seated position. Macon stared down at her, as if silently asking for permission to continue. When Joanna didn't protest, that was enough for Macon to move on top of her, straddling Joanna's legs. Macon looked down at her as she licked her lips and moved those lips to Joanna's again. Joanna's hands went to Macon's back this time, while Macon's pressed into the back of the sofa on either side of Joanna's head. Joanna had never been straddled before on a sofa like this. After taking a moment to appreciate her position, she found she liked it. Macon's lips continued at their fast pace. It felt to Joanna that they couldn't get enough of her own lips, or maybe it was that Macon was trying to get as much as she could because this might end soon.

Joanna moaned this time as Macon took her bottom lip between hers, sucking on it hard. Joanna knew it would be swollen later, but she didn't care. She ran her hands up under Macon's shirt. When she felt a bra there, she stopped. Macon's hands had moved to Joanna's stomach and were about to travel under her shirt, but they stopped at Joanna's pause.

"I'm sorry," Macon said and shot back off her, almost toppling over the table as she stood up and then moved away from Joanna, touching her lips as she did.

"What?"

"I'm sorry. I thought–"

"I did," Joanna interrupted, knowing what she was

about to say. "I did, Macon."

"You don't."

"I do."

"You don't, Jo. You think you do, but you don't. I can't do that; not with you."

"Do what? Kiss me?"

"I can't *just* kiss you." Macon ran both of her hands through her dark hair.

"Why not?"

"Because I don't just want to kiss you."

"So?" Joanna stood.

"So? Joanna, you're straight! You like men. And I think when you hit my bra clasp a second ago, your brain finally remembered that I'm not a man."

"I didn't need to feel your bra to realize you aren't a man, Macon. I kind of knew that going in," she retorted. "And I kissed you back."

"You're just confused or something." Macon started to pace, and Joanna stood watching her.

"I'm not confused."

"So, you're suddenly into women?" Macon stopped.

"I don't know," Joanna replied frustrated. "I've never thought about it before you."

"I'm not an experiment, Jo."

"I know that. God, Macon! Do you really think I'd treat you like that?"

"I don't know what to think. One second, I'm playing the violin. Then, you're kissing me, and I'm kissing you back."

"Make, you played *Somewhere.*"

"I know."

"Why?"

"Because you love that song." Macon shrugged.

"I love that you know that about me." Joanna smiled at her. "Macon, I've been thinking lately... No, that's wrong. I haven't been thinking. I've been feeling. And I don't know what it all means, but I've–"

"Don't, Jo."

"Let me finish."

"Please, don't." Macon implored.

"Why not? I'm trying to tell you that I–"

"Because I won't be able to handle it when you change your mind," Macon interrupted and nearly yelled.

"What? Change my mind?"

"Jo, I wouldn't be able to handle it if something happened between us and you changed your mind. If you couldn't do it, or didn't want to be with me, I don't think I could take it." Macon paused, and Joanna noticed that the brightness in her eyes had gone. "I want you," she added. "I want you so much, sometimes, it nearly kills me not to have you. I've never felt this before, and I know it's real."

"Then, what–"

"Because I want you, but I don't just want you. I want to be with you. You might think you want it tonight, but if you wake up tomorrow and you can't be with me, then I–" She looked away. "Jo, it's too hard."

"So, you like me, but you're afraid I don't or can't like you?"

"It's not *like*, Jo." Macon turned back to her. "*Like* is something you feel when you're in an eighth grade about the girl or boy in your pre-algebra class. I don't *like* you. I *want* you." Her eyes had changed back to their former dark green shade. "I want to touch you. I want to taste your skin. I want to hear the sounds you make when you come. I want to feel your skin against my lips." She took a step toward her. "I want to bury myself inside you and come with you when I do." She paused. "I want you like crazy."

"Make–"

"And I also want to hold you after you come down, and I want to kiss your temple while you lie against my chest. I want to run my fingers up and down your back and listen to your breathing. I want to watch you sleep and hug you, kiss you before you leave for a shoot." She looked skyward for a moment and then lowered her eyes back to Joanna. "I didn't realize it until Keira pointed it out to me."

"What? Keira?"

"In her office, the other day. That's why I was so mad at her. I didn't want to believe she was right, but she is." Macon let out a sigh. "I want to be with you, Jo, but you're unavailable to me. I've been trying to get over it, but you don't make it easy."

"Macon, I'm here." Joanna tried to take a step toward her, but Macon held out her hand.

"I need you not to be."

"What? Why? Don't do this; don't push me away right now." She took that step.

"Jo, you don't want me; not like that."

"Let's just talk. I don't know what happened tonight, but—"

"Please go," Macon said.

"Make—"

"Please, Jo." Macon lowered her head.

"I'll go now, but this doesn't mean we're done with this conversation, Macon. We have things we need to talk about, to figure out. We kissed tonight; we more than kissed tonight."

"Please," Macon implored again.

Joanna couldn't stand hearing that hurt tone coming from Macon. She reached for the purse she'd dropped when she'd entered, opened the door, and turned back once more to see if Macon was watching. When she discovered she wasn't, Joanna left the apartment.

CHAPTER 10

GREENE STARED AT THE CEILING above her bed all night, trying to get her brain to quiet and her heart to stop thumping long enough for her to get some sleep, but sleep never came. She was just going through the motions as she showered around eight in the morning and left for orchestra rehearsal at the normal time, but. When she got there, she took her usual seat and played through the rehearsal with no real emotion. She got called out by the conductor once – which hadn't happened to her since she first started – and then packed up to go, stopping at Rose's office.

"Hey," she greeted.

"Miss Greene, how are you?"

"I'm in."

"I'm sorry?"

"For the tour, I'm in," she said and stared at the floor. "When do I leave?"

"That's great news. I'll call the coordinator right now and let her know. You'll leave for Sydney next weekend."

"Can I leave sooner?" she asked.

"Sooner?"

"I just think it'll be better if I get there a little earlier, check out everything, meet the people."

"Oh, when do you–"

"Sunday," Macon interrupted. "We have the performance tomorrow night. I can leave this Sunday."

"You'll be ready by then?"

"Yes."

"I'll have my assistant reach out once the flights and hotels are confirmed." She smiled at her. "Miss Greene, this is amazing news: great for the orchestra and great for your career; six major cities in thirty days."

***

The offer had come out of nowhere but, at the same time, it had been expected. Usually, once a season or so, she'd get an offer like this to visit cities and sit in on their symphony. When she'd been a student at the conservatory, she'd been at the top of her class. In their performances, she'd been noticed by many in the field. Some of them had kept up with her and continued to ask about her. She'd had offers to move to just about every major symphony in the country, and a few international ones as well. She'd always turned them down, until now. Now, she wanted to leave. No, she wanted to flee.

Joanna's kiss had been better than she could have ever imagined. And the thought that they could have gone further last night – that Greene could have taken things further and could have had her and then lost her come morning when Joanna said she was straight and regretted the whole thing – stung worse than not having her like that at all. Greene couldn't risk that.

She received the flight confirmation for her flight from San Francisco to Sydney. With that came her hotel confirmation for Sydney for a week, followed by Rome for four days, Vienna after that, Paris, and London, with her last stop being in New York; and then home, to rejoin the orchestra.

Greene did her best not to think about Joanna all night again, but she'd failed miserably. By Saturday evening, she was getting ready for the performance. She was forced to push Joanna out of her mind so she could focus on the music. She thought about how different it would be on tour, where she was a featured soloist and would perform two or three pieces with the orchestra and at least one on her own, or with only a piano or bass and cello. In Paris, she'd have a quartet piece, and a viola would join in that, but she was still the named musician. This, as Rose hoped, could be the beginning of her solo career. Or, it could go horribly wrong, and she'd never tour again.

She played her solo, and then they finished the performance, bowed, as was the custom, and headed backstage to pack up and say her goodnights and also her temporary goodbyes. It took her longer than usual to make her way out to the street to head home and sulk.

"Macon Greene, can I have your autograph?"

Greene turned to see Joanna standing there, with a bouquet of colorful flowers and a hopeful smile on her face.

"What are you doing here?" she asked.

"I saw the performance."

"You were in the audience?"

Joanna walked toward her and said, "These are for you."

"Jo–"

"And before you start interrupting me, like you did the other night, just shut up." She passed Greene the flowers. "Macon, I don't know what's going on with us, but I do know that I haven't been able to stop thinking about you since that kiss, or I guess those kisses, since there were more than one. I don't want things to be awkward between us now. We never go this long without talking to one another."

"I'm leaving, Jo."

"I'll come with you. I–"

"I'm leaving San Francisco."

Joanna's face immediately changed as she asked, "You're what?"

"It's just for a month. I'm going on tour: six cities in thirty days."

"When? Why didn't you tell me?"

"I accepted the offer yesterday."

"After we kissed?"

"They offered it to me before."

"But you accepted after?"

"Yeah," she admitted.

"When do you leave?"

"Tomorrow."

"Tomorrow?" Joanna looked around as if checking for an answer somewhere on the street. "You leave tomorrow? For where?"

"Sydney."

"You're going to Australia tomorrow?"

"Yes."

Joanna shook her head back and forth in disbelief.

"Were you going to tell me?"

"I haven't told anyone about it yet. I was going to call everyone tomorrow."

"Everyone including me?"

"Yes, Jo," she confirmed. "I was going to call before I headed to the airport."

"So, you would be calling to say goodbye." Joanna was angry, and Greene knew it was all her fault. "We kissed, Greene. You kissed me. I kissed you back. I wanted to keep going. You're the one that pulled away, and now you're doing it again."

"You called me *Greene*. You never call me that."

"Well, I'm not feeling like myself much right now."

"Yeah, that's what I'm worried about." Greene lowered the flowers to her side.

"What's that supposed to mean?"

"It means it happens, Jo. A lesbian kisses a straight woman; the straight woman thinks she wants it and then changes her mind. I can't do that with you. I want too much with you. I told you that."

"This isn't some lame lesbian movie you watched ten years ago, Macon." She returned to Greene's first name, which always sounded so good coming from her. "I'm not some character; I'm real. I have real feelings. And, yeah, I'll admit, I don't have them all figured out right now, but you're not exactly giving me a chance, either."

"I can't be around you and not be with you, Jo. And I don't think I can be with you either."

"Because you're scared. You're scared of so much, aren't you? You're scared of letting anyone really see you. You're terrified that if they find out who you really are, they'll leave." She paused, turned, and then turned back. "But you're the one that's leaving. Remember that, Macon. You're the one leaving for a month."

"You're the one that wanted me to go on tour."

"I'm the one that wants you to be *yourself*. I don't care if you're a famous violinist or if you're, I don't know, a high school guidance counselor, Macon. I don't care. I want you to be you. I want you to be happy," Joanna argued. "If you don't want to go on this damn tour, don't go. In fact, stay and talk to me. But if you want to go, then go. I'm done trying to convince you to be an adult and just talk to me about what's going on." She turned once more. "Don't expect me to be waiting around when you get back though." She started walking.

***

The next morning, Joanna received a text. She was sitting at her desk, staring at pictures of another newborn in a basket, when it flashed across the upper right-hand corner of her screen because she'd linked her phone to her computer a long time ago. She clicked on the notification to read the message on her screen.

"My flight takes off in a few minutes. I'm going to be

in the air for the next fifteen hours. I didn't sleep last night, Jo. I'm sorry. I'm scared. I've been here before, and I didn't care about her like I care about you. I'm sorry."

Joanna read and reread the message before clicking away the messages window and returning to her editing.

***

Three days later, Joanna was heading out of the coffee shop she used to frequent with Macon and heard her name called from behind her.

"Russell?"

"Hey, I'm getting one of those myself. I didn't know you come here," he said, referencing her cup.

"Yeah, not often," she returned.

Russell was about 6'3" with short dark hair he had in a semi-spike. His eyes were gray. He had a slight five o'clock shadow seemingly all the time. He was dressed in a gray suit that matched his eyes and a pinstripe shirt with a light blue tie. His shoes matched his black belt and were clearly expensive.

"I'd offer to buy you one, but you've already got your own there."

"I was just on my way to a shoot."

"Listen, I can take a hint, I promise." He smiled at her. "I get it: you're not interested. I've stopped my incessant texting, and I'll leave you alone. I just thought we got along well when you did the work for the magazine, and I had to try."

"I'm sorry, Russell. I've been busy lately. I've been working pretty much non-stop. I didn't reply to you; that was rude, and I'm sorry."

"So, you wanted to reply but couldn't?" he asked, and Joanna realized she'd given him and in.

"I kind of stopped dating when I started working in photography full-time. It takes a lot to get a business up and running."

"Do you maybe want to grab a drink with me tonight? No pressure." He held out his hands, palms forward. "You can totally say no. I know it's last minute. It can just be two people getting to know each other outside of work; nothing more."

She thought first of Macon, who was probably on a beach somewhere in Sydney, watching girls in bikinis walk past while she sipped on a fruity drink. Actually, it was nighttime there; she was more likely asleep. Joanna had added Sydney time to her world clock feature on her phone the day after Macon's message. She'd also looked up the tour she was on since it was listed on the orchestra's site, and added Paris, London, Vienna, and Rome. Even though some of those times were the same, she liked having the names of the cities Macon would be in on her phone. She would have added New York, too, but it had already been there. She then thought about how she had no romantic feelings thus far for Russell, but he was an attractive man who had been nothing but nice to her since they'd met a few months ago.

"Okay."

"Okay?"

"Sure. Tonight."

"I'll pick you up… or wait, no. I'll meet you there. It's not a date. Sorry."

"I'll meet you there," she said. "Where and what time?"

***

Greene woke on her fourth day in Australia. She still hadn't adjusted to the time zone. She had left her hotel room only for food and to go to the hall where she'd met some of the people she'd be working with. She used one of their music rooms to rehearse for a couple of hours each day. That had been her life since she'd arrived in one of the most beautiful cities on earth.

She hadn't heard back from Joanna. She wondered if she'd ever talk to her again. The way she'd acted with her that night, and the night they'd kissed, had probably been inexcusable. Joanna deserved better.

"Macon Greene, right?" a girl in her mid-twenties with an Australian accent asked the moment Greene exited the soundproof music room, carrying her sheet music and her violin.

"That's me," Greene replied.

"I know. I've seen all the posters." She referenced the promo posters that had been put up around the building. "I'm Gail, Mr. Abernathy's assistant."

"Nice to meet you."

"He sent me to check on you; make sure you had everything you needed."

"I'm good. Thanks." She started walking with Gail following and then joining her.

"Great. I'm glad to hear it. He wanted to coordinate with you to make sure you get a chance to see the sights. I think he's hoping you'll finish the tour and leave San Francisco to come here."

"What?"

"Oh, no. He doesn't think you'll stay here. I mean, he might. I think he'd love it if he could get you to stay on, but he hasn't put a plan in motion to win you over or anything. I'm sorry. I'm just a little nervous," she admitted and then promptly delivered a nervous laugh. "I'm sorry. You're just, like, really pretty. I saw it in the posters and in pictures but, up-close, you're even prettier. I tend to get nervous around pretty girls."

"Oh."

"Sorry, I heard you were gay. Is that just a rumor and I'm completely wrong?"

"No, I am," Greene replied.

"Me too," she replied with a smile. She was a cute girl. She had curly, strawberry blonde hair and light blue eyes. But the blue eyes reminded her of Joanna's eyes. "Do you maybe want to hang out tonight? There's this lesbian bar some of my friends and I go to. It's called *Betty's*. You might like it."

"No, thanks," she said and shifted her violin case over her shoulder.

"Oh, okay."

Gail was disappointed. Greene felt bad that she'd disappointed her.

"What time?"

"Sorry?" Gail lifted her eyes to Greene's.

"No promises. I'm still trying to get used to the time difference. I might fall asleep when I get back to my hotel, but I might try and make it."

"We'll be there around nine." Gail smiled again.

"Nine. Okay."

"See you then," she said as Greene began walking off.

"Maybe."

CHAPTER 11

"HAVE YOU heard from her?" Keira asked as they sat at lunch the following Saturday.

"She sent me a text before she took off. That's it," Joanna replied.

"I got one of those, too." Keira took a drink of her iced tea. "I still cannot believe she just took off like that. It's so unlike her."

Joanna hadn't told Keira, or anyone else for that matter, about the kiss or their fight after. She wasn't sure what Macon would be comfortable with them knowing.

"Yeah," she agreed half-heartedly.

"I really thought she would have told you before she just up and left."

"Why?"

"Because you're the best friend," Keira argued. "You two have been crazy close."

"Crazy close," Joanna repeated for some reason.

"What's up with you?" Keira laughed. "You seem different."

"Nothing. I'm fine."

"It bothers you, doesn't it?"

"What?"

"That she left and gave you no notice."

"It's her job. She can do what she wants."

"You want to maybe try telling me the truth there?"

"I miss her; that's all. We spent practically every day together, and now she's gone."

"I get it, but are you sure that's it?"

"Yeah, why?"

"Did something happen with you two?"

"No."

"Nothing? Really?"

"Keira, what's this about?"

"I don't know. It just seemed like something was up at After Dark."

"No, we just enjoyed the exhibits."

"Until she fled," Keira returned. "For the first time, but not the last time in the same week."

"She got upset with me because I was asking her questions that night."

"Questions about?"

"Keira, I know what you're getting at. Just say it."

"Did she try something?"

"No, *I* did," she confessed. "I tried something. She rejected me. Happy?"

Keira's eyes were big. She'd been lucky she hadn't been drinking her tea, because she coughed out her surprise.

"You tried something?"

"I kissed her, and then she kissed me back. And it was good, but she freaked out and sent me away. When I tried to talk to her about it, she rejected even the conversation and then ran off to Australia. She couldn't get much farther away from me right now. So, yes, something happened. But, no, it's not going to happen again."

"Wait. Didn't you tell me this morning you went out with Russell this week?"

"I did, because I told her I wouldn't wait for her to get her ass back here, and she seemed to think I wanted men and wouldn't ever want her for real. I said yes to drinks, and then we went out again last night, and he tried to kiss me."

"Tried?" Keira dropped the fork she'd been holding still onto her salad plate.

"He leaned in, and, yes – our mouths connected. Technically, it was a kiss. But I didn't kiss him back, and he pulled away as soon as he realized. I told him it wasn't going anywhere between us. I didn't tell him why, though, because I don't even know myself."

"Because you have a thing for Greene?"

"She won't *let* me have a thing for her even if I do. So, what's the point? I just know Russell's not the guy. I tried to force something that's not there just to see if she was right. But I can't imagine kissing anyone other than her right now."

"So, you liked it?"

"I loved it, Keira. She's…" Joanna looked away from Keira. "I've never thought of a woman the way I think about her."

"And you think about her like that? Like you'd do more than kiss her?"

"I have, yeah."

"You have?"

"I don't understand it. We've been friends; I love her as my friend. She's such a great person. But, recently, I've been thinking about her in that way you shouldn't think about friends, especially when you've always considered yourself to be straight and that best friend is a gorgeous gay lady."

"You think she's gorgeous?" Keira chuckled.

"Have you seen her? She's hot," Joanna said. "She's *beautiful,* and she's hot," she clarified.

"And you want to have sex with her? You could have sex with her? With a woman?"

"It doesn't matter. She doesn't think I can. Actually, she thinks if I did – if we did – I'd snap back into my apparent straightness right after or the next morning."

"You should talk to her."

"I tried. She left."

"She cares about you, Joanna. I know it; Emma knows it. Hillary can see it, and she's hardly around these days. Hell, even Mason and Maggie noticed. It's obvious."

"And you warned her not to be with me."

"No, I warned her to take care of herself, because I thought she was falling for a straight woman who would turn her down if she did anything. I was wrong. I knew it last Thursday night for sure."

"What? How?" Joanna glared at her.

"I saw you two in the room: she was teaching you how to play, and you were enjoying it. When she moved back, your face changed. Emma caught it first. She said you were smiling and happy, and then you weren't when Greene stepped back. Then, you two were doing something at the door; she put her hands on your waist. I saw your reaction, and it hit me that it's not just one-sided."

"It is, though, because she doesn't feel it enough to try."

"She does." Keira placed her hand on top of Joanna's on the table. "She does. She just doesn't know how to tell you, or show you. She's not exactly the relationship type, Joanna. She dates a lot, but she doesn't do relationships."

"You guys all make these assumptions about her; you know that? You assume that because she flirts with a woman at a bar, or because she goes out with one a few times, that they're hooking up and then she drops them. But she doesn't."

"She hasn't recently. Honestly, she stopped when she met you."

"And I stopped dating when I met her."

"Until Russell."

"Russell was a mistake, and nothing happened."

"So, I'm curious: if you and Greene don't happen, would you be open to dating another woman?"

"I don't want another woman."

"But would you be open to it?"

"Are you trying to ask if I'm bisexual?"

"I'm just trying to figure it out probably in a similar way that Greene is."

"I don't know. I just know that I like her in a way I hadn't expected. When I kissed her, it felt good. It felt right. I haven't had that in a long time; maybe ever."

"Then, you should really tell her that."

"I tried. She's not interested."

"Try again. Nothing good seems to come easy," Keira advised.

***

"You were amazing, Greene," Gail told her.

"Thanks."

"Did you have fun the other night?" she asked as they made their way down the hall after Greene's first of three performances with the symphony.

"At *Betty's*?"

"Yeah."

"Sure. Your friends are nice." Greene headed to the outer doors.

"We have what, three more days here?"

"Four days and three nights," Greene corrected.

"Right." Gail pushed open one of the doors for them. "I was thinking that maybe you'd want to hang out tonight."

"Tonight?"

"Yeah, it's only 9:30. I'm starving. We could grab a late dinner and then maybe go back to my place, or there's always your hotel; I have two roommates."

"Oh."

Greene's phone chimed with a text message. She'd gotten a few when she'd first arrived from her friends, checking on her and also expressing their anger with her departing so quickly. She pulled the phone out of her pocket with a jump in her heart rate, hoping to see Joanna's name there, but she frowned when she saw Keira's name instead.

Keira: *You're going to lose her if you don't stop acting like an asshole.*

"Everything okay?" Gail asked.

"Yeah, sorry." She went to stuff the phone back in her pocket, but it chimed again.

Keira: *She's going on dates, Greene.*

Greene shoved the phone back into her pocket and stared at the poster on the wall that had her picture on it, advertising the show.

"Do you need to make a call?"

"No, it's nothing." She looked over to Gail, who appeared confused. "Listen, Gail… I can do dinner, and I can hang out, but that's it, okay? If you're looking for more than a friend, I can't be that for you."

Gail seemed a little shocked at that response, but she smiled all the same.

"Something you want to talk about?" She nodded toward Greene's pocket where she'd just stuffed her phone. "I can listen. I'll admit that I did want more. I had fun the other night with you. But if you're not interested, that's okay, too."

"I'm not," Greene returned. "But it's not about you."

"I get it. Another woman?"

"Something like that." Greene made her way to the parking lot, with Gail at her side. "How about we just go to the hotel restaurant? We can eat and charge it to the room."

"Sounds like a plan to me."

CHAPTER 12

JOANNA THOUGHT back to the night with Russell as she stared blankly at her computer screen. She'd had a wedding shoot she needed to edit and get turned over to the client, but she'd been putting it off. He'd been a perfect gentleman. He'd asked her out officially, and they'd gone to dinner the next night. Again, he'd pulled out her chair and opened doors for her. He offered his arm to her as they walked. He probably would have offered his jacket had she not had her own. He'd been a perfect first date. They'd shared a great conversation about her work, his work, and how they intersected. They spoke about their upbringings, schools, and hobbies. When their conversation died out over coffee, he'd paid the bill, and they'd stood to go. He'd walked her home, and at her front door, he'd kissed her.

As she sat staring at her computer, she glanced at the time. It was six minutes after five. She'd been at the office for most of the day, meeting with existing and potential clients and scolding Keira for a certain text message she'd sent to Macon without telling her. Joanna had asked her politely to send Macon another one, clarifying that she was not dating anyone. She'd gone on one mistake of a date, and it had ended there. She wasn't exactly waiting around for Macon Greene, but she couldn't seem to move beyond what it had felt like to kiss her and be kissed by her either. She couldn't remember how it felt to touch the last man she'd been with, or even how Russell's brief kiss had felt against her lips – and that had only been a few days prior. She could remember every single sensation from her all too brief encounter with Macon: there were her soft and full lips, and they moved so perfectly against her own; there was the feel of Macon's hands on her skin, and the feel of Joanna's hands on Macon's back; Macon's bra that she'd almost undone but had hesitated. That hesitation was likely why Macon was in Australia, where it was six minutes after ten in the morning.

Her phone rang. She removed her headphones that had been plugged into the computer as she listened to the *West Side Story* soundtrack for the thousandth time. She glanced over at it, preparing to tell whoever it was that she was busy, when she saw Macon's face and her name and number.

"Hey."

"Hi," Macon said. Joanna closed her eyes at the sound of her voice. "What are you doing?"

"In my office, editing. What are you doing?" She leaned back in her office chair.

"I'm lying in my hotel room. I have rehearsal in about an hour."

"Sydney?"

"Last show," she replied.

"Then?"

"Rome."

"Have you ever been?"

"No," Macon said. "I've never really been anywhere. I'll be in all these cities for the first time, except for New York."

Joanna stared at her floor for a moment and asked,

"How are you?"

"Are you dating someone?" Macon asked almost at the same time.

"I'm going to murder Keira," Joanna grunted. "No, I'm not. I went on *a* date; one date. And it was a mistake."

"With whom?"

"Macon, you left. Why–"

"I know," she interrupted. "I know, and I'm sorry."

"You're sorry?"

"Can we start over?"

"Why do we need to start over? How would we even do that, Macon?"

"I like when you call me *Macon*. No one else can do that; only you." Joanna could hear Macon smiling through the phone.

"I don't want to start over with you. I just want you to be honest with me."

"About how I feel?"

"About that. About why you ran. About how you are there." She hesitated and closed her eyes. "About if you're dating anyone or–"

"No," Macon said immediately. "No, I'm not. And I don't want to date anyone."

"Have you–"

"No, I haven't slept with anyone, Jo. I don't want to do that either."

"I didn't know. You just left. You were angry."

"I don't deal with my anger with sex. You know that about me."

"I do."

"Did you go out with a guy?" Macon asked.

"Yes. Because I did express my anger with you–"

"With sex?" Macon asked.

"What? No," she rejected. "Macon, it was Russell. I ran into him, and he asked me out. I was upset with you, but I was also trying to figure out–"

"Why you kissed me?"

"Yes," she confessed. "I thought, stupidly, that if I went out with him, and felt about him how I feel about you, that I could somehow get past it."

"How *do* you feel about me?"

"Right now? I'm a little annoyed," she admitted. "And I can't stop thinking about you."

"I can't stop thinking about you."

She smiled at the sound of Macon's voice saying those words.

"Macon, he kissed me. It was a peck really, and I pulled away."

"Oh."

"I stopped him, because he wasn't you," she revealed and stood. "Macon, I kissed you, and it opened this whole new world to me, because *you* opened this whole new world to me. God, when I first met Emma, I had to admit that she was the first lesbian I'd really gotten to know. Then, I met you. I felt like I had a real friend – and not one of those friends from work, or friends you have on Facebook or sometimes see after a few years, but someone I would be friends with forever." Joanna paused and walked to her bed, sitting on the end of it. "But I think it might have always been more than that, and I just didn't know."

"For me too."

"I don't know what that makes me, but I don't think that makes me straight, Macon. I've never felt how I felt when you kissed me. It was, God… it was perfect. I could do that for hours, I think: kiss you like that."

"You could?"

"Yes." Joanna practically giggled. "Never tell me how many women you've kissed like that, by the way."

Macon laughed. Joanna adored the sound of it.

"I've never kissed anyone like that, Jo," she shared. "I've kissed a lot of women, but I've never kissed anyone like that."

"Like what?"

"Like it's all I want to do for the rest of my life," Macon offered.

Joanna smiled at that and bit her lip to hold back a gleeful yet embarrassing outburst.

"So, you only want to kiss me? You don't want anything else?"

"Oh, I want *everything* else." Macon's voice had grown sexier, deeper at that. "But do *you* want everything else?"

"I want you to touch me, if that's what you're asking."

"You do? How?"

Joanna flopped back onto her bed, leaving her legs hanging over the side.

"I don't know," she replied, suddenly embarrassed.

"Yes, you do."

"You really want to know?"

"Yes."

"I had this dream one night." Joanna toyed with the strings of her sweatpants.

"About me?" Macon asked.

"About you."

"What were we doing?"

"We weren't doing anything; I was just lying there. *You* were doing things."

"I was?"

"You were between my legs." Joanna felt the redness in her cheeks burn as she remembered what it had looked like to have Macon between her legs, but more importantly, what it had felt like.

"I was?" Macon was breathing a little harder now.

"Yeah."

"Do you want me to do that to you?"

"I don't know."

"Oh."

"No, Macon. It's not like that." Joanna stopped playing with the strings at the sound of Macon's disappointment. "It's not a woman thing. It's because I haven't done that before."

"No one's gone down on you?" the woman replied, surprised.

"No one ever seemed to want to," she answered the question with a new surge of embarrassment.

"But I bet every guy you dated expected a blow job, right? Wait... Don't tell me. I don't want to know." She paused, and her breathing increased again. "I want to do that to you, Jo."

"You do?"

"Yes," Macon gasped out.

"What else do you want?" Joanna asked and toyed with those strings again.

"You, in every way I can have you," Macon returned. "God, I can't believe we're talking about this, and I'm not there to touch you."

"Like I'd let you." Joanna giggled and felt like a schoolgirl.

"What if I kissed you first?"

"Maybe."

"And if I ran my hands up and down your sides?"

"Maybe," she said between quick breaths.

"And if I kissed your neck and ran my tongue along your collarbone?"

"It's possible."

Her fingers had stilled. Her hand was now flicking at the waistband of her sweatpants.

"And if I lowered you onto the bed, climbed on top of you, and spread your legs with my hand so I could rest my hips between your legs and rock into them?"

"Jesus." Joanna breathed and slid her hand just under the waistband and over the purple panties she had on under them.

"Yeah?" Macon asked, and Joanna realized the woman was breathing just as hard as she was.

"Yes."

"And if I took off your shirt and your bra?"

"Macon, this isn't fair."

"Why not?"

"Because you're there."

"I know."

"And I want you here."

"Pretend that I am," she suggested.

"How?"

Macon didn't answer right away. Joanna wondered if she'd said something wrong. Had she embarrassed herself without even knowing? She'd never talked like this before, and not just with another woman, but with anyone.

"Jo?"

"Yeah?"

"I'm touching myself," Macon admitted.

"You are?" Joanna couldn't believe it. She was listening to Macon while she was doing things to her own body. The jolt of electricity flew through her and down to the spot between her legs. She grew instantly wetter after having been turned on since this conversation had turned heated. "What are you doing? I mean, what—" She stopped. "I've never done this, Macon."

"We don't have to now," Macon said, but Joanna could recognize her short bursts of breathlessness into the phone.

"No, don't stop," she replied. "Just tell me."

"I've been thinking about doing things to you since I woke up this morning. I wasn't going to do this, but then we started talking, and I couldn't stop myself."

"Then, don't."

"Jo, I want you."

"Where is your hand right now?"

"In reality or in my mind?"

"Both." Joanna's hand moved under her panties, but she held it there.

"I'm stroking my clit right now, slowly," Macon replied. "But I'm thinking about doing that to you."

"Touching me?"

"Yes." It was a gasp.

"Will you, when you get back?"

"Yes." Another gasp.

Joanna slid her hand down further and cupped her own sex.

"Make, you sound…" She couldn't describe how good Macon sounded.

"Jo, I'm sorry," she said. "I'm sorry I left. I should be there. I should be there with you, touching you like this."

"Or, I could be touching you," Joanna suggested.

"Yeah?" Macon asked.

"How do you like to be touched?"

Joanna bent her index finger to find her clit and start stroking it. She found it hard and swollen. She was wetter than she'd been in a very long time.

"Slow at first," Macon replied.

"Like you're doing now?"

"Yes." Macon gasped again. "But I need to start going fast."

"Where is my mouth, Make? Where do you want it on your body right now?"

"My nipple."

Joanna's eyes shot closed and then open as she slid her two fingers up and down hard while picturing Macon's breasts in her mind, or at least what she thought they'd look like. She'd never touched another woman's breasts, but when Macon said those words, she pictured her lips around a hard, erect nipple, sucking it into her mouth. Her strokes turned harder and faster in an instant.

"So, my fingers are stroking your clit, and my mouth is sucking on your nipple."

"Yes." Macon's word was louder this time, and somehow, the one-syllable word sounded clipped. "Yes."

"Are you–"

"Yes," she repeated. "I'm almost…"

"Oh, my God." Joanna stopped touching herself

because she wanted to listen. She needed to listen. "Please… I want to hear you."

"Jo," Macon said her name right before she moaned, then cursed, and then breathed into the phone.

Joanna couldn't believe what she'd just heard; what she'd participated in. She'd heard Macon come for her and while saying her name. Joanna's hand was still unmoving. She no longer felt the need for her own orgasm. She wanted Macon to do that again, and again, and she wanted to hear it in person; to see it in person.

"Macon?" she checked after a long moment of silence.

"I'm sorry. I shouldn't have–"

"Stop," Joanna interrupted her. "That was… God, that was hot, and it was beautiful at the same time."

"It was?" Macon asked.

"I want to do that again," she said.

"Me too. I want to hear you. Will you–" There was a sound Joanna couldn't identify. "Shit. I just looked at the time. I've got to go, Jo. I'm sorry. I'm going to be late for rehearsal."

"It's okay."

She heard Macon start moving around the room and suspected she was trying to find clothes for the day or grabbing a towel so she could go shower.

"No, it's not. I don't want to stop right now, but I have to go. The car will be here in twenty minutes," Macon explained. "Can you tell me something though?"

"Yeah?"

"Did you start?"

"Yes."

"Jesus Christ," Macon exclaimed. "I hate myself right now."

Joanna laughed out at that response.

"Because?"

"Because I'm not fucking there. Because I ran here. I miss you, Jo. I really fucking miss you."

"I miss you, too."

"I didn't scare you with that, did I?"

"No, Make. I'm not scared. I'm not scared of you."

"Can I call you tomorrow morning your time so we can talk?"

"Talk?" Joanna toyed and realized her hand was still between her legs.

"Talk, yes. If other stuff happens, so be it." She laughed. "I want you to catch me up on what I've missed."

"And I want you to tell me about your first tour."

"You know what it felt like when we kissed, Jo?"

"What?"

"Like I'm yours," Macon admitted. "It felt like I'm yours."

CHAPTER 13

GREENE CHECKED her phone for about the fifth time since they'd wrapped up. It was four in the afternoon. She'd wrapped up the rehearsal and had used one of the music rooms to work on the new piece she'd need for Rome. She'd been mad at herself because she'd planned on wrapping up early enough to give Joanna a goodnight phone call, even though they'd agreed to a phone call in her morning. This whole time difference thing was confusing. This time of year, they were seventeen hours apart but on different days. All she knew for sure was that what they'd done this morning she'd also never done with anyone.

She hadn't planned it. But talking to Joanna about that, turned her on in a way she'd never been turned on, and before she knew it, she was touching herself. She'd fallen asleep only in her underwear and a t-shirt the night before. After talking to Gail and thinking about Joanna more and more, she couldn't resist calling her. She needed to hear her voice, even if Joanna was dating someone.

Greene made her way back to the hotel and checked the clock. It would be around midnight in San Francisco. She knew Joanna would be asleep, but she couldn't resist calling. Even if she got her voicemail, she'd be able to hear her outgoing message.

"Hey there," Joanna greeted in her sleepy voice.

"Hi." Greene smiled as she laid back in bed. "Were you asleep?"

"I was, yeah. Someone told me she was calling me in the morning. I wanted to get a good night's sleep," she replied.

"I'm sorry."

"Don't be," Joanna said. "Is everything okay?"

"Everything's fine. I just wanted to hear your voice."

"Oh, if your friends could hear you now." She laughed.

"What's that mean?"

"You are a smooth talker, Macon Greene, but you are also very romantic and sweet."

"I am?"

"Yes, you are. It's one of my favorite things about you."

"You know what one of my favorite things about you is?" Greene asked.

"No, what?"

"How forgiving you are, especially where I'm concerned."

"And you're cute, too? I have got to tell Keira."

Greene laughed and said, "I'm serious."

"I know you are. Where were all these words when we were in the same room, Macon? It would have been nice to look at you while you said them."

Greene had to agree with that. It would be nice to look at Joanna while they talked. That was something she could fix, though. She hit a button on the screen of her phone and waited.

"Okay," she said.

"Are you trying to FaceTime?"

"Yes. If you want to see me while I say these things, you should probably accept."

"Macon, I was asleep. I look–"

"Accept the FaceTime, Jo," she ordered gently. A moment later, she saw Joanna's face appear on the screen; she had turned on the lamp next to her bed to illuminate herself for the call. "God, you're gorgeous."

"Stop."

"No, you are, Jo," she told her. "Remember when we watched that movie, you got drunk and slept over?"

"Of course, I remember."

"I watched you sleep. Technically, I woke up before

you, and I saw your early morning bed head and your eyes as they opened. You're beautiful, and that doesn't change when you wake up."

"I miss you," Joanna said.

"I miss you, too."

"No chance I can convince you to come back, now that we're doing whatever it is that we're doing?"

"I wish. I'm contractually obligated to be here now. I'm sorry. I shouldn't have accepted the tour. I should have just talked to you about what I was scared of and how I felt."

"I'm glad you're there, Macon. You should be on tour. You're so good at what you do. Everyone should see you play."

"I want to be there with you, though."

"Then, finish the tour and come home to me." She said with a smile.

"Home?"

"Yes, Macon. Come home to me, here, in San Francisco."

She smiled as she watched Joanna's mock frustration unfold on the screen.

"I'm not going to date anyone else, Jo."

"Oh," she replied, confused. "Was that an option or a possibility?"

"No, that's not what I meant. I don't mean that I was, but I'm not now. I mean that I never was; I was never going to date someone or do anything with any woman even before this morning when we talked."

"So, why are you telling me now then?"

"Because I don't know if you will." Macon hesitated. "I mean, will you date a guy or another woman, or would you be open to–"

"Macon Sage Greene, are you kidding me right now?"

"What? No." Greene stared at her curiously.

"I'm not going to date anyone. You're crazy if you

think I'd do what we did this morning and then go find someone else to date until you get back."

"Okay, okay." Greene laughed. "I'm sorry. I just wanted to be clear about my intentions and find out yours."

"What *are* your intentions then?" Joanna lifted an eyebrow.

"To make you my girlfriend when I get home," she answered honestly.

Joanna didn't say anything at first. She just smiled back.

"Why not now?"

"Because when I ask that question, I want to be able to kiss you after you say yes."

"Why are you assuming I'd say yes?"

"You'd totally say yes," Greene replied.

"Maybe I wouldn't. I like to keep you guessing."

Greene laughed at her again, and then her laughter subsided into a smile.

"You should get some sleep. I still want to talk to you in the morning, you know?"

"Is this what we're going to do while you're gone? Talk twice a day?"

"Is that okay?"

"It's kind of the best we can do right now, I guess."

"We can FaceTime like this, too, so I can see your face."

"And I can see yours." Joanna smiled.

"Yeah."

"It's like five there. What are you doing for dinner?"

"I'll order room service or something when I get hungry."

"And then after that?"

"Take a long bath to wind down."

"Wind down?" Joanna's eyebrow was lifted.

"Yeah, I've been a little keyed up all day. I wonder why." Greene laughed lightly at her.

"No idea. I should get some sleep, though. I kind of had an eventful afternoon." She wiggled her eyebrows.

"How eventful?" Greene glared.

"Pretty eventful. Like two times kind of eventful." Joanna must have noticed Greene's eyes get really big because she started laughing. "Goodnight, Macon."

"You're kidding, right? You're going to sleep after you tell me that?"

"Yup. Call me tomorrow."

"I will." Greene was still laughing when Joanna's face froze for a second and then disappeared as she hung up. "Fuck!" She tossed the phone on the bed, knowing she'd have to do something other than take a long bath to calm herself down now.

***

"So, you are dating?" Emma asked Joanna as they sat at the bar.

"I guess. I don't really know." Joanna took a drink of her rum and Coke.

"You guess?" Emma laughed.

"Yeah, I guess." Joanna laughed back, because it did sound funny. "We're not exactly in the same place. The time differences have made things complicated, but I guess we're long-distance dating. Macon said she wants me to be her girlfriend, though. She just wants to ask in person."

"Seriously?" Emma's eyebrows lifted. "That's kind of remarkable and adorable."

"Remarkable?"

"I've only known her as long as you, but according to Keira and Hillary, Greene was never one to settle down; not that you two are settling down or anything."

"You guys crack me up sometimes."

"How so?" Emma asked.

"What do you think she does every night?"

"Huh?"

"With women? What do you all think? She goes out to the bar and takes a different girl home each night?"

"Not each night, no."

"But often?"

"I guess, yeah." Emma took a sip of her wine.

"So, let me run this by you," Joanna requested. "We all come here and have some drinks, she talks to a girl, and then what? She comes back to our table, right?"

"Yeah."

"And then she and I leave together, or I leave, and she follows pretty closely behind, right?"

"Are you trying to tell me you two have been–"

"No, we haven't." Joanna laughed again. "She has one show night every week, at least; she rehearses for hours a day and, sometimes, completely loses track of time and misses a dinner or drinks, right?"

"Yeah."

"And the rest of the time, she's usually with me or with all of us. I spend nearly every night with her. Not like that," she added at the end. "I have lunch or dinner with her almost daily. We watch TV or talk until it's time for me to go home or for her to leave. I know she goes home because she texts and sometimes even calls me because I insist on her letting me know she's gotten home safe. She makes me do the same. Sometimes we talk for another hour or so before we both go to bed."

"And you *guess* you're dating?"

"My point isn't that we've been dancing around this for a while now. My point is that you guys must think she has more hours in the day than the rest of us. When exactly is she supposed to be hooking up with all these women?" Joanna asked and took another drink.

"I guess I never thought about it like that."

"None of you have. I think someone said something years ago in their little group of friends about her hitting on a lot of women or having sex with some of them and it somehow turned into this thing that she's hooking up with every woman in the city."

"But she's not? Or at least she hasn't since meeting you?"

"Since before that even. I'm not going to tell you anything I think she should probably be the one to explain, but Macon isn't this Lothario you all make her out to be. She's nice to women, yes. She might flirt back. She might even kiss a few of them. But she's not taking them home with her. In fact, she told me she'd never had a woman in her apartment: a woman she wanted to sleep with or has slept with."

"You've been in her apartment. She wants to sleep with you," Emma posited.

"Well, that's a recent occurrence."

Emma nearly cackled at that and said, "If by *recent* you mean since the moment Greene laid eyes on you..."

"She did not–"

"Oh, yeah, she did." Emma turned her entire body on her stool to face Joanna. "Keira doesn't know this, because Greene asked me not to say anything. She knows how my girlfriend is: she's like a dog with a bone, sometimes. Back then, neither of them knew you well. Keira might have tried to test the waters with you; see if you'd be into the idea of converting our wayward flirt of a friend into having a serious relationship. Once she knew you were straight for sure, though, she would have tried to intervene, to prevent Greene from getting too involved, because she wouldn't want her to end up getting hurt." Emma smiled at the accurate description of her girlfriend.

"What did Macon say?"

"She told me she thought you were hot," Emma offered. "Then, she said you weren't hot."

"Wait. What?"

"She said you were hot again, and then corrected herself and said you're somehow both hot and beautiful and, normally, she only notices the hot part."

"That sounds like her," Joanna said.

"She wanted to ask you out, but she'd overheard you talking about an ex-boyfriend one night. Then, you were off limits."

"She wanted to ask me out?"

"From the beginning. I think she kind of turned it off. It seemed like she wanted to, but she couldn't. She tried to put it behind her and see you as just a friend. As time went on, I wondered if she'd been successful at that, because from where I was sitting, it didn't seem like that."

Joanna smiled. The smile faltered when she thought about how she must have caused Macon pain over the past year.

"I didn't know."

"How could you? Greene is good at hiding when she needs to. It's not like you're the first straight woman she's been into," Emma revealed. "That came out wrong. Sorry."

"No, what do you mean? The girls she's flirted with?"

"No, I mean Liv."

"Liv?"

"You don't know?"

"About someone named Liv? No."

"Oh, maybe she should be the one to tell you. I thought you knew. I only know because Keira told me."

"Tell me."

"You should talk to her, I think. It's not my place."

"You brought it up, Emma," Joanna persisted.

"Because I thought you two had discussed it."

"Well, we haven't, obviously. She told me about Daniella, but not much about her other relationships other than they were short."

"Just ask her about it the next time you talk. I'm sure she'll fill you in."

"I'm kind of wondering why she hasn't already," Joanna said.

***

"Hey there, world traveler," she greeted Macon.

"Hey," Macon replied. "How are you?"

"I'm okay," she answered. "You?"

"I'm good. We have an early rehearsal. I wanted to give you a quick goodnight call before I have to head in."

Joanna looked at the clock and noticed it was after eleven her time, which meant it was after eight in the morning in Rome.

"You're sweet."

"Don't tell anyone."

"I plan on telling everyone," she replied playfully. "How was rehearsal?"

"It was good. The orchestra is nice, and they're like every other orchestra, so they can obviously play. Gail thinks they're better than Sydney. And I think sections might be better than Sydney but, as a whole, Rome is better at performance."

Joanna had heard the name Gail a few times and knew she was along on the tour with Macon as the coordinator's assistant. She knew she was young and nice, but that was about all Macon had revealed about her.

"Gail, huh?"

"Yeah, we hang out sometimes. She doesn't know anyone here either."

"Right." Joanna stood from her sofa and moved to the front door to make sure it was locked for the night. "Is she gay?"

"Yes."

"And you guys hang out?"

"We do." Greene laughed lightly. "Are you jealous?"

"No."

"Jo…"

"Do you think she's interested?"

"In me?"

"No, in the fucking wallpaper of your hotel room, Macon. Of course, I mean you."

She *was* jealous. Yeah, definitely jealous. Macon

127

could only laugh for a few minutes, or at least it felt like it was a few minutes.

"Jo, she tried the first time we hung out, but I wasn't into it. That's me being completely honest with you. She's the hit and run kind of girl, and she's about ten years younger than us."

"So, she's backed off?" she asked hopefully.

"I told her about you back in Sydney. She asks about you all the time now."

"Oh, so now she's into me?" Joanna smiled as she headed to her bedroom.

"She better not be," Macon said. "She's fun to hang out with; it's not like I have any friends wherever we go. But she knows I'm not into her like that. I think she's in that phase where she wants to pick up a woman a night."

"Gross."

"Yeah, but it's cute that you're jealous."

"I'm not jealous." She flopped down on the edge of her bed, laid back, unbuttoned and unzipped her jeans. "I just know how women are around you."

"And you know I'm not interested."

"I know," she replied softly and slid out of the jeans she'd been wearing all day. "I know, Macon. I didn't mean that you would do anything. It's just hard picturing someone else around you when I can't be, especially when they're into women."

"What are you doing right now? What am I hearing?"

"I'm changing for bed."

"You can't do that when you're on the phone with me," Macon exclaimed.

Joanna stood and kicked her jeans the rest of the way off.

"Why not? You called to say goodnight. I'm changing so that I can get some sleep."

"And now I'm picturing you in your underwear near a bed. Thanks, Jo."

Joanna laughed and tossed the jeans into her laundry

basket, on top of the pile of other dirty clothes.

"You know what I miss?"

"Your pants? Put them back on. Add a sweater or maybe a parka to that, too," Macon suggested and received laughter in return from Joanna.

"I sleep in my panties and a t-shirt, mostly," she informed. "Sometimes, I sleep naked if it's hot enough outside."

"Fuck, Jo. I'm in public here."

Joanna couldn't believe she could have this kind of effect on someone as beautiful as Macon Greene.

"I miss you doing laundry over here." She changed the subject. "I miss having lunch and talking while things are in the washer."

"Me too."

"When you get back, I bet you'll have a lot of laundry. Think maybe you'll pay me a visit to use the machines?"

"No, Jo," Macon replied, and Joanna's playful smile disappeared. "I plan on paying you a visit to take you on a date."

"A date, huh?" The smile returned.

"Our first date," Macon corrected.

"That sounds nice."

"Too many more days here without you."

"Twenty more, to be exact," Joanna said.

"You're counting the days?"

"Since you left, yeah."

"I miss you."

"This is the longest we've gone without seeing one another," Joanna added.

"Never again."

"Never again," she agreed with a smile. "Have a good rehearsal. Let them hear you, Macon."

"They always hear me. It's kind of hard not to, when I'm the only one playing."

"No, Make. I mean let them really hear you; play for

them how you played for me that night."

There was silence for several moments. Joanna worried she'd said something wrong.

"I was going to make a comment that if I played like that for them, they'd all jump up and kiss me. But I think what I'd rather say is that I don't want to play for anyone else how I played for you."

"Save the kissing for me, but give them that part of you, Macon. I've seen it now. I saw it that night. I saw it when I went to the performance. It's beautiful. You're so beautiful when you play."

"I'll try."

"Don't try, honey. Do it. Let yourself go. Let them see that part of you. You don't have to be scared to let it out."

"Did you just call me *honey?*"

"I've called you that before. I think I called you *sweetie* once or twice, too."

"You have. I had to remember we were just friends every time you did that."

"Well, we're not just friends anymore, are we?"

"I guess not," Macon agreed with her.

"Macon, I want this. I want us."

"I believe you. I'm sorry I didn't before."

"Don't be. Just have the best time playing on your first ever world tour, and then come back here so we can really start this."

"I will. I should get ready. I have to shower and change."

"Shower, huh?"

"Yeah, now you know how it feels. You live with that image now. Picture my hands running all over–"

"Okay. I get it." Joanna laughed. "I'll just say, 'have a good day,' and hang up now."

"Goodnight, Jo."

"Have a good day, Make."

CHAPTER 14

"HOW'S VIENNA?" Joanna asked.

"Your face is prettier," Macon replied while smiling back at her.

"You're sweet to me." Joanna rolled her eyes. "But it is nice to see you when we talk. I've missed those eyes."

"Now, who's sweet?" Macon wiggled her eyebrows at her. "I'm exhausted. I might not be up for long."

"It's late there; I understand. How was the performance?"

"It was the last one. It went well. All of them recently have gone really well."

"Recently? Why?"

"Because I listened to you," she admitted, and Joanna smiled when she did.

"How so?"

"You told me to let it out, to just be me out there; and I did. I guess people like it."

"Of course, they do, Macon. You're so good. I've been watching the videos the orchestras have posted of your performances on their sites. Some have been posted on YouTube already, and there are only good comments. One has ten thousand views, and it was posted like two days ago."

"What? Really?"

"Yeah, really."

"I didn't know. They keep me pretty busy here. If I'm not rehearsing with the group, I'm in a solo room. If I'm not doing that, I'm eating or sleeping. I haven't even seen these cities I've been to."

"That's no good. You need to try to make time for a little sightseeing. These are beautiful places, Make. You should see them."

"I will," Macon replied. "I have something I need to talk to you about." She turned serious.

"That doesn't sound good." Joanna pulled her knees into her body and placed her socked feet on the desk chair.

"They want to extend the tour," she replied.

"Extend?"

"Two more weeks."

"Oh."

"I know," Macon replied. "It would be two weeks in Boston. They want me to perform at Berklee, since that's where I went. They've got me doing a few shows in other places, too. I haven't been back since I moved."

"So, you're going to Boston?"

"Not yet. I mean, they asked me in Rome, but I wanted to talk to you about it first."

"And now you're in Vienna and only have one more show before you head to Paris."

"I know. I waited because Gail had to get me all the details. I didn't want to talk to you until I saw it all in writing. If I didn't want to do it, there was no point."

"But you want to?"

Macon squeezed her lips together as if trying to stop herself from saying it.

"I think I do, yeah. I had a great time in school. I loved the city. Some of my old teachers will be there. They want me to teach some talented current students," Macon explained. "Temporarily," she added.

"Are you sure it's temporary?"

"I don't want to live there."

"I mean the tour. Will it extend further?"

"No, this is it. I have to get back home to finish up the season. It's in the contract."

"I can do another two weeks," Joanna said.

"Yeah?"

"I don't want to. I miss you, but I understand. I want you to do this for yourself. You're too good to just sit in an orchestra."

"You're biased."

"Maybe. I've gotten a private performance." Joanna smiled at her. "So, two more weeks. I guess we'll push our first date back. I'll cancel the reservations."

"You made reservations somewhere?" The woman seemed surprised.

"Maybe."

"Where?"

"You get that information when you get home and we can actually try this whole dating thing in person and not on screens."

Macon laughed and took a moment to respond.

"I can't wait to see you in person."

"Me neither." She softened at the words and the sight of Macon's face as she said them.

"You know that thing we did when we talked the first time?"

Joanna's face reddened at the mention, and she replied, "Yes."

"I want that for real with you, Jo."

"Me too."

"Are you sure?"

"Yes, I told you–"

"I know. But saying it and going through with it are two different things. We haven't talked about that yet: sex."

"I think we talked a lot about it that night," Joanna countered.

Macon smiled at her softly and said, "You know what I mean. That was different. That was us speaking in hypotheticals; when I'm here and you're there."

"So, you're worried that when we're in the same room, I won't want to go through with it, or that I'll be scared or won't like it after?"

"Jo, if we do that and you don't–"

"Who's Liv, Make?"

"What?"

"Liv, who is she?"

"Who told you about Liv?"

"Not you," Joanna returned.

Macon looked away from the screen for a moment before meeting her eyes again.

"I would have told you about her."

"But you didn't. Why?"

"Because she was a mistake."

"She was straight?"

"Yes. And I dated her anyway, believing that she wanted me, and thinking we could have a real relationship one day."

"What happened?"

"We were friends for a while first; kind of like you and me. I met her when I first moved back. I knew she was straight. I still liked her, though, and thought that maybe it was even more than that. One night, she broke up with her boyfriend and invited me over as a shoulder to cry on. She kissed me. I kissed her back. I left right away because I knew what it was about." Macon paused. "She apologized, and then a week later, she asked me to come over again. She told me she wanted to try to be with me and that part of the reason she'd ended it with her ex was because of me. I stayed over that night, but we didn't sleep together. She wanted to take things slow. I understood. We dated for a few weeks, but I was already more than smitten." She looked away again and then met Joanna's eyes once more. "When we finally slept together, she didn't reciprocate, which was fine. I got it. I didn't have a problem with it the first time, or the second time, or even the third time."

"Oh."

"Yeah... By the fourth time, I thought I should say something or ask her if I could do anything to help, to make it more comfortable for her or something." There was a longer pause this time. "When I went to her apartment one night to surprise her with dinner, the front door was unlocked. I went right in and found her kneeling on the floor of her living room, with her ex-boyfriend standing right in front of her, minus his pants."

"Jesus, Macon." She leaned forward. "I'm so sorry."

"Not many people know about that; maybe only Keira. I'm guessing she's the one that told you."

"It was Emma, actually. But I think that comes with the coupling: the telling of secrets."

"I guess." Macon nodded and looked far off.

"So, you're worried I'd do that to you?"

"That specifically – no." Her face told Joanna she had something else to say. "Jo, I thought I had intense feelings for her. Seeing that hurt like hell. Hearing her tell me after that she just couldn't do the girl thing but she really liked me as a friend hurt even worse, because I should have known. I should have known she wouldn't have been able to commit."

"And with me?"

"I don't want to be wrong again, Joanna. But I also can't be wrong again; not with you. You are different. This isn't some crush I have, or even intense feelings. This is real. It feels real to me. The fact that you've been entertaining the idea of trying this with me has been so miraculous, that I've been trying to put the worry away."

"Entertaining the idea? Really? Macon, I listened to you come on the phone and then got myself off after, because I was so turned on," Joanna reminded her. "Hell, I probably would have had sex with you that night had you not sent me away."

"You would have?"

"Yes, and I would have reciprocated, too. Trust me." She watched as Macon's eyes grew darker and wondered if her own were doing the same. "I don't know what's going to happen with us. I don't know if it's for a while or forever. But I do know that I want you. I don't just want to be touched by you, either. I want to touch you, too. I'll probably be bad at it at first, but you can teach me what you like. I miss you like crazy, Macon." Her eyes were welling up with tears. "You know the saying, *'You don't know what you've got until it's gone'*… That's how I feel right now: like if I would have figured this out sooner, we would've had time together before you left. You wouldn't be worrying about this stuff right now. I miss going for dinner with you all the time, or you doing laundry here. I miss *7Ups*. We still have points to earn and prizes to win." She watched as Macon smiled. "I want all that back when you get home. I want to add to all the things we used to do."

"Yeah?"

"I want to fall asleep next to you again and wake up next to you. I want you to grumble about the alarm clock again. I want to make you coffee. I want to kiss you before you head off to rehearsal. I want to come up behind you while you cook and hold you. I want to make love to you. I want you to climb in the shower *with* me. And I want to be your girlfriend. I want all that that entails, okay?"

Macon smiled back and wiped a tear off her cheek as Joanna did the same.

"Me too."

"Go to sleep, beautiful; and think about everything I just said, okay?"

"I will."

"Call me when you can?"

"I don't call anyone else," Macon replied and smiled, wiping one more tear.

***

"It's her, isn't it?" Keira asked when Joanna smiled at her phone.

"Yeah, but it's like two in the morning there. I

wonder what's up. I should get it."

"Tell her I said hi and that she could call someone she's not trying to sleep with maybe one day, since other people miss her."

"I'll let her know." Joanna climbed inside the elevator on her way out of the *Worthy Bash* office after a meeting. "Hey, what are you doing up?"

"I just got back to the hotel."

"From?" she asked, looking at her watch to make sure she'd done the calculations correctly. "It's after two, Macon."

"We went out after the show," she said, sounding a little slurred.

"Are you drunk?" Joanna laughed as she arrived in the lobby.

"Yes."

"Where did you guys go?"

"They took me to a bar to celebrate my last show in Paris and bought me drinks. I didn't want to be rude, so I took them all."

"Oh, Make."

"I know. Then, Gail suggested we go to this lesbian bar over by *Moulin Rouge*, so we did. She ended up meeting some girl and made out with her in a corner while I sat there and did nothing." She rambled. "I did nothing, okay? Some girls tried to buy me drinks, and one asked me to dance, but I didn't do it."

"Okay." Joanna laughed again and made her way outside.

She didn't feel like walking home, so she'd ordered an Uber from upstairs, and it arrived just as she'd exited the building. She climbed in and put her phone on mute for a second to say hi to the driver before he started driving.

"I made sure Gail got back to the hotel safely, and now the alcohol is really kicking in, and I am very drunk."

"Oh, babe. I'm sorry."

"I have a flight tomorrow. I'll just sleep it off."

"Your flight is to London, not New York, Macon. It's super short. You need to drink a lot of water before you go to sleep, take some aspirin right now, and do the same in the morning. Have a big breakfast with lots of protein. It'll soak up all the crap you drank tonight. You'll feel better."

"You're very smart," Macon stated a little louder than was necessary.

"It's common knowledge, Macon."

"Is it common knowledge that I can't wait to see you?"

"I don't know, but I would assume it's not; and that's probably especially true since you haven't talked to anyone else since you left."

"I know. I know. I don't have a lot of time, Jo. I'm working. What time I do have, I just want to talk to you. I'll apologize to them when I get back, okay?"

"Okay." She smiled at Macon's words. "I'm almost home. I was just at *Worthy Bash.*"

"Getting interrogated by Keira Worthy, I assume."

"She does have a lot of questions about us."

"What are your answers?"

"You really want to know?" she asked suggestively and then remembered there was a man driving this Honda Accord in the front seat.

"Yes."

"That I want you." She'd covered her hand to try to keep the driver from hearing. "That I can't wait to see you because I want you."

"You can't say stuff like that to me right now."

"Why not?" She smiled and blushed as the driver turned down her street. "Right here is fine," she requested as he was near the front of her building.

"What's going on?"

"I'm in an Uber. He's dropping me off now."

"Home?"

"Yes."

"So, you'll be alone?"

"Yes."

"In your apartment?"

"Yes, Macon." Joanna climbed out of the car and laughed.

"And I'm alone in my room."

"And you're drunk."

"Drunk and horny," she replied, and Joanna laughed wildly as she walked hurriedly to her building.

"Romantic."

"I'll be romantic when I see you. I watched a bunch of girls make out at this sexy lesbian club while I had to sit there, thinking about how much I wanted to touch you. My body is on fire right now."

"You're overheated because of the alcohol." She unlocked her front door.

"Trust me; it is not because of the alcohol. Jo, I kept thinking about how you dreamed about me. I couldn't stop."

Joanna felt the blush creep across her cheeks as she made her way through her living room and into her bedroom, dropping her bag by her desk.

"I can't believe I told you about that." She sat on the edge of her bed and kicked off her shoes.

"I'm glad you did," Macon replied. "Jo, tell me what else you want. Tell me how you want to be touched."

"Are you–"

"Not yet."

"But you want to?"

"Yes," Macon replied immediately.

Joanna stood and ran her hand through her hair before she moved to her side of the bed, laid back on top of it, and bravely unbuttoned and unzipped her jeans.

"Did you just–"

"Yeah," she interrupted. "I did."

"Is this okay?" Macon asked.

"Yes," Joanna agreed, feeling herself instantly wet.

"But I want you to tell me how I should touch you."

"You do?"

"Tell me, Macon." She slid her hand between her legs and moved her fingers to her clit, waiting for Macon's words.

"No, wait." Macon seemed to snap out of something.

"What? Wait? Macon, come on."

"I need to get myself in check." Her deep sexy voice had disappeared. "I'm on my way to London, and then New York."

"So?"

"So, I think we should wait."

"You think we shouldn't have phone sex right now?"

"I haven't heard you yet, Jo."

"Heard me?" Joanna tried to piece it together. "Oh, heard me when I come?"

"Don't say *come* right now." Macon laughed.

"You're the one that started this." Joanna laughed back and removed her hand.

"I know I'm going to regret this later, but I want to wait until I can be with you in person."

"Okay. You can still do it, though. I've kind of already heard you."

Macon laughed loudly and replied, "True. That wasn't exactly planned. I still think I'd like to wait, if that's okay."

"Of course, it's okay," Joanna confirmed.

"I should probably try to get some sleep."

"You're going to hang up on me, get off, and then go to sleep, aren't you?"

"No." Macon responded. "I'm going to force myself to go to sleep while I'm this turned on, and then I'm going to resist doing anything else to myself until I can get to you."

"And then I can do it for you?" Joanna asked, trying to be brave. "Or to you? Is it for you or to you? To you, right?"

"Oh, my God. You are so adorable." Macon laughed. "You can do whatever you want for me or to me. How about that?"

"You're making fun of me."

"I'm not, I swear. I just think you're cute."

"Okay. Goodnight, Macon Greene." Joanna laughed.

"What are you going to do tonight?"

"Not myself."

Macon burst out laughing again and said, "Now, I feel bad."

"Don't. I can wait for you."

"I promise, I'll make it good."

"You can't say stuff like that to me."

"Noted," Macon replied. "I'll call you tomorrow."

"Sleep well."

"I'll do my best. Jo, I'm…"

"Macon?" she asked after a few seconds of silence.

"Nothing. I'll call you tomorrow. Goodnight, Jo."

"Goodnight."

CHAPTER 15

"SO, WHERE IS our violinist on her world tour today?" Emma asked as she and Keira sat across from Joanna at one of their usual bar hotspots.

"She's in New York, finally. She had her second show tonight and just texted that she's back in the hotel," Joanna replied. "One more tomorrow night, and the next day, she's off to Boston for two weeks."

"She texts you, huh? No text for her friends?" Hillary entered and sat next to Joanna.

"Sorry."

"She could text me that, you know?" Hillary retorted in Joanna's direction.

"Don't shoot the messenger." She held up her hands in defense.

"You're the girlfriend now, dear. You're linked," Hillary stated.

"Oh, we're not–" Joanna started. "We haven't taken that step yet."

"I just assumed, the way these two have gone on and on about you and her." She pointed at Emma and Keira.

"We have not gone on and on," Keira defended.

"You told me you wouldn't be surprised if they get married one day," Hillary professed.

"You did?" Joanna nearly choked out as she'd taken a sip of her drink one second too soon.

"So, no on the wedding then?" Emma laughed at her reaction.

"We've kissed once," Joanna replied, taking a real drink now.

"And how was it?" Hillary nudged her shoulder.

"Right." She shrugged her shoulders with a smile. "It just felt right."

"Boring," Hillary said. "What did it really feel like? This is your first kiss with a woman, right?"

"Oh, yeah, I totally forgot. You're bi," Joanna announced loudly.

The three of them laughed at that statement.

"I am, yeah," Hillary replied and smiled at her. "But I can understand how you'd forget it: I'm usually surrounded by lesbians." She pointed at the two across the table. "But if you need to talk, I'm here." She said more quietly to Joanna.

"I might take you up on that."

"I need a drink. Want to walk with me?" She nodded toward the bar.

"Sure." She stood along with Hillary.

They walked together to the bar – which wasn't as crowded as it normally was – and took two stools, knowing Emma and Keira had no problem keeping one another company for a few minutes as they ordered and talked.

"So, how are you handling this revelation of sorts?" Hillary asked.

"That's the thing: it doesn't feel like a revelation."

"Feels normal?"

"Yes," she answered.

"And I assume you're not ready to label it anything?"

"I don't know. I don't really care. Is that wrong?" she asked.

"No, it's not wrong. Human sexuality is a fluid thing

that most people never open themselves up to experience. Some people are raised to hate anything other than the hetero norm: others are raised to be open-minded and understand that it's okay to be different. Then, there are people that actually open themselves up to the possibility of love coming in from a totally different place; and that's you with Greene."

"She's amazing." Joanna blushed at the thought. "I honestly never thought I'd be interested in a woman. But I kissed her, and it felt…"

"Right?" she repeated Joanna's earlier word.

"It felt like home. Does that make sense?"

"Yeah." Hillary ordered her drink when the bartender approached. "How *else* was it, though?"

"You mean you want the not-boring details?"

"Yes." Hillary laughed and grabbed her wine glass when it was presented in front of her.

"You can't tell her this." Joanna squinted at her with a shy smile. "I mean, we've talked about it some, and I'm sure I'll tell her sometime at least…"

"I'm sworn to secrecy." Hillary mimicked locking her lips and throwing away an invisible key.

"She played for me," Joanna admitted.

"For you? Like, only for you?"

"Yeah."

"She doesn't do that. Keira and I have asked for a private concert for years."

"She did for me." Joanna smiled. "And it was one of my favorite songs. She knew that because we'd gone to see *West Side Story* together, and she knew I'd bought the performance soundtrack and that I'd listened to the song over and over, because she'd been there to hear it. It was like I suddenly remembered that she'd been there for a year. We'd spent practically every single free moment together. And it hit me in that instant that I wanted it to be that way. I wanted to spend every moment I could with her; and that wasn't normal for people who were just friends. Then, I really watched her play. She's so beautiful when she's playing – like, really playing; not just sitting in the orchestra playing what they tell her to play. She let go that night. And I think I fell in love with her then. She doesn't know that part. Please–"

"I won't say anything." Hillary laughed.

"I just stood up and kissed her. It wasn't anything major; I just kissed the corner of her mouth, because I was too terrified to actually kiss her lips. Then, I did. I got up the courage and I kissed her on the lips, and then I pulled back to check to see if I was way off-base – when she pulled me back in, and we really kissed. I mean, we *really* kissed. It was hot, sexy, and slow. And then it was fast and, somehow, even hotter. It was the best kiss of my life."

"Damn, sounds good. I'm kind of upset I didn't try to get Greene to kiss me once so I could experience that."

"Why do you assume she's the one that made it so good?" Joanna tossed back with a wink.

"So, are you offering?" Hillary joked.

"Uh, no. I'm not." She laughed at her.

"All that really matters is that you're honest with yourself about how you feel about her, and that you're honest with her about it. Greene can be a patient person. She is a pretty good listener. Even if the hormones are going crazy – thanks to that hot kiss you two shared – if you need to slow things down, or you need to talk through stuff before you take certain steps – like that pretty big one – you should."

"I know; she's good like that."

"She is. She doesn't let a lot of people in. And even when she does, she doesn't let them in far. It's different with you; I can tell. So can Keira and Emma."

"I hope so. I guess I'm a little nervous about the whole thing. I don't have a clue how to…" Joanna paused, embarrassed. "You know."

"I'm sure you'll be fine." Hillary winked at her.

"What if I'm not?" She lifted a shoulder.

"You've had other first times with men, right?"

"Obviously."

"Were you nervous with them?"

"Yes, but this is like that times ten."

"Why?"

"The woman part."

"And?"

"And I want to take care of her, you know? I want to make her feel good. I want to see her like that. I don't know if I'll be able to. With guys, it's not exactly a concern."

"Men don't take a lot of work is what you're saying."

"No, not usually." She hesitated. "I was nervous for each first time with all the guys I'd had sex with. But this is…" She allowed herself to think before she spoke. "This is Macon, and she's not just a woman. She's–"

"You're in love with her, and it matters."

"Yes. I know she's worried that I might freak out or not like it, but I know that won't be the case with her. I don't want her to worry more if I'm unable to perform, so to speak. I don't want her to think I'll be phoning it in."

"She won't think that."

"How do you know?"

"Because Greene knows you. And besides, you won't be phoning it in, will you?"

"What? No," she exclaimed as Hillary stood.

"Then, she'll see that. She'll probably feel it, too." She took another drink while Joanna stood.

"I hope so."

"And look, it's been a while for me, so if it's good, please give me the details so I can live vicariously."

***

Joanna arrived home around midnight, and she was ready to crash, but there was one more thing she needed to do for herself before she went to sleep.

CHAPTER 16

GREENE HAD an interesting first few days in Boston. It had been strange: being back there after all this time. She'd taken the train with Gail, because she was sick of flying. She'd taken the T a lot in Boston, because she hadn't had a car and she'd enjoyed it most of the time. She'd taken the trains to and from New York and Rhode Island a few times while she'd lived there and liked that she could relax while someone else was in control of the trip. Since moving into San Francisco proper, she'd rarely taken BART, because her world was really just a few blocks. She could walk to work when the weather was nice, which it often was, and she could walk to the few bars her group frequented. She could get to Keira and Emma's by foot, along with Hillary's place. Though she was rarely there these days. Most important to her now was Joanna's place. She could easily walk there, even while carrying her laundry. Her world had been rocked recently with this trip. She'd enjoyed almost all of it. What she didn't enjoy was the time away from Joanna.

She'd spent her first day in Boston just getting settled in and checking out the old hall she'd played in hundreds of times. The next day, she'd gone on a short sightseeing trip to visit a few of her old haunts. She'd had a late afternoon rehearsal and then met up with a few old friends that night. The third day of the trip had her back on campus, talking to current students and advising as she could. She found that she really enjoyed that work and considered maybe getting more involved with her alma mater from home if she could or, perhaps, partnering with a university in the city if any of them were interested. Most importantly, though, Greene felt that her playing had improved. By traveling and working with these different people and hearing their music, she'd improved her own. She'd been surprised to find how good it felt to truly let go when she was on stage. She had Joanna and their growing connection to thank for that.

Greene had always lacked confidence, despite being called a prodigy and one of the best in the world. Her preference had always been to sit in the back and play whenever she could get away with it. She soloed when asked but never suggested or asked for one herself and only followed the notes when she delivered it. Technically, she'd played in front of her parents as a youth, but not really in front of them. They'd hear her in her room as she practiced, but she never performed for them. She never did the recitals the normal young musicians deliver to demonstrate her skill, because her teachers could see the skill and Greene had no desire to perform by herself in front of small groups of parents like that. Her teachers chalked it up to stage fright which she'd eventually grow out of, so they didn't press.

When she moved on in her playing career, she knew it wasn't stage fright; she could play in front of thousands. It wasn't that. She'd always preferred to be in the back. She suspected there was an initial cause for this behavior. It could have been her first actual violin teacher that told her she slouched when she played. She was three and didn't know what that word meant. It might have been when her second teacher told her she was playing her age and she expected more from her. She'd been four then. It also might have been when her mother opened her bedroom door when she was six, to find her watching TV instead of practicing, and told her she shouldn't be lazy. If she was going to keep ahead of all the other students, she needed to practice every single night. There wasn't time for TV back then. Her mother had closed the door after Greene had picked up her instrument. Five minutes later, she'd knocked loudly and, through the door, yelled that Greene was off-tempo.

By the third night in Boston, Greene was ready to show her old school that she still had the stuff. She played the three pieces they'd arranged for her at her old hall. They played a few pieces with the school orchestra, and it felt, in a strange way, like home to her. She knew none of the musicians she was playing with by name, but it felt good all the same. When the performance finished, she received her accolades and even some long-stemmed roses. She'd given them to Gail to give to a pretty girl she'd spotted in the woodwind section, and then headed out the back to get to her hotel and call Joanna. They hadn't spoken that morning due to Greene's schedule, and she'd missed her already.

"You've turned me down for an autograph once; I'm kind of hoping you won't again."

Greene turned around on the street and immediately relaxed into a smile.

"You can have all the autographs you want," she said to Joanna in response. "What are you doing here?" she asked after she took the woman in.

Joanna was wearing a black dress with matching heels, making her a little taller than usual. Her hair was pulled back into one of those wrap-around braids. She held a single red rose in both hands in front of her body. And she looked more beautiful to Greene than all those beautiful cities she'd just visited, combined.

"I flew out this morning. Got here just in time to see you out there." Joanna motioned with her thumb to the hall and then moved it back to hold the rose in front of herself.

Joanna was nervous. Greene could sense it even from ten feet away. She didn't know what to do. In all her fantasies of the next time they saw one another, it was never on a public street in Boston. They were all at Joanna's place, because Greene knew she would go straight there from the airport, not bothering to stop at her own apartment first.

This was different, though. Joanna stood ten feet away from her as people moved around them on a city street. She didn't know what to do; she didn't know if Joanna would want to kiss her in public like this. They hadn't exactly discussed her opinion of public displays of affection.

"I can't believe you're here," she said out of her own nervousness.

"Are you going to come closer to me, or are we staying this far apart for my entire trip?" Joanna asked with a small laugh.

"How long is this trip?" Greene asked and took a few tentative steps toward her.

"Well, today is Friday," Joanna took a few steps toward Greene, pulling a small roller behind her, then continued, "and tomorrow is Saturday."

"I know the days of the week, Jo." She laughed.

"I'm here until Sunday. My flight is at four. I have a job on Monday, or else I'd stay longer."

"So, I have you for two days?"

"You have me for longer than that, but I'm here for two days." She smiled as Greene stood a foot from her. "This is for you, superstar."

"Thank you." Greene took the rose from her and brought it to her nose to sniff it. "Where are you staying?" she asked – again, out of nerves.

Joanna laughed wildly at that and turned Greene around to face the direction she'd originally been walking to.

"Where am I staying?" Her laugh quieted. "I didn't book a hotel, so if I'm not staying with you... I guess I'm on the streets."

Greene smiled as Joanna took her free hand and

stood beside her. Joanna used her other hand to grip her bag handle.

"With me, huh?"

"Yes, with you, Macon." Joanna's head went to her shoulder.

Greene reveled in the feel of her closeness and her ability to express herself like this in public after all.

"I was going to grab something to eat before heading back. I didn't have dinner," Greene explained. "Any chance you want to hit up one of my old favorite places before we go back?"

"I haven't eaten all day. I skipped breakfast because of the early flight. And then my layover was supposed to be two hours, but we were delayed because the fog wouldn't allow us to land. I barely made my connection. I came here straight after."

"Good. Dinner's on me." Greene tossed her a smile, shifting her violin case over her shoulder. She took the rose Joanna had given her and slid it into the top compartment of the woman's bag. Then, she took the handle of the roller from Joanna, shifted it to the side where her shoulder was already bearing the violin, and held out her free hand. Joanna lifted her head off Greene's shoulder to watch. "I missed you," Greene admitted softly.

"I missed you. Why do you think I flew across the country to see you when you're coming home in a week and a half?" Joanna's head went back to Greene's shoulder, and they walked on.

***

Joanna hadn't ever held hands with a woman while walking down a street. She definitely hadn't rested her head on a woman's shoulder while she walked down a street. But, God, it felt good to see Macon again. It was too good to not be touching her in as many ways as possible.

Their meeting had been awkward. She thought that maybe she shouldn't have approached Macon outside. She knew the hotel she'd been staying at; she could have just met Macon there. But she'd watched her perform, and she could swear she'd fallen more in love with this woman. Macon was somehow even better than that night she'd watched her play *Somewhere*. She'd been gorgeous on that stage and was now even more so, as they walked in silence down the street.

"This is weird, huh?" Joanna finally said after a few blocks.

Macon only laughed and squeezed her hand.

"Yes, it's weird," she agreed. "It's you, so it's not weird. But… it's you, so it *is* weird."

"That makes no sense." Joanna lifted her head and glanced at Macon.

"Here it is." Macon pointed at the restaurant they were now next to. "It's a local place, not a chain. Back when I was still in college, I found it when I needed a break from rehearsal one night." She motioned for Joanna to walk inside, which Joanna did, pulling Macon along with her. "I know how much you like Mexican food."

"I do." She smiled at Macon as they made their way into the waiting area of the seemingly small restaurant.

It was decorated in the typical Mexican restaurant garb and flare. There were four chairs against the wall that were occupied by waiting patrons. Joanna, with Macon's hand still in her own, stood next to her, wondering where they were going to sit and wait for their table in the crowded ten-table restaurant.

"Hi, Marcia," Macon greeted the older, rotund woman, who approached from one of the tables.

"Verde," the woman exclaimed and moved to Macon.

Macon let go of both Joanna's hand and the bag as the woman engulfed her in a hug, letting her go moments later.

"It's nice to see you again, too." Macon laughed. "Marcia, this is my friend, Joanna."

"Hola, Joanna." Marcia nodded with a sweet smile in Joanna's direction. "Give me two minutes; I'll clean a table for you."

"No hurry. We can wait if–"

"No, no. You won't wait. One minute." She headed back into the restaurant.

"You're a regular."

"I *was* a regular, yes." She turned to face Joanna. "I came back after that first time and met Marcia. Her family owns the place. She's great, and the food is great. She used to let me occupy a table all night if I needed some time away from everything."

"That's nice of her."

Macon smiled at her, and Joanna's world was suddenly all about that smile. She'd never thought that about a man's smile before. She somehow knew Macon's smile was about her and for her; for *only* her. She smiled back and hoped that hers conveyed the same emotion until the exuberant Marcia returned and sat them at a small two-person table, helping roll Joanna's bag until it was against the wall behind her along with Macon's violin case. Before they could even sit, a server placed a bowl of chips and salsa on the table, and another one brought them two glasses of water. Macon sat down across from her. Joanna instantly grabbed for the water, not caring for her sudden case of dry mouth at seeing the woman for the first time in almost two months.

"So, can I just start by saying *I'm sorry*?" Macon asked.

"Sorry?" Joanna suddenly felt nervous, and the water had done nothing to eliminate her dry mouth.

"I know we've talked a lot since then, but I want to apologize in person for how I acted that night and before I left. I should have just trusted you. I let my fear get the better of me, and I'm sorry."

"Oh, Make. We're good on that. I understand. Part of me wishes you wouldn't have left because I missed you like crazy. I don't just mean because of the obvious. I mean because I got so used to having you around. Most of my plans outside of work involved you; even some of my work plans involved you. It felt like my arm was missing or something." She paused as Macon laughed and took a chip. "But, at the end of the day, I'm so glad you went. Honey, you are so talented. God, I thought you were good that night at your apartment. But you're even better now. I'm not exactly sure how that's possible."

"Thank you." Macon smiled at her and ate the chip sans salsa.

There was a moment of companionable silence. Then, the waiter returned to take their orders. Joanna hadn't even looked at the menu and just motioned for Macon to suggest something. She ordered for them both, and the waiter left to grab their drinks first.

"I'm glad I went, too," Macon finally acknowledged.

"Yeah?"

Their beers arrived. Macon had ordered them both a Corona with lime, and Joanna shoved her lime into the yellow liquid, following Macon's lead.

"I feel like I needed to go for myself: to have this experience. But I also kind of feel like it worked out for us."

"It did?" She gave Macon a one-sided smile and a lifted eyebrow.

"We've talked a lot, Jo. I mean, we've always talked a lot, but... this time, we talked about us and what we could be. And because I wasn't here, we didn't have the physical part to – I don't know – get in the way of all that."

"Get in the way?"

"You know what I mean." Macon laughed.

"So, you think you and me being in the same place would have created some physical situations that would have–"

"We wouldn't have stopped having sex, Jo," Macon interrupted her and gave her a wicked grin. God, it was a hot, wicked grin. "Right now, I'm having a hard time not touching you."

"Then, why aren't you?" Joanna tossed back to her and tried to meet that grin with a wicked one of her own.

"Fuck, Jo. You can't say stuff like that here." She laughed and took a long drink of her beer.

"Why are we eating dinner here when we can go back to your hotel and order room service and just be alone?"

"Is that what you want?" Macon asked.

"I don't know." Joanna let out a deep sigh. "I can't wait to be alone with you, but–"

"But we haven't been alone together since we started this."

"Yes."

"And you're worried that we might jump into bed together because I'm back now, and that–"

"We should maybe take our time to get to that step," Joanna interjected. "I can interrupt you, too." She wiggled her playful eyebrows at the woman.

Macon smiled at her and reached her hand across the small table. She held it still there, with her palm up in invitation. Joanna smiled back and placed her hand in Macon's.

"I will go as slow as you need to."

"So, you're not worried I'm going to freak out anymore?" Joanna asked.

"I didn't say that." Macon looked concerned. "I believe you when you say you want this. I believe you, Jo. I don't compare you to Liv. Honestly, I can't believe our idiot friend brought her up." She allowed her thumb to play across Joanna's skin. "I might be worried about that until–"

"After, when I don't run away?"

Macon smirked at her and leaned forward.

"Do you want to just sleep tonight?" she asked.

Joanna thought about it. Macon's hand was perfect in her own: it was warm, and soft; it was right. She met Macon's eyes: they were flickering with candlelight like her olive skin from the small beige tea candle inside the ornate red holder on the table. Her red lips were still adorned with her red performance lipstick. She had a black dress with a V-cut on, revealing a slight amount of cleavage. And her hair was down but half-pinned back.

"You're gorgeous," she whispered.

Macon licked her lips. Joanna felt the muscles in her lower body tense and release suddenly. She licked her own lips in response. Macon's eyes moved down to watch the action. Her smile reformed, and her wicked stare returned. Joanna knew the woman was picturing something in that beautiful mind of hers.

"So, you don't want to just sleep?" Macon asked.

The food arrived at their table before Joanna could answer. She was glad for the reprieve, because she wasn't sure she knew the answer to that question. She knew she wanted Macon; just staring at her made her want her. She also wasn't sure if she was ready just yet. Macon had been right: they'd talked and talked while she was away, but they hadn't spent time in the same room with one another to just enjoy the steps like holding hands, or sliding a hand up someone's thigh, or wrapping it around someone so they could nervously rest their head on the other's shoulder while they watched a movie.

They'd done that as friends, but not like this: not as more. They hadn't had a real kiss as two people who had admitted they were attracted to each other and wanted to pursue something real. That kiss hadn't then progressed into a full on make-out session, with tongues battling and quick heated breaths intermingling. They hadn't stumbled onto a bed and fallen into one another. She hadn't felt Macon's breast in her hand or yet tweaked a nipple with her fingers. She hadn't nervously slid her hand across Macon's stomach while kissing her neck. She hadn't heard

Macon's sounds from beneath her, as her own lips grazed Macon's toned flesh and moved lower and lower.

"Everything okay, dear?"

Joanna looked up and realized that Marcia was standing there at their table, and she was staring at her.

"I'm sorry?"

"She just asked if your food tasted okay." Macon was clearly trying to hold back a smile, then nodded at Joanna in silent understanding that she knew what she'd been thinking about.

"Oh, yes. Everything's great." Joanna smiled and nodded at Marcia, lowering her reddened cheeks to the food she'd barely touched.

"Verde, you must tell me about your travels," Marcia requested.

"She's called me that since she found out my last name was Greene," Macon told Joanna. "Where should I start?" she asked the woman who was clearly interested in hearing Macon's stories.

"The beginning, of course," Marcia encouraged.

Macon gave Joanna an apologetic look, but Joanna merely smiled back and started eating while Macon regaled the old woman with her tales.

CHAPTER 17

GREENE HADN'T EXPECTED Joanna to magically appear in Boston just for her, but the woman was always surprising her these days. She also hadn't expected Marcia to want to talk her ear off while they were trying to enjoy their meal and catch up. As she pulled Joanna's bag down the street toward her hotel, she knew they hadn't finished their conversation at dinner. Now, they were walking in silence the few blocks, because it was a nice night and neither wanted to call for a car. Joanna's arm was slung through her own. And while her head wasn't on Greene's shoulder all the time, because she was glancing around at the buildings and sights of the city, every now and then, she'd place it there temporarily, and Greene smiled each time.

"Greene, oh—" Gail was about fifteen feet in front of them and had a look on her face that Greene couldn't quite make out due to the darkness and the distance.

"Hey, Gail," Greene replied, and they continued to move in the direction of the hotel she could now see at the end of the block.

"Oh, Gail!" Joanna lifted her head, acknowledging. "Gail?" She turned that head to Greene and gave her a look that said she had no idea Gail was attractive.

Macon knew Joanna's faces and expressions well enough by now. She'd figured out the main ones fairly early in their friendship. Her nose would crinkle when she was telling a lie or about to tell a lie. Her left eyebrow rose a little higher than the other when she was intrigued and really listening. Her smile didn't always reach her eyes. Greene had noticed that expression commonly when they were in a lesbian bar and women tried to pick her up or buy her a drink. She'd politely decline with that smile and, sometimes, a handshake before returning to Greene and their friends. She had a nervous tell where she'd run her finger or a couple of them over her right eyebrow once, and then again, a few moments later, if the feeling hadn't righted itself. She knew many of Joanna's expressions already, and that included the one that was making Greene laugh right now.

"Gail, this is Joanna. Joanna is glaring at me because she thinks you're pretty," she said as they made their way toward Gail.

"Macon!" Joanna poked her in the ribs, causing Greene to laugh more.

"What? I know that look," she returned.

"Joanna, it's so nice to meet you." Gail practically launched at Joanna, forcing them to disconnect.

"You too." Joanna hugged her back.

"Okay, she's mine," Greene said and playfully pulled Gail apart from her. "What are you up to tonight?"

"Well, not bothering you two." Gail wiggled her eyebrows and pointed with two fingers at them. "Did I know she was coming? I feel like that was something I should have known so I could get your room set up or something and tell the hotel to have champagne or wine brought up for you."

"I didn't know she was coming."

"I surprised her."

"How romantic." Gail smiled at them both. "It was so dark there for a moment, I thought Greene had picked some woman up after the show. That didn't seem right to me because she talks about you non-stop."

"Hey!" Greene said in mock-defense.

"Hey, what? I wasn't going to let you take some random back to your room when you had this one waiting for you at home." She pointed at Joanna. "She's gorgeous, by the way." She turned her attention to Joanna. "You're gorgeous. If you ever change your mind about—"

"And we're going inside," Greene interrupted her with a laugh and took Joanna's hand again. "Goodnight, Gail."

"Have fun, you two. Will I see you for breakfast tomorrow? Oh, probably not, huh? Room service?" She started to walk past them. "It was nice meeting you. I assume I'll see you both at some point tomorrow."

Gail walked in the direction they'd just come from after squeezing Greene's shoulder and giving her a smile.

"So, that was Gail?" Joanna asked.

"That was Gail. She's probably on her way to pick someone up. She does that a lot."

"And you don't, right?"

"No, Jo," she replied. She placed her hand on Joanna's cheek. "I'm still at number nine. I'm kind of hoping I'll end at ten." She leaned forward and placed a chaste kiss on Joanna's lips, not wanting to do much more than that in public.

She pulled back to see that Joanna's concerned expression had vanished. It had been replaced with a look of surprise and the large, expressive eyes and lifted eyebrows that went along with it. She didn't say anything in response. She just took Greene's violin case off her shoulder and placed it over her own while taking Greene's hand. They walked side by side toward the hotel and then into the lobby while Greene realized that she was letting someone else hold her violin. She hated letting anyone hold her violin, only allowing it in rare and necessary circumstances. She had no problem trusting Jo to carry it for her, knowing she'd protect it and keep it safe. She could only hope she'd do the same with her heart.

***

"So, first thing," Macon stated the moment she opened the door to her hotel room.

"Yeah?"

Joanna followed her inside, still carrying Macon's violin case, while Macon rolled her small suitcase over and leaned it against the wall. The room was a nice one. Macon had been provided with a suite. She had a small sofa and a chair with a table in a living room, along with a large flat screen mounted to a wall, and a full kitchen off to the left with a refrigerator, a stove, and even a dishwasher. Everything was shiny and clean. And there was even a welcome note on the refrigerator to the hotel's VIP guests, which Macon obviously was. Macon stood a few feet away from her, with two pieces of paper held out.

"We should order our breakfast now. We have to hang these from the doors before 5 a.m., and it's already 11 p.m. I don't know about you, but I don't plan on waking up before five tomorrow, nor do I want to have to worry about this later."

"Oh, sure." Joanna was a little thrown off by this. When Macon had said *first thing*, she'd thought they'd throw their stuff down and run at each other a moment later. But Macon, apparently, had tomorrow's menu in mind instead. "You can order for me. You know what I like." She held out the violin case. "Where do you want this?"

"Oh, yeah. Sorry." Macon placed the order forms on the coffee table and headed to her.

The woman took the violin case, entered what Joanna assumed was the bedroom, and emerged a few moments later, while Joanna moved to sit on the sofa. She'd been traveling all day. From the airport, she went straight to the performance, leaving her suitcase for the checkroom to hang onto so she wouldn't have to worry about it during the performance itself. After that, she went to dinner with Macon in a busy restaurant. It was now after eleven, and despite that only being after eight Pacific time, Joanna was exhausted and needed to sit.

"So, whatever you're getting is fine," she added when Macon returned to the room and stood just inside the arched doorway to the bedroom, taking in Joanna's new position.

"Eggs and bacon?"

"Sure."

"Wheat toast instead of white, coffee, and orange juice?" Macon moved to sit down next to her.

"You know me well." Joanna lifted both shoulders and offered what she could only assume was a tired smile.

Macon smiled, but she didn't look back at her as she completed both their forms and provided her name and room number atop each. She stood and walked to the door, opened it enough to hang the forms, hung them up, and closed it behind her. Then, she stood there and stared at Joanna from about fifteen feet away. Somehow, it felt even further away than when she'd been halfway around the world.

"Are you tired?" Macon asked and leaned against the wallpapered wall.

"Yes," she answered.

"Do you want anything from the minibar? A drink? A snack or something? I think there's rum. I know there's a Coke." Macon started talking faster and walked toward the minibar, which was stocked under the TV.

"Hey, Macon?"

"Yeah?" She opened the tiny refrigerator that was lined with overpriced alcohol, other drinks, and snacks.

"Are you nervous?" she asked.

Macon closed the fridge and stood. She turned around to face Joanna but didn't move toward her.

"That obvious?"

"Yes."

"I'm sorry."

"You don't have to apologize. You can just tell me what's going on."

"I don't know." Macon wrapped her arms around herself. "I guess I'm afraid to touch you."

"What?" Joanna stood. "You're afraid to touch me?"

"Not like that." Macon released her arms. "I'm afraid that if I touch you, I won't want to stop. And now that we're in this room alone, and there's a bed – a really nice bed – I don't want to push you if you're not ready for something."

"So, you're afraid if you kiss me – and I mean *really* kiss me, not like outside there – that you won't want to stop?"

"No, I *know* I won't want to stop," she corrected. "I'm afraid I won't be able to. If I go too fast, I might freak you out or make you feel pressured. I don't want that."

"Babe, come on. It's me." Joanna moved around the table and toward Macon, instantly noticing that Macon wrapped her arms around her body again. "You won't push me too far, Make. You know me too well for that."

She reached out to Macon and placed her hands on Macon's arms, pulling them gently apart and then placing them at Macon's sides before placing her own hands on the woman's hips. Macon looked remarkable in that dress. It was soft and thin. Joanna could feel the woman's toned muscles and her hip bones jutting out just slightly. She rubbed her thumbs over them and watched Macon's eyes close as she took another step into her.

"Maybe we can just sleep tonight," Macon suggested.

"Is that what you need?"

"I think so." She opened her eyes. "And no, it's not; at all." Her green orbs were dark and hungry.

Joanna knew exactly what she meant. She felt the

same way. It was the right decision for them to just sleep tonight. If not because of how tired she was, because it would be nice to just hold one another in a new way after being apart for so long. She also knew just by the simple touch of her hands to Macon's hips that she wanted more. All it would take was Macon making the first move. Joanna wasn't sure she had it in her to make that move herself. She'd already placed her hands on Macon's hips and was running her thumbs there, indicating she was clearly thinking about more than just sleep. Macon's stare was telling: she wanted it, too. They both wanted more than just sleep tonight.

"Can I maybe go take a shower, change, and get ready for bed?" she asked after a moment of staring into Macon's dark green eyes.

"Yeah." Macon swallowed and took a step back. "I'll go in after you. I'll change out here."

"Okay."

Joanna returned to the living room and wheeled her suitcase into the bedroom. Macon sat on the end of the bed, watching as she pulled out the items she'd need for her shower along with the shirt and pants she'd be sleeping in. Joanna felt Macon's eyes on her as she moved to start the shower and then returned to the bedroom to zip up her suitcase and place it against the wall.

"The shower is nice; it has good pressure," Macon stated after several moments of silence. "Just watch it: it gets pretty hot."

"Thanks." Joanna stood in front of her and stared down at the unsure eyes. "Will you do me a favor?"

"Sure." She seemed hopeful for a second there.

"Will you unzip me? I can probably do it, but—"

"Yes." Macon nodded and stood. "I can do that."

Joanna chuckled softly at her and turned around, showing Macon her back. The zipper of the dress was on the side, but it was easier to access from the back. Macon seemed to need a moment. Then, one hand moved to the zipper while the other one was placed on Joanna's hip, seemingly there to steady herself. She pulled down on the zipper slowly until it was all the way down. Her still hand slid up Joanna's other side and then back down while her other hand moved to the strap of the dress. She slid it down over Joanna's shoulder.

"Thank you," Joanna whispered.

"Will you…"

Joanna turned around to see her staring at where her hands were currently on Joanna's body, as if she needed to see them to believe they were there. Joanna wondered if that was actually true. Macon's hands were on her hips now. She was running them up and down, not going too far in either direction.

"Turn around," Joanna directed, knowing Macon needed the same kind of assistance.

Macon released her hips and turned around in place, allowing Joanna to see the long gold zipper on the back of Macon's dress. Joanna's hand shook slightly as she lifted it to the zipper and pulled it down. She could see the clasp of Macon's bra beneath, as well as the expanse of olive skin on her back. The zipper ended at the small of her back. Joanna stilled her hand there for a moment. She swallowed and worked up the courage to then move her hands up to the wide black straps on Macon's shoulders, sliding them down the woman's arms as she did. Macon gave her arms a quick shake. The dress fell to the floor, revealing the black bra and matching underwear beneath. Joanna found herself swallowing once more when Macon turned around, inches from her.

"You should probably take that shower now," Macon suggested in a whisper after she took in Joanna's stare.

Joanna's eyes moved to Macon's. Then, they lowered to her lips as Macon licked them. They lowered to her long neck, her breasts, and her stomach. Joanna ventured them lower only for an instant, trying not to focus too much on the thin fabric that separated the rest of Macon's most private parts from her view. She met her eyes again and slid the straps of her own dress off her body, letting it intermingle with Macon's on the floor.

"Just so it's fair," she said and walked into the bathroom.

She closed the door quickly behind her and leaned back against it. Her breathing was fast and shallow. She knew she'd never wanted anyone more than she wanted Macon. Her panties were more than soaked. She was grateful she'd brought in a new pair to change into after the shower. She dropped them and her bra to the floor and climbed inside the steaming shower, allowing the water to coat her skin.

She cleaned herself quickly, finding it difficult to stand because of a pounding in her chest that was somehow connected to the one between her legs. She then gave herself an extra five minutes to get her brain and body together, climbed out, and toweled off. She changed and brushed her teeth. She blew out a breath as she exited the bathroom. She found Macon sitting on the bed, changed into a pair of shorts and a t-shirt that she'd seen many times before.

"Hi," Macon greeted sweetly.

"Hi," she greeted back. "It's all yours." She motioned to the bathroom.

"Thanks." Macon stood quickly and rushed into the room.

Joanna only chuckled more at this woman's nervousness on her account. She couldn't understand it. Macon had been with women before. This should be more awkward for Joanna, because she was Macon: she was gorgeous, smart, funny, talented, and sexy as hell. Joanna couldn't figure why she was so nervous around her all of a sudden. A few minutes later, Macon emerged and found Joanna in the same position she'd been in on the bed moments earlier.

"All good?" Joanna asked.

Macon's foot was tapping rapidly on the carpet; she was biting the side of her mouth in nervous contemplation.

"No," the woman said and moved quickly to the bed where she straddled Joanna as she'd done on the sofa in her apartment nearly two months ago.

Her lips moved to Joanna's. Joanna was captured by this woman in every way. Macon's lips were hungry. Her tongue was moving against Joanna's. Joanna's hands were holding Macon's back to pull her closer against herself. Macon's hands were buried in her hair. Joanna was regretting the decision not to dry it. It would be easier for Macon to run her hand through the strands if they were dry. But after that thought, all other thoughts escaped her. Macon was pressing for her to lie back. Macon fell on top of her. Macon's skin was hot. She lifted her head to look down at Joanna.

"And now?" Joanna asked her with a smile.

"Good," Macon replied. "Can I?" she asked before moving her mouth to Joanna's neck.

"Yes," Joanna agreed easily as hot lips kissed and sucked at her skin, and then teeth nipped at her earlobe.

Joanna's legs were still hanging off the end of the bed as she gripped Macon's hips to try to make sure she didn't fall off. Macon pressed further into her body. Joanna felt Macon's center press into her stomach. Even though Macon had on shorts and a t-shirt, that was bunching up due to their movement, she could feel how wet Macon was.

"Are you okay?" Macon checked as she moved her hand under Joanna's shirt.

"Can we–" she started to ask, but Macon halted all her movements immediately. "No, Make. I don't want to stop. I just want to move up the bed."

"Oh." Macon smiled down at her and then lifted herself up.

She didn't climb off Joanna, though; she lifted

enough for Joanna to slide out from under her and up the bed, to rest her head against the pillows. Macon sat back for a moment and watched Joanna move before she followed and laid out on top of her, placing her hands beside Joanna's head.

"Better," Joanna said.

"I've always wanted you like this," Macon revealed. "I just didn't know it." She pressed her forehead against Joanna's. "How did I not know?"

"I didn't know either." Joanna ran her hands up and down Macon's back under her shirt, feeling the heat of Macon's skin against her own palms and fingertips.

"It's different for you."

"Why?"

"Because you weren't gay before me. Not that you're gay now," Macon added the last part quickly and lifted her forehead to check Joanna's reaction. "I just mean that I'm the first woman for you. I don't care what you are: gay, straight, bi, or somewhere in-between. I just–"

"Make?" Joanna smirked at her.

"Yeah?"

"Just kiss me." Joanna giggled at her and moved her hand to the back of Macon's neck, pulling her back down into herself.

Macon responded with a slow, deliberate kiss that deepened the longer it went on. Joanna spread her legs so that Macon could settle into her. Their hips lined up perfectly, meaning that their centers did too. Macon's hips rolled slowly into her; almost imperceptibly. God, Joanna was okay with what Macon was doing with her hips and her hands that were sliding back up Joanna's shirt. They stilled on her stomach, just below her breasts. Macon must have felt she needed permission.

Joanna wanted to give it to her, but she didn't want to stop kissing Macon to do it. She took her free hand and met Macon's arm. She gave it a slight nudge in the right direction, and after another moment of hesitation, Macon took the hint and slid it to cover her breast.

"God, Jo," she exclaimed after a brief disconnect of their lips.

She then ran her tongue along Joanna's bottom lip. Joanna moved her hand into Macon's dark, soft hair. Macon moaned into her mouth. Joanna's eyes shot open at the sound. She immediately flashed back to hearing Macon on the phone over a month ago and decided that, in person, it was so much better. Macon's hand, that had initially stilled on her breast, was now moving.

Macon squeezed, and squeezed. Joanna recognized that her hips wanted to lift to meet Macon's, which were still slowly rolling down into her. Macon's fingers were now playing with her nipple. They weren't twisting or squeezing; they were just running against it up and down. Then, Macon placed one finger on either side of the hardened pebble and gave it a slight squeeze, the pressure of which caused Joanna's hips to jerk up and into Macon. It was as if electricity had jolted through her body down to her toes. Macon repeated the action with her lips, leaving Joanna's and gliding back to her neck.

Joanna couldn't stand not touching her anymore and moved her hand back under Macon's shirt but around the front. She wasted no time in grasping Macon's breast with it. She squeezed immediately. Macon's reaction was to lift up and detach her lips from Joanna's body. Joanna wondered if maybe she'd done something wrong at first, but Macon sat up with both of her legs between Joanna's and clasped Joanna's hand to her chest. She reached for Joanna's other arm, and without words, Joanna knew what the woman wanted. She moved her hand to Macon's other breast and grasped them both while Macon's eyes closed and took in the sensation of Joanna's hands on her body.

After a few moments, Macon's hands topped hers. Macon coaxed more pressure out of her before she half-lowered herself back on top of Joanna but still allowed space for Joanna to play with her breasts while her hips returned to their work. Joanna worried she might come just from watching and touching Macon like this. But the hips rolling into her made her worry even more; they were going faster. Macon moved one thigh between hers. Joanna gasped at the additional pressure before she used her fingers and thumbs to play with Macon's hard nipples. Macon's hands were too busy holding her body up and in place as she moved her center above Joanna's thigh and then down into it with another thrust.

Joanna knew there was no turning back now. Macon's expression told her she was building toward release. She wouldn't stop that for anything. She had one of her own building as well and wondered who would come first.

"Make," she panted out when she felt Macon's thigh hit her clit in just the right way.

Then, Macon stilled. Joanna figured the woman had come and just did so silently, but Macon lifted up and looked down at her with such concern and wonder at the same time.

"I don't want it like this," she said after a moment and was clearly short of breath.

"What?"

"I want all of you," Macon explained. "I don't want us to come together for the first time fully clothed like this."

"Then, take–" Joanna began and tried to tug at Macon's shirt.

"No, Jo." Macon sat back up, still straddling one of Joanna's thighs. "We said we wouldn't tonight. And as much as I want to right now – and trust me, I do want to – what we said before I essentially attacked you with my lips was true."

"But you're almost there; I can tell," Joanna replied.

"I've been almost there since I saw you on the street a few hours ago." Macon smiled at her. "You turn me on just by being around, Jo." She leaned back down and kissed her gently on the lips before rolling off her and staring up at the ceiling. "Um... Am I a major bitch for stopping us? I mean, were you..." She turned only her head to Joanna, who was still staring up at the ceiling, reeling from the loss of warmth and pressure. "Were you-"

"Turned on?" she interrupted Macon and then blew out a deep breath. "Yes, Macon. I was and still am incredibly turned on, and about to come." She turned her head and gave Macon a smile that told her while she'd been absolutely serious, she also understood Macon's reasoning.

"I'm sorry." Macon turned onto her side to place a gentle hand on Joanna's cheek. "If you can tell me this is what you want right now, I will happily tear your clothes off. But I'm also happy with us just doing this and me getting to touch you." She moved that hand to Joanna's hip and ran it lightly under her shirt and around her back. "Like this," she added. "I've never gotten to do this. I would love to do just this until we fall asleep."

"Fine. But if our friends ever ask about our first night together after your whirlwind world tour, you'd have to tell them that *you* were the one who stopped us from having sex for the first time." She winked at Macon and loved the smile she got in return.

"My reputation will take a major hit."

"Babe, I think your reputation flew out the window the moment you and I decided to do this." She moved her body closer to Macon's and ran her hand up the front of Macon's shirt, placing it between her breasts. "Earlier outside, when Gail and I hugged, you apparently felt it was a little too long. You said I was *yours*."

"I did." Macon laughed.

"Did you mean that?"

"I told you I'd ask you to be my girlfriend when I saw you in person," she stated without answering the question.

"You did say that, yes." Joanna smiled.

"Are you sure you're ready for that? For me to be

your girlfriend? You've never had one of those before."

"Ask me."

"Will you–"

"Yes," she interrupted Macon and smiled before leaning in and capturing the woman's lips in a sweet kiss.

"What if I was going to ask you something else?" Macon laughed when they pulled apart a moment later.

"Were you?" Joanna lifted an eyebrow.

"No."

"So, I have a girlfriend?" Joanna asked her.

"Yes, you do." Macon pointed at her and squinted. "Off limits now."

Joanna could only laugh at that as she asked, "And you?"

"I've been off limits since I met you, Jo."

CHAPTER 18

"MACON?" Joanna rubbed the woman's back gently.

"Huh?"

"Babe, breakfast is here," Joanna said.

"What time is it?" Macon still hadn't opened her eyes.

"It's eight. You ordered it for eight. I heard the knock."

"I thought I wrote down nine." She opened one eye to see Joanna sitting on the edge of the bed next to her.

"You wrote down eight. But it smells really good. I poured you coffee." She smiled down at her.

"Does it have a heart in it?" Macon rolled over onto her back and smirked up at her.

"It's not that kind of coffee, and I still can't believe I did that." She moved to stand, but Macon's hand was on her arm.

"Hey, come here," she invited with a soft, still groggy voice that Joanna found sexy.

Joanna leaned down. Macon's hand went to the back of her neck, pulling her in for a brief good morning kiss.

"Morning," Joanna greeted.

"Sorry I got us out of bed earlier than expected," Macon replied and pecked her lips again.

"Well, my alarm went off the last time we spent the night together. I guess we're even."

"And you made me an artful and delicious coffee when that happened. What am I supposed to do for you today?"

"Well, that's a loaded question." Joanna stood. "After breakfast, what's on your agenda?" She walked into the living room of the suite toward the table that room service had set for them. "And I know I surprised you. I don't expect you to change any of your plans for me. I can check stuff out myself or just hang out here."

"I'm supposed to go to campus. I'm meeting with three violin students. They've each prepared a piece they want me to review. Then, I have to practice in one of the music rooms for a couple of hours, but I can skip that today."

"No, don't." Joanna turned back to see Macon following behind her. "You should practice if that's what you were planning on doing."

"I don't want to miss time with you while you're here," Macon said, then lifted Joanna's still somewhat messy hair away from her neck and kissed the back of it.

"I could watch you practice."

"Not exactly what I had in mind there, Jo." Macon wrapped her arms around Joanna from behind. "I was thinking we could eat our breakfast and go check out a few of the sights, then grab lunch before I have to do the reviews at two. That won't take more than a couple of hours. Then, we can walk around some more, come back here to change, and go to a nice dinner somewhere, taking a romantic after-dinner stroll along the water later; maybe in the North End. There are some amazing Italian restaurants there. We can come back here after that and – I don't know – watch a movie and just be together." She squeezed Joanna tightly. "I don't care what we do, honestly. I just want to be with you." She kissed Joanna's shoulder.

"You should still practice."

Macon laughed and released her.

"Fine. I'll practice for one hour," she agreed. "You know what's weird but also not?" Macon asked.

"What?"

"That, despite the addition of the physical element to our relationship, everything else is still the same. You still call me on shit, and we still banter back and forth."

"Did you think that would change when we started dating?" Joanna picked up her orange juice and sipped.

"I don't know. I've never really had that with any of the women I've dated. You know I haven't exactly been in many long-term relationships."

"And this is long-term for you?"

"Is it not for you?"

"You know how last night you said you're hoping to end at ten?"

"You're bringing up sex again? Really?"

"I'm hoping to end at eleven." Joanna stabbed at her eggs and didn't bother to check on Macon's reaction, knowing she'd be smiling at the thought of being Joanna's last lover.

"You sure you only want to be with me? There are other women who love women who would love to have their chance with you. I know because I've seen them hit on you in the bars. You sure you want to settle down with little old me?"

Joanna knew she was only kidding, but the thought of being with anyone other than Macon was completely unappealing to her.

"Make?"

"Yeah?" Macon took a bite of her eggs.

"Don't do that anymore, okay?"

"Do what?"

"Don't suggest I would want to be with anyone other than you, okay? You're who I want. I don't need to know what it's like to have sex with another woman. I don't need to hold another woman's hand or kiss another woman. I want you. I need those things with you. You are exactly who I want. You are perfect for me," Joanna stated confidently and watched Macon practically melt as she did.

"Okay," she replied.

"I'm sitting across from my best friend, who is now my girlfriend. We're having breakfast after she surprised me and flew across the country for me. We have this whole day planned together. I can stare at her all the time now, and it doesn't matter if she notices, because we're together. I can even check out her ass without having to look away when she turns around, because it's okay if she catches me. I can even tell her that I have an early show tomorrow: a matinée that starts at noon. And my parents will be there, because they're flying in late tonight and staying through Wednesday so they can see me play back in Boston. I didn't mention it because I didn't want to make you feel like you have to meet them if you don't want to. And they can be assholes sometimes, so you should really feel fine saying no, and I won't mention you were in town this weekend," Macon rattled off.

"Your parents are coming into town tonight?"

"Their flight doesn't land until after eleven. They're going straight to their hotel, which is several blocks away from this one, because they're members at the Camden chain." She took another drink of her coffee. "They don't know about you, because if my mom knew about you, she'd have to meet you immediately, and it would be more about my career than you."

"What do you mean?" Joanna sipped on her own coffee.

"You know my mom is not a fan of gay."

"I remember." She finished her bacon.

"I've never introduced her to any of the women I've dated mainly because of that. It wouldn't have been fair to them when I wasn't sure if the relationship was serious enough or going to last. When I did tell my mom I was dating someone, though, she only wanted to know how it messed with my rehearsal schedule. She only cares about my playing. If I brought a man home, she'd open the door and bake him a damn cake; but a woman is an inconvenience to my playing."

"I'm sorry, Make." Joanna placed a hand palm up on the table and waited for Macon to place her hand on top. "My flight is at four. I can head to the airport before the show, or I can still go but just be in the audience. I'll say goodbye to you before. I don't have to meet them if you don't want me to."

"I do." Macon squeezed her hand. "I'm being selfish because I don't think she's going to be welcoming. But my dad and I have an okay relationship. I guess it would be nice if they knew about you; about us."

"If you want me to meet them, I will. I can deal with the attitude."

"Yeah?"

"For you? Anything." She winked at Macon.

***

"I just want to say one thing before you start practicing." Joanna stood and walked to Greene, who had only just turned to face her after the student exited.

"Okay?"

Joanna wrapped her arms around Greene's neck and pulled Greene into her.

"You are so hot when you teach," she suggested. "I've been sitting there, watching you watch them. Your hand moves at your side sometimes, as if you're the one playing. Then you stand, and you use words I don't know. They play again. It always sounds better, and they worship you, Macon. Those students worship you."

"So, I'm hot when I teach? That's what I took away from that." Greene smiled and wrapped her arms around Joanna's waist.

"Yes, you are very hot when you teach." Joanna pressed her lips to Greene's neck just below her earlobe. "You're even hotter when you play, though." She kissed the same spot again.

"We can go; I don't have to rehearse. We can head

177

back to the room, and–"

"Nope." Joanna pulled back. "You're rehearsing."

"Jo…"

"I'm going to leave you to it. I'll just walk around for a bit and take some pictures. I'll meet you back here in an hour."

"You just said I was hot when I played. You're not going to watch?"

"I want you to be focused. Maybe I can get a private show later, though?" she asked.

"Absolutely." Greene laughed and pulled Joanna back into her.

"You know I'm crazy about you, right?"

"I guess I do now." Greene kissed her cheek.

"And that has nothing to do with your talent with a violin, Macon."

"Okay?"

"I just want you to know that. I'm with you because of who you are. And, of course, a part of who you are is a musician and has been your whole life, but I love your sense of humor, and how smart you are. I love how caring you are, and how you sometimes care so much about someone else that it's to your detriment. I love watching you play whether it's in the back of an orchestra, at the front of the stage on your own, or in your apartment where it's just for me. Tomorrow, if you decided you never want to play again and you want to take up – I don't know – marine biology or something, I'd still be here." She kissed Greene's lips gently. "I'm not getting into any water where there are sharks, though."

Greene wasn't sure what she was happiest about after Joanna finished that speech. She stared into those baby blues and ran her hands through Joanna's light hair that was down. Joanna had used the word *love*. She hadn't said those three special words or anything, but she *loved* parts of Greene, and that was a start.

"Jo?"

"Yes?"

"Tonight, when we get back to the hotel, can we turn our phones off and spend your last night here together?"

"We already planned–"

"I mean *together*."

"Oh," Joanna replied, and her hands were now on the back of Greene's neck, running soft fingers over the tiny hairs there.

"I want to make love to you." Greene pulled the woman in and whispered in her ear. "I want to touch you all night."

"So, no more waiting?" Joanna asked into Greene's ear.

"No more waiting."

CHAPTER 19

GREENE WAS NERVOUS as she heard the beep of the hotel door accepting her card key. The mechanism clicked, indicating that it was unlocked. They'd enjoyed a day of exploration in between her work activities. They'd finished their evening out with dinner at a small Italian restaurant on the water. It was after nine when they finally returned to the room.

"How about a shower, and I can order us a movie and make us some drinks or something?" Greene suggested when they entered.

"You don't want to join me?" Joanna asked suggestively as she tugged on Greene's hands toward the bedroom. "Or we can take a nice, long bath together. You can lie behind me and be naked. I can also be naked."

"That's an option? You, me… naked in a bathtub?" she asked.

Her phone rang in her pocket, and she scolded herself for not turning it off the moment she'd left the rehearsal room. She pulled it out and squinted at it when she saw her mother was calling.

"Who is it?"

"My mom. She's supposed to be on a plane." She glanced at Joanna. "Maybe it's a good thing, and they got caught up and aren't coming in after all." She accepted the call and offered Joanna two crossed fingers to provide them luck. "Mom?"

"Macon, we're here."

"Here where?" she asked.

"Boston. Your father and I are here. We caught an earlier flight."

"What happened to the luncheon you couldn't miss?" Greene asked, feeling her heart speed up, and not at all for the right reason.

"It was rained out. Someone didn't plan on the weather, and it was outside with no tents. Who does that?"

"I don't know, Mom. So, did you guys just land, or—"

"No, we're in the lobby of your hotel. We changed ours to this one."

"What? Why? You're at the Camden."

"We were at the Camden. But this is a sister property, and your father has discovered that we still get points here because of it. I guess Camden bought out this brand. I don't know, Macon. We're downstairs. We just need your room number. We're in room ten-fifteen."

"It's late, Mom. Why don't we just have breakfast tomorrow? I just got in, and I'm exhausted." She gave Joanna what she hoped was an apologetic expression.

Joanna leaned in, kissed her cheek, and pointed to the bathroom. Greene wasn't sure if she had to go or if she wanted to give Greene some privacy.

"We're just going to say goodnight. Your father could use a drink. Bourbon helps him sleep. The minibars have that here, right?"

"I don't know. Have him order from the bar or something, Mom."

"I'll have him get one. But do you want one, too, or do you want something else? A beer, maybe?" she said that last part with a little bit of disgust in her voice. "I'm getting a martini. Why don't you just meet us down here? We'll sit and drink. Then, we'll leave you alone."

Greene had three choices: she could allow her parents entry into her room; she could go down to the bar herself and save Jo from the meeting tonight, but then would have to explain to her parents why she'd done that tomorrow; or she could go down to the bar with her girlfriend, have a quick drink with her parents, and come back upstairs.

"Give me five minutes. I'll meet you down there."

"We're checking in. Your father just got the key. We'll go up to our room and freshen up. We–"

"Freshen up? Mom, you said a quick drink."

"And it will be. I'm exhausted, too, Macon. But your parents just flew across the country to see you. The least you could do is give us fifteen minutes to get settled and meet us for one drink."

"I'll be down in a minute." She ended the call before her mother had a chance to make her agree to anything else, and went in search of her girlfriend who, it turned out, was sitting on the bed, staring at her own phone. "Hey, sorry."

"Where are you going in a minute?" Joanna asked, obviously hearing the whole conversation, or at least Greene's side of it.

"My mom wants me to meet them at the bar for a quick drink."

"Oh." Joanna sat the phone on the bedside table and turned back to her. "I can hold off on the whole bath thing until you get back."

"Or, you could come with me?" Greene asked.

"You sure?"

"If you don't come tonight, they're just going to wonder where I was hiding you tomorrow, when you do meet."

"I don't have to meet them at all, remember? It's up to you, Macon. I don't want you to feel pressured just because I surprised you here."

Greene walked around to Joanna's side of the bed and sat on the edge. She took her hand, lifted it to her mouth, and kissed each knuckle individually.

"This is not how I planned on us spending the rest of our night."

"I know." Joanna ran her hand through Greene's hair. "But it's okay. Honestly, I'm fine with whatever you decide."

"If I say I really want you to come meet them because I've never introduced them to anyone and I like the idea of you being the first, and they treat you like a second-class citizen, am I going to pay for that later?"

Joanna laughed and leaned forward, pressing her forehead to Greene's.

"That depends: will you be defending my honor or throwing me to the wolves?"

"Defending, of course."

"Then, you will not be paying for it later." Joanna kissed her nose. "Let's go get this part out of the way. I think I can hold my own against your mom."

"Maybe you can. She's not your mom, so she can't do the parental guilt thing with you."

"You're so cute." Joanna pecked Greene's lips. "My big, bad girlfriend is afraid of her mommy."

"Oh, just you wait, Joanna Isabella."

***

Joanna and Macon sat at the hotel bar at a table for four. Unfortunately, it was only the two of them so far. They'd been sitting downstairs for twenty minutes now, and she was starting to think they'd been stood up.

"I'm sorry," Macon said for at least the fifth time. "Let's just go back upstairs. I'll text them it's too late." She reached for her phone.

"Babe, it's fine. We can wait." She took Macon's hand under the table.

"I can't believe they're making us wait like this."

"Macon, let's just give them five more minutes, okay?" Joanna requested.

"I'm at least getting you a drink. Me trying to be polite and waiting for them is over." She stood. "Rum and Coke?"

"No, just water. I don't feel like alcohol."

"Are you sure? You'll need it." Macon gave her an

expression that said she knew what she was talking about. "I'm getting a shot and a beer. I'm going to finish both of those, then I'll get a glass of wine or a more appropriate drink according to my mother; like a dry martini. I'll sip on that until we end this little meetup." She was still holding onto Joanna's hand even though she was standing. She ran her thumb over it. "Are you sure you only want water?"

"How about I just sip on that martini with you so we can finish it faster?"

"Macon?"

"Mom, hi," Macon greeted a woman who had come up behind her and was standing next to a man Joanna assumed to be her father. Her mother looked like a shorter and slightly heavier, but not by much, version of Macon. Her eyes weren't as bright. Her hair was slightly darker. Her skin was also just a touch on the darker side, which led Joanna to believe that this was the Italian half of her parentage. "Dad," she greeted her father.

"Hi, honey." Her dad was only slightly taller than Macon, and he reached out his hand for a shake, which Joanna thought a little strange.

"Hi," Macon replied, shook his hand, and then looked to her mother, who did, in fact, hug her daughter. "Hi, Mom."

"Sorry, we're a little late. I had to hang up a few things for this week, and one of my dresses was already wrinkled, so I wanted to iron it before we came down."

"You could have called and told us you'd be late," Macon suggested.

"Us?" Macon's mom asked. It was then that she noticed Joanna, who had stood up behind Macon. "Hello?"

"Mom, Dad, this is Joanna." She reached for Joanna's hand. "My girlfriend."

"Oh," her mother said.

"Girlfriend?" her father asked. "Did we know you were seeing someone?" "Hello, dear," he greeted Joanna, and his tone was a little more forgiving than Macon's mother's.

"It's nice to meet you both," Joanna told them with a smile and held out her hand for them to shake.

Macon's father took it first. His handshake was firm, like he used it for business and didn't know how to adjust it for personal encounters. Macon's mother was very clearly giving her a once-over.

"How long have you two been together?" her mother asked and went to sit down at one of the chairs without so much as an introduction to Joanna. "Do you live in Boston?" she asked Joanna, who sat down alongside Macon and immediately took Macon's hand into her lap, because she needed to be touching her girlfriend now for encouragement.

"Mom, calm down. We've been together for–" She stopped, and Joanna met her eyes. "How long have we been together?" She laughed.

"You don't know how long you've been a couple?" her father asked as he sat down. "Is there a waiter here or do I have to go to the bar to get a drink?" He seemed to be asking no one in particular, and then waved his arm to the bartender in that way that often drove Joanna crazy.

"It's not like that; we've known each other for over a year. I've talked about her to you guys before," Macon said.

"We've heard about Keira and Hillary. And I remember someone else with a K name. Kelly?" her mom asked.

"Kellan; she moved to Lake Tahoe to be with her girlfriend," Macon explained. "And Joanna; I've mentioned her a lot over the past year or so."

"Joanna? The photographer?" her dad chimed in just as the bartender approached, seeming a little out of place beyond the safe confines of his wooden bar. "I'll take a Macallan 18; neat. My wife will have a Bombay Sapphire martini; perfect."

"With olives on the side," Macon's mother requested.

"Macon?" Her father looked at Macon.

"Oh. Jo?" Macon asked Joanna.

"A water for me, thanks."

"Water?" her mother questioned.

"I'm feeling a little dehydrated; we walked a lot today," she replied and then gulped at the stare Macon's mother gave her, as if she was wondering if she was an alcoholic and lying about it.

"She'll have a Pellegrino then," Macon's mother ordered for her.

"Mom, she'll have whatever water she wants. Jo, tap?"

"Yeah." Joanna loved Macon even more in that moment; not for telling her mother off, but for knowing her well enough that she'd want simple tap water tonight and nothing complicated.

"I'll have a—"

"Please don't say a beer, Macon Sage," her father said. "At least not in your mother's presence, or I'll have to hear about how uncivilized our daughter is all night."

"What if it's a French beer? Is that better?" Macon directed at her mother.

"Lord, Macon." She turned to the bartender. "She'll have what I'm having."

"I'll just have a water," Macon said. "Like my girlfriend, Joanna, who is sitting right here and is meeting you two for the very first time. You could at least pretend you care."

"I'll get your drinks." The bartender seemed all too interested in leaving this conversation.

"He could have asked if we wanted pretzels or something. We should have just stayed at the Camden," she said to her husband and then looked at Macon. "And, honey, it's not exactly like we were prepared to meet your friend tonight. You don't tell us anything about…" she hesitated, "that part of your life."

"She *was* my friend, Mom. But now, she's my girlfriend; we're a couple."

"A couple that doesn't know when they started dating?"

"It was six weeks ago." Joanna leaned forward. "It was right before she left on tour. We'd been dancing around it for a while, I think. It took us both realizing it was more than friendship, and when we finally admitted it, it felt right." She turned to make sure Macon agreed, and when Macon smiled back and squeezed her hand under the table, Joanna knew she did. "Your daughter is one of a kind."

"We know that, dear. She's always been the most talented violinist in—" her mother started.

"No," Joanna interrupted. "That's not what I mean." She made sure her glare gave away that she wasn't done. "Macon is a remarkably gifted violinist. But, to me, that's the least important thing about her." She took her hand from Macon's and placed it on the back of Macon's neck instead. She knew it might be too much, but she didn't care. "She is beautiful, and I don't just mean in the obvious way." She smiled at Macon. "She's so sweet. She brings me lunch because she knows I forget to eat sometimes. She helped me figure out that I wanted to leave my old job and do photography full-time. She inspires me and makes me laugh. She challenges me. I'm better because I know her." She rubbed Macon's neck and watched her eyes close, but only briefly before she seemed to remember she was sitting in front of her parents.

"Well, that's nice," her father said as the bartender arrived, carrying their drinks.

"So, a new relationship then?" Macon's mother asked. "And you've been on tour since then? Did she go with you?"

"No, Mom. She didn't. She just came to Boston for the weekend. She surprised me." She placed her hand on Joanna's thigh.

Macon's father passed the martini to his wife as the bartender left the water glasses in front of Macon and Joanna.

"And things are good?" her father asked and took a long drink, as if needing the burning liquid to recharge his batteries and go on.

"Things are great," Joanna replied for her. "We haven't had a lot of time together, obviously, since she's been away, but I'm very happy."

"And you don't mind her going on tour?" her mother asked in an accusing tone.

"No, I don't. I miss her. I'll miss her when I leave tomorrow, because she won't be back for another week and a half, but I want her to be happy. If she wants to go on tours, then I want that for her, too."

"She should be touring more; at least six months out of the year, Macon." She turned to her daughter and drank half of her martini in one gulp before she tossed an olive into the drink and ate another one from the small dish of five or six the bartender had provided. "Maybe even nine months. You need an agent at this point, since this tour has been so successful. It can be hard on a relationship," she added, "to be with someone who isn't around much."

"Well, I'm a photographer, so I can always grab my camera and go with her," Joanna fired back.

"And you make good money at that? What do you photograph?"

"Mom!" Macon exclaimed.

"It's okay." Joanna laughed. "I have my own business. I do everything myself, and that means I have no employees to pay, so that's helpful. I'm really just getting started though, but I make ends meet fine. I had a gallery show a while ago and sold some prints. I mostly shoot weddings, newborns, and families."

"She's being modest," Macon said. "She does that stuff, but she also does a lot of urban photography. She just walks around and sees things no one else does, captures it, takes it home, and edits it into something amazing. She goes on hikes sometimes and does the same with nature photography. I have one of her flower prints in my apartment."

"Editing? Isn't the point of photography to take the picture so that it's perfect and leave it at that?" Macon's father asked, but Joanna didn't sense that he meant anything offensive in his tone.

"That's the goal. But, sometimes, it can be fun to manipulate them, too; take something you shot in color and make it black and white or crop something out that was just on the edge."

"I guess that makes sense." He drained his glass, and Joanna noticed Macon's mother's glass was also empty.

"So, you and Macon will just travel the world together then?"

"Mom, the tour is ending. I'm going home soon."

"I know. But there will be another one, Macon. I'm sure they'll be reaching back out to you soon to schedule the next."

"I have a contract with the orchestra, Mom. I have to finish that, and then I'll think about what I want to do next. Right now, I just want to get home. I miss it there, and I miss Joanna."

"Yes, but Macon, your career–"

"Is fine the way it is, Mom. We've had this discussion a million times. We've been having it since I was sixteen years old. I wanted to stay in high school like a normal kid, and you wanted to ship me off to Julliard."

"You were never a normal kid, Macon," she argued.

"Because I wasn't allowed to be."

"Normal kids are not as gifted as you were. And if we didn't honor that gift and push you to practice and–"

"Okay, I think it's time we call it a night," her father interrupted. "I'm tired, and your mother is tired. I'm sure you're both tired as well."

"I was–" her mother tried again.

"Dad's right. I'm tired, Mom. I really don't want to have this fight again, and definitely not in front of Joanna, who you've managed to be rude to without even realizing it, which is exactly what I thought you'd do. So, we're going upstairs to bed. I'll just see you two after the performance tomorrow."

"Macon, I thought we'd have breakfast at least," her father protested, though lightly, and stood up at the same time.

"We're going to have breakfast in our room. She's leaving tomorrow. I want to have time with her alone before she goes."

"She's staying here?" her mother asked and stood.

"Mom, where the hell else would she be staying?" Macon stood as well, disconnecting their bodies, but she reached out for Joanna's hand. "I'm an adult. She's an adult. We're together. We're staying in the same damn hotel room, Mom. We share a bed. That's how this thing works."

"I don't need you to tell me that," her mother whispered while looking around at the relatively empty bar, as if to see if anyone had heard Macon's words.

"Seems like you do," Macon reminded. "Mom, we're going to bed. And tomorrow, I'm going to spend time with Jo until I have to go to work. After the show, I'll see her off to the airport. Then, the three of us can go to dinner or something. But please don't spend this entire trip trying to browbeat me into doing things I don't want to do, and don't pretend you want to know about my love life when we all know you're not interested because I'm gay." She took Joanna's hand. "Let's go?"

"Sure," Joanna replied. "It was nice to meet you." She was then pulled away from the table by Macon.

"I am so sorry," Macon said the moment they entered the elevator and the door closed behind them.

"For what?" Joanna asked her and placed her head on Macon's shoulder as the elevator ascended.

"She's such a bitch, and he's not that much better. I shouldn't have brought you. I should have just gone myself, answered the two or three questions they'd ask about work, and then come back up to the room. I'm so sorry, Jo."

"Hey, you don't have to be sorry. You warned me. I wanted to go; that's number one. Number two is that you didn't just sit there and let them interrogate or denigrate me, Macon. You stood up for me, and you left when it was time to leave. I'm okay. We're okay."

"I just want to scream at her sometimes."

"Why don't you?" Joanna suggested as the elevator dinged and arrived at their floor. "Seriously."

"I don't know." Macon sighed as they walked down the hallway hand in hand. "She's still my mom. I just wished she tried to understand me instead of always making me feel like I'm not enough."

They arrived at the door. Joanna stopped Macon before she could use the key to open it.

"You're enough for me." She turned her so that they were facing one another. "You're enough for me, Make. I don't care about how your parents treat me. I can deal with that. You're enough for me."

"Thank you." Macon laid her head on Joanna's shoulder. "I am so tired.

"Let's get some sleep then."

"What? No, I didn't mean–"

"Babe, we're both exhausted; and after that fireworks show downstairs, I don't think either one of us is in the mood."

"I guess not." Macon lifted her head. "I guess we'll wait a little bit longer then."

CHAPTER 20

"So, YOU TWO didn't go through with it?" Emma asked as they sat at lunch the following Friday with Keira and Hillary.

"Go through with it?" Joanna tossed back like that sentence sounded ridiculous. "Emma, really?"

"You two have been apart for a while now, and we know you have the hots for her," Keira egged her on.

"Well, she *is* my girlfriend. It kind of makes sense that I have the hots for her."

"I knew it!" Emma pointed at her. "They are official. You owe me twenty, Hill."

"Fine. Fine," Hillary acquiesced and reached for her wallet.

"You guys bet on me? On Macon and me?"

"We weren't sure if you'd come back official or still in limbo since you hadn't had a lot of time together," Keira replied. "And *they* bet on it." She pointed at Emma and Hillary. "I didn't."

"Did you really just rat me out like that?" Emma laughed and wrapped her arm around Keira, placing it over the back of her chair.

"I'm not going down with you two," Keira returned.

"I can't believe you losers bet on us."

"It's actually a good thing," Hillary offered. "We are betting *on* you. We're on your side."

"You didn't think we'd be a couple?"

"I thought you had two days together on that little trip and that you guys would talk and get to know this new part of your relationship. I figured you'd come back and feel good about it, but that you wouldn't be official yet. I thought that would come later. However, Keira does owe me twenty for betting that the two of you would have sex," Hillary elaborated.

"What?" Emma laughed in Keira's direction.

"Fine. Just give Hill back the twenty, and we break even."

"So, you bet that Macon and I would have sex in Boston?" Joanna asked.

"The way you'd been talking about her, I thought you'd *only* have sex in Boston."

"You two had a side bet going on, and you didn't tell me?" Emma teased her girlfriend. "How can we ever get past this betrayal?"

"I guess I'll just have to make it up to you then." Keira lifted suggestive eyebrows.

"God, I need a girlfriend," Hillary said. "If you two are still acting like this after being together for over a year already, and you and Greene are now an item, I'm the new fifth wheel."

"You're not a fifth wheel," Joanna encouraged.

"Not now. But when Greene comes back in a week, I will be."

"What about the coffee shop woman?" Keira questioned.

"Still with that, Keira?"

"Who's the coffee shop woman?" Joanna asked.

"She's this incredibly attractive woman who has been going to the same coffee shop as our beautiful little Hillary here forever, and she stares at her. They've never spoken, because neither of them, apparently, has the guts to start a conversation. It's now just ridiculous," Keira explained.

"I think if she wanted me, she would have said something by now, don't you?" Hillary asked Keira.

"*You* want her. You haven't said anything," Emma joined.

"I don't want her. I don't even know her," Hillary retorted.

"Because you haven't talked to her," Keira replied and laughed. "We could do this all day."

"Around and around," Emma said.

"Anyway, I don't know about the coffee girl, but I think I am finally ready for something real; something lasting." Hillary took a sip of her ice water. "I feel good. I'm healthier now. I love my job and my students. I still need some new friends that are actually nice to me, but other than that… I think I'm ready."

Joanna's phone buzzed in her pocket. She pulled it out to see that Macon had texted her.

"Is that her?" Keira asked. "She's been back in the states for over a week now, and she still hasn't called any of us. Put her on speaker so I can yell at her."

"It's a text."

"That says?"

"To call her," Joanna answered.

"So, call her." It was Hillary this time.

Joanna rolled her eyes, dialed, and said, "Fine. But be nice to her. I want her to come home, remember?"

"Hey, beautiful," Macon said into the speaker, and Joanna's face turned a bright shade of red.

"Thank you, Greene. I changed moisturizers. It's so nice of you to notice."

"Keira?" Macon asked, and everyone other than Joanna laughed.

"Babe, don't blame me. We're all at lunch, and they wanted me to put you on speaker."

"Oh." Macon sounded disappointed.

"Nice to talk to you, too, Greene. It's only been what? Like two months?" Keira said.

"Yeah, sorry. Things have been–"

"Busy?" Hillary interrupted her. "You seemed to have more than enough time to call Joanna over here."

"She's my–" She stopped. "Jo?"

"They know, Make."

"She's my girlfriend, Hill. And I *have* been busy. I was actually just calling my girlfriend to tell her something when you idiots jacked her phone. Can she have it back now so that I can tell her something?"

"You haven't spoken to us in months, and we're the idiots? Nice, Greene." Keira laughed. "I guess we can just yell at you next week."

Joanna took the phone off speaker and put it to her ear immediately.

"Everything okay?"

"Yeah, everything's fine," Macon told her. "So, they know about us?"

"They know we're officially together, yes." Joanna watched as three sets of eyes stared at her. "Talk amongst yourselves," she ordered and stood to flee the table and the scrutiny as they laughed at her.

"Are they giving you a hard time?"

"I can take it." Joanna walked toward the door of the restaurant to have some privacy from the group. "What's going on?"

"They want to extend the tour again. They want me in Chicago after this, and then LA before I hit Canada."

"What?" Joanna made her way outside and suddenly felt like she couldn't breathe.

"I'm kidding." Macon laughed.

"Macon Sage Greene!" she practically yelled.

"I'm sorry. I couldn't resist."

"I hate you right now." Joanna laughed back.

"I just called to tell you that we're going out after the performance tonight, since it's the final one at the school. I won't be able to make our goodnight call."

"Oh, okay."

"I miss you, Jo."

"I miss you too. You'll be home soon though, right?"

"Yes, I'll be home soon. I can't wait to see you."

"Me neither."

"I should go. I have to rehearse."

"Okay. Hey, Make?"

"Yeah?"

"I'm really happy," she told Macon. "I just wanted you to know that I'm really happy right now. I can't imagine how much happier I'm going to be when we're actually in the same city."

"I'm really happy, too, beautiful. I'll call you tomorrow?"

"Have fun tonight, but not too much."

"I'll save my too much fun for you," Macon offered.

CHAPTER 21

JOANNA WOKE at six as usual and made her coffee before she took a quick shower. She didn't have a shoot that day, but she did plan on spending most of it at home editing. She had not scheduled any actual work because she would only be unfocused and counting down the minutes for Macon's arrival. Her flight would land at 7:14 p.m. It would take her about forty-five minutes to get off the plane, get to baggage claim and grab her bags. Joanna would be standing there as soon as she entered, and she could not wait to get to hug Macon.

She climbed out of the shower and dried her hair. When she turned off the hair dryer and slid it into the drawer, she heard a sound coming from the front door of the apartment. Her heart started racing. She worried she'd left her phone in the kitchen and had no way to call for help. She gulped and stuck her head slightly out the bathroom door but didn't have a clear view. She moved out into the hallway. That was when she saw her.

"Macon?"

"Hi, beautiful. I'm home." Macon smiled at her from just inside the door.

"What are you doing here?"

She ran toward her, not waiting for a response, and watched as Macon dropped her shoulder bag to the floor. Her violin case was already there next to her luggage.

"I took the red-eye. I couldn't wait." Macon pulled Joanna into her.

"God, I'm so glad you're here." Joanna wrapped her arms around Macon's neck and squeezed her tightly.

"I also had to do laundry." She laughed into Joanna's

hair. "You smell good." She pressed her lips to Joanna's neck. "You smell really good. You smell like home," she added softly, and her lips pressed to that spot again.

"Laundry, huh?" Joanna had her hands in Macon's dark, soft hair.

"Yeah, laundry," Macon said again and kissed the spot just a little lower. "I came to your place first so I could—"

"Do laundry?" Joanna pulled back and stared into her eyes.

"Yes," she whispered.

Joanna saw how exhausted Macon was in her eyes. The woman probably hadn't slept well on the plane. But she could also see something else. She knew what was about to happen, because it had been building between them all along. Macon's hands moved to her hips, around her waist, and then gripped her ass. Before she knew it, Joanna was lifted off the ground. She had no choice but to wrap her legs around Macon as her lips met Macon's in a heated kiss. Macon walked them both backward, until Joanna's back was against a wall and she was tugging at Macon's shirt.

Macon held her in place but shifted her own body to allow Joanna to hastily pull it off and toss it to the floor. No words were spoken between them as Macon watched Joanna pull off her own shirt, which she'd only thrown on after her shower. She hadn't bothered with a bra. Macon's eyes went to Joanna's breasts as she held her pressed to the wall; her stomach against Joanna's center. Joanna reached around Macon's back and unclasped her bra.

She knew she wouldn't be able to get it off entirely, given their positions, but she still slid the straps down Macon's shoulders. Macon moved into her, pressing their breasts together before Joanna had a chance to even look at them. It didn't matter, though, because how they felt pressed against her own was enough to make the pulsing between her legs quicken.

Macon's nipples were moving against her own as her lips and tongue played with Joanna's neck. All that movement only provided her center with much-needed friction. She felt her own hips lift and fall against the wall to try to increase it, until one of Macon's hands moved to her breast. Macon held onto it tightly while she continued to practically thrust into Joanna. Joanna could barely hang on and had her palms pressed to the wall behind her. Macon's fingers played with her nipple, holding it so she could bring her mouth to it and return her hand to Joanna's ass, which allowed Macon to use both hands to lift Joanna just slightly higher.

Macon's lips engulfed her nipple. It had already been erect, and now it was painfully so. As Macon sucked it deeper into her mouth, Joanna couldn't think about pain; only the sensations rushing through her body. Her wetness had now soaked her underwear through. She felt one of Macon's hands move to her jeans to try to undo them. Joanna moved Macon's hand back to herself, to hold her in place, and moved her own hand to her jeans. She had to try several times but finally got the button undone and then unzipped them.

She used both hands to push the jeans down slightly, and though they weren't off entirely, they were down far enough that Macon seemed satisfied for the moment. Macon's tongue bathed Joanna's nipple while she pressed further into Joanna. She moaned into Joanna's breast as Joanna's wetness coated her abdomen.

Joanna needed more. She pressed her hands into Macon's back, pushing the woman even further into herself. Her own back was hurting from being pushed into the wall, but she felt like she could be absorbed by it and she wouldn't mind as long as Macon was pressing into her like this.

Macon's mouth moved to her other breast and paid it the same attention. Joanna's breathing was so fast, she felt like she might hyperventilate. Without saying anything,

Macon lifted her from the wall and carried her through the open door of her bedroom. She then dropped Joanna unceremoniously onto the bed. She yanked her own bra away from her body, then slid the jeans down her legs and kicked them off. She was dressed only in pastel purple boy shorts.

Joanna could see how wet she was through them. Her eyes stayed on that spot as she lay back, lifting herself on her elbows to take in the view before she watched Macon reach for her legs, pull them toward her, and then reach for the waistband of her underwear. Macon met her eyes. Joanna nodded. Macon's hand went to work and pulled the underwear down over her thighs, her knees, and then past her ankles, dropping them to the floor.

Joanna observed Macon's eyes as they immediately took her in. Macon's tongue slid slowly over her lips as she did. Joanna was certain she'd never been more wanted in her entire life. Within seconds, Macon had removed the last remaining article and climbed on top of Joanna, moving back with her to the top of the bed, where she captured Joanna's lips once more. Macon lowered herself. Joanna could feel every part of this woman pressed against her own skin. It was better than she'd imagined it would be.

Macon's lips were on her throat, then her collarbone. It was all happening so fast, Joanna couldn't keep up with the sensations she was experiencing. Then, Macon's hips were rolling into her. Her own hips were lifting up without her even realizing it. Macon had a thigh between hers. Macon's center was pressed into her thigh, and she could feel it. She could feel how wet Macon was; how turned on she was. Joanna gasped. Macon stopped for a moment and looked down at her; she didn't say anything. She just looked down with such reverence, Joanna knew that if she didn't want to do this, this was Macon giving her an out. This was Macon telling her silently that it was okay.

Joanna pulled her back down and kissed her while

her free hand went to Macon's hip and moved it back and forth, indicating that she wanted the woman to slide that wetness over her skin. Macon did. As her own thigh pressed into Joanna's center, she rubbed herself against Joanna's thigh. Macon grunted once, and then again, before she began to speed up. Joanna felt like she could come at any minute, and she hadn't even really been touched yet.

Then, it happened: Macon's fingers slid between their bodies. She wasted no time; her fingers moved into Joanna's wetness. Macon seemed directionless at first, but she was only coating her fingers, because then two of them slid inside her. Joanna moaned at the feeling of being filled by Macon, and then moaned again, because Macon's hips were pushing her thigh against her own clit while Macon's fingers seemed to be dancing inside her body, moving in and out with each roll. Joanna was holding onto Macon's back; her fingernails were practically digging into the woman's skin because she was so overwhelmed by all the emotions and sensations of this moment. She couldn't believe this was happening: that a woman was touching her intimately. But that thought lasted only a moment, because it wasn't just *a* woman. It was Macon; the woman she loved. Joanna loved her. She'd possibly been in love with her since they'd met and hadn't realized it. Now, they were finally together. Macon was moving down her body while still pushing deep inside her.

Macon kissed her breasts and sucked on her nipples before using her tongue to flick each of them in turn. Joanna watched her watch them as they hardened, and Macon captured each one again before kissing Joanna's stomach and running her tongue around Joanna's belly button. Macon kissed just below it and then lower still. Joanna knew where she was going. She'd never done this before. Macon's tongue slid between her folds. Joanna's hips lifted up and then lowered back down as Macon repeated the motion.

Macon's eyes were open. They were on Joanna as she licked her up and down before she sucked Joanna's hard clit into her mouth.

Joanna let out a whimper and decided not to be embarrassed by that. She practically yelled as Macon twisted her right nipple at the same time she thrust inside her and sucked hard. Macon moaned, too. The vibrations caused Joanna to crest; she was there. She was right there, ready to tumble over the edge. But she didn't want this to end yet. It hadn't been long enough. She couldn't focus on each sensation because they were all happening at once. Macon was taking her in every way she could. She was giving Joanna what she'd never had. Macon was claiming her at the same time. She was saying Joanna was hers: her body, her heart, and her soul. Joanna screamed Macon's name as she came. Macon only slowed when Joanna's hand met the back of her head and coaxed her up. She continued further, though, as if not wanting to stop, until Joanna's trembling ceased. She removed her fingers and lifted herself up to hover over Joanna.

"Okay?" she asked softly.

"Okay?" Joanna wanted to laugh because she'd never been more okay in her life. "Are you kidding me?"

"Jo?" Macon kissed her, and Joanna tasted herself on her lips.

"Yes?"

"I love you," Macon whispered just above her lips, and Joanna saw the reverent look in the woman's eyes return.

"I love you, too." Joanna smiled up at Macon and couldn't believe she'd finally said it. "And that was way more than okay," she added. "Macon, that was…"

"What?" Macon asked and kissed her neck.

"Perfect," she replied, and Macon looked back up at her.

"Perfect?"

"Perfect, babe. God, I can't believe we just did that."

She ran her hands up and down Macon's back.

"Me neither. I've wanted to do that forever." She climbed off Joanna and moved to her side, running her fingertips over Joanna's hot skin. She then met Joanna's eyes. "Are you okay?" Her expression showed concern.

Joanna didn't answer. She rolled onto her side and then climbed on top of Macon, straddling her hips. Macon gripped Joanna's hips instantly, holding her reassuringly in place. Joanna had dreamed of this many, many times over the course of Macon's tour. She'd thought about how she'd touch Macon, and in what order she'd do things. She recalled the sounds Macon had emitted over the phone and used that memory to drive her fantasy forward. She'd pictured it a hundred ways and had never been able to narrow down what she'd do in reality. Now, Macon was beneath her. Her chest was heaving either from what she'd just done to Joanna, or from the realization of what Joanna was about to do to her. Joanna's brain was racing. Her hands were still on Macon's stomach, and she wanted to move them. She wanted to touch Macon everywhere, but she didn't know what to do first.

"I–" she stuttered.

"Hey, it's okay. You don't–"

"Stop," Joanna ordered gently. "It's not that."

"Okay. What's wrong?" Macon asked and ran her hands up and down Joanna's sides.

"Nothing. Nothing is wrong. Make, I love you," Joanna said and laughed softly. "I'm so in love with you." She watched as Macon's smile extended to her eyes. "I've thought about this so much: this moment, and how I wanted to touch you. Each time, it was good for you, you know? I just don't know about now. I don't know if I'll be able to–"

"Oh, Jo," Macon whispered. "I just showed up, and things started, but we can slow them down."

"I want slow," Joanna replied and nodded.

"Okay. Just come down here then and let me hold

you." She placed her hands on Joanna's back, coaxing her to lie down.

"No, that's not what I meant, Make," she corrected and leaned down to whisper into Macon's lips, "I meant I want slow." She pressed her lips to the corner of Macon's lips and rolled her hips into Macon. "Slow, Macon," she repeated and kissed the other side. "I don't want to forget any part of this." She lifted to check Macon's expression, which was clearly surprised. "And I'm not going to stop. I'm not going to be scared off. I'm not going to wake up tomorrow and want to run. You're it, Macon. You're it," she repeated and began a slow, deliberate kiss.

Joanna's hips wanted more; they craved it. They wanted to move down. Her hands did, too. They wanted to move between Macon's legs, but they didn't. Joanna used all her will power to hold them steady on either side of Macon's head while she continued their easy kiss. Her tongue danced with Macon's, and Macon's hands were on the move. They rubbed Joanna's back up and down before moving to her sides and repeating the movement. Macon slid them up Joanna's abdomen and grasped her breasts, causing the woman to gasp, but Joanna still remained focused on keeping things at her pace, despite Macon's best efforts to hasten her movements.

She could never be finished exploring this woman's mouth. She wondered if they were, perhaps, made to kiss one another, because that was what it felt like to Joanna. She'd never had a single kiss come close to matching any of the ones she'd shared with Macon. She moved her lips to Macon's jawline and placed soft kisses along it.

Macon's hands were becoming more insistent against Joanna's breasts, and her hips were beginning to move up. Joanna moved her lips to Macon's throat, continuing gentle kisses as she lifted her body up and away from Macon's hips. Just as Macon let out a moan of protest, Joanna sucked her pulse point, and that moan turned to one of pleasure. Macon's hands stopped squeezing, and her fingers started working on Joanna's nipples instead.

Joanna felt the now all too familiar pulse between her legs begin to pulse faster. She considered telling Macon to stop touching her so that she could continue on with her full focus. But she didn't want to give into her, knowing Macon was trying to distract her. She sucked on Macon's pulse point harder. She knew she'd leave a mark, but that only made her happier. She wanted to mark this woman. She wanted Macon and the rest of the world to know that Macon was hers. They belonged to each other now. She lowered her lips to Macon's collarbone and placed another mark there.

Macon let go of Joanna's nipples and moved her hands to Joanna's ass, pressing her back down into her own hips. Joanna rubbed her center over Macon's abdomen. Her wetness spread across the skin there. Macon attempted to spread her legs, but Joanna held her there with her thighs as she continued to move her lips and tongue over Macon's neck. When she could wait no longer, she lowered her mouth to Macon's breast, taking one hand to the other breast while she flicked a hardened nipple with her tongue.

"Yes." Macon's hips rose and fell once, and then again.

Joanna smirked into the nipple as she flicked it again, harder this time. Her hand squeezed the other breast before she sucked the nipple into her mouth, and then she knew that this was what she wanted for the rest of her life. She was making love to a beautiful woman. It was the most she'd ever felt; it was all at once. It was what she wanted forever. She moved to the other breast and tried to spend the same amount of time on that one, but her own body craved contact. She felt Macon's responses growing feverish. Her gasps and moans were louder. Her hips were rising insistently. Macon needed contact, and Joanna needed to be touching her.

She lowered her lips to Macon's abdomen and placed

both hands on Macon's breasts, continuing to squeeze them while alternating gentle and hard pressure to keep Macon off balance. When her lips moved to Macon's hips, that was the moment she knew what she wanted to do first. She kissed and sucked both of those beautiful hip bones before moving lower, to the woman's thighs. Macon gasped once, her head shot up, and Joanna knew she was about to tell her that she didn't have to do that if she wasn't ready. But Joanna kissed the inside of her thigh and then licked up and around, moving just above the top of Macon's curls to the other thigh, where she licked down. Macon's head shot back down. She didn't say anything after all.

Joanna could smell her arousal. She could almost taste Macon; and she wanted to. She hadn't been sure how she'd feel when she got to this point, but she knew now. She opened Macon's legs by placing both of her hands on the inside of the woman's thighs, used her fingers to spread Macon, and moved her mouth to Macon's center. Macon gasped first, and then moaned deeply as Joanna's tongue slid between her folds and moved up and back down.

"Oh, my God," Joanna whispered to herself more than to Macon.

She repeated the action. Her thumbs opened Macon to her even more before her hands went to Macon's breasts. She grasped them tightly, because she couldn't hold back anymore. Her lips engulfed a hard, swollen clit, and she sucked. She found that this action – even more so than any others – turned her on like crazy. While her hips were almost at the edge of the bed due to their position, Joanna found herself trying to hold back grinding them into the comforter that was bunched there. She halted her sucking to lick around Macon's clit and taste more of her.

She lowered her mouth to Macon's entrance, and slid her tongue hesitantly inside. Macon's hand went to the back of Joanna's head to encourage her further. Joanna dove deeper once, twice, and then three times before she used her tongue to slide herself back up and suck on Macon's clit even harder than before. Macon's hips lifted. Joanna moved one of her arms instinctively over the woman's hips to hold her in place. She had no idea where she'd learned that move, but it worked: Macon remained still, squirming beneath Joanna as her sounds grew louder. Then, they became non-existent. Macon came with small whimpers. Her hand in Joanna's hair relaxed. Joanna slowed her actions until the hand fell away entirely. She looked up and saw that Macon's eyes were still closed. She noticed something glistening on her cheeks. She lifted herself up and moved to hover above her, recognizing tears. She kissed each of Macon's cheek first, and then, her still closed eyelids.

"Macon?"

Macon didn't respond, but her eyes opened. They were bright, yet still filled with desire. She smiled wide when she realized Joanna was above her again. Joanna slid her thigh between Macon's and moved her hand between them. Macon's smile shifted into an O-shape when Joanna's hand lowered and entered her.

Joanna's fingers stilled at first. She'd already had so many firsts today, but this was somehow different and even more intimate than what she'd just done; she was inside another person. They were, in fact, one at this moment, and had been earlier, when Macon had been inside her. She knew then that she'd never felt whole before today.

Joanna moved her hips, pressing her thigh and her fingers into Macon's body. Her breathing picked up as she moved slightly faster, and then faster still. Macon's hands were on her back, pushing Joanna further into herself. She used her thigh to apply more pressure, moving even deeper. Macon's sounds got louder again as Joanna tried something Macon had done to her earlier: she curled her fingers in time with a thrust. Macon seemed to come undone beneath her. Joanna did it again, and again, and Macon came hard into her hand. She could feel Macon's muscles clench around her fingers. She could only smile and look down at her own hand. There was almost a sense of derealization, that she wasn't the one actually doing this; but Joanna knew that wasn't the case. As Macon began to come, her own center pressed into Macon's warm and muscled thigh. She came as she rocked herself into Macon.

Only when they both came down entirely did she remove her fingers, choosing to slide them up through Macon's wetness before she moved her hand back beside Macon's head, along with her other hand to hold herself above her. Macon was still breathing hard, as was Joanna. They both stared for long moments before Macon's smile returned and caused one in Joanna as well.

"I love you," Macon whispered against Joanna's lips and kissed them gently.

"I love you," Joanna replied and lowered herself on top of Macon, needing the woman's arms around her; and Macon knew that, so she provided.

They remained in that position until Joanna felt the breathing beneath her slow and then completely even out, and she knew Macon was asleep. She waited until she could be certain that Macon was out and not likely to wake up if she moved; then, she slowly, very slowly extricated herself to lie beside her. Macon stirred, but only slightly, and then she rolled onto her side. Her arm went lazily over Joanna's waist, and she pulled Joanna into herself.

Joanna wasn't tired. She'd slept the night before, unlike her exhausted girlfriend. She just rubbed Macon's back while she slept, revelling in how good it felt to have these moments with the one person she was supposed to be having them with all along.

CHAPTER 22

GREENE WAS IN THAT special space that only existed when someone was between sleep and wakefulness. She was smiling, she could tell that; maybe not on the outside, but definitely on the inside. She knew that her body was completely relaxed. Actually, her entire being was relaxed. That was a first. She recognized that she should be awake, though, because there was something happening. She wanted to be fully present for it. Her eyes remained closed as she tried to understand what it was that was happening. They opened instantly when she realized that someone's fingers were between her legs, sliding up and down. She glanced over to see Joanna watching her own fingers in action, before realizing Greene was awake and turning her eyes to hers.

It was as if Joanna had wanted her to wake up before she entered her, because the moment she realized Greene was up, her fingers slid down and inside her. Greene's hips lifted to allow her better access. Joanna slid on top of her, placing that thigh back where it was the last time they'd done this. Greene loved that she was being possessed entirely by this woman. She kept her eyes open this time as Joanna laid her head against her shoulder and thrust inside her, moving harder and faster each time.

Greene's hands went to Joanna's lower back before sliding them up and into her hair, loving the feel of it as it fell over her skin. Joanna breathed heavily into her ear and kissed her neck while she worked her thigh against Greene's center to try to create the friction Greene so clearly needed. Once she'd achieved just that, Greene felt the orgasm overtake her from the inside first, before it felt as if it was attacking her outside in the best way possible. She came hard. Before Joanna could even begin to slow down, Greene had flipped them and hovered over her. Joanna's fingers were still buried inside her, but they were still. Greene rocked against Joanna, encouraging her to continue. Joanna lifted an eyebrow and gave her a knowing grin as Greene's hips rolled and her center rubbed against Joanna's abdomen.

Joanna's head went back at the feel of it while her free hand held onto Greene's waist; she invited Greene to take whatever she wanted from her fingers buried inside. Greene moved her hand to cover Joanna's and pressed the woman's palm into her own center, showing her what she needed. Joanna lifted herself up, held onto Greene's hip as she did, and pressed her palm into Greene's sex while her mouth took her breast and she sucked on a nipple.

"God! Yes, Jo!"

Greene gripped the back of Joanna's head with both hands as she rocked, needing another orgasm before she could feel sated. Joanna's teeth nibbled at her nipple, and her fingers curled inside. That, in combination with the palm against her already throbbing and sensitive clit, was enough to carry her over again. When she came, Joanna slowed but didn't stop her sucking. She seemed to be enjoying Greene's breasts. Greene had no problem with that. She just coaxed Joanna on further by playing with her hair as the woman moved from one nipple to the other to deliver the same focused treatment.

"I love your breasts," Joanna acknowledged between breaths and sucks.

Her free hand moved from Greene's hip to the other breast. She didn't squeeze; she just held it. She ran her thumb gently along Greene's nipple. Greene felt the tingle all the way down to her center. She lowered her body down, and Joanna laid back, allowing Greene to lie on top of her.

"Jo, that was..." She didn't have a word. *Amazing*

didn't sound right; it sounded cliché, almost. *Remarkable* wasn't right either. "You know what? Fuck it. That was the best fucking sex I've ever had; not romantic, but true," she said when she caught the shocked expression on Joanna's face.

Joanna laughed wildly. And with one hand still inside Greene, she could only place the other against her cheek.

"Which time?" she asked.

"Every time. I am crazy in love with you."

"That might have something to do with it." Joanna smiled up at Greene and slid her hand out of the woman's body, placing it on her hip instead.

"You're my first, Jo."

"I think you've said that backwards: you're *my* first." Joanna gave her a light laugh.

"No, I meant what I said." Greene pressed her forehead to Joanna's. "I told you before that I've never been in love. I've never been with someone I've loved. Now, I have."

"You also told me it never seemed right. You've never felt that thing… that you thought you'd know. Do–"

"Yes," Greene interrupted, because she knew the question. "That's why I teared up before."

She had hoped Joanna wouldn't notice that she'd cried as she came the first time by Joanna's touch. They were happy tears. They were tears she couldn't prevent or hold back, because they'd been waiting to come out for years, hoping she'd find someone she loved as much as she loved Joanna Martin. Touching Jo had nearly made them emerge: being inside her like that for the first time, being the first person to taste Joanna on her lips and touch her in that way had almost brought Greene to tears. But she'd needed to be focused on Jo and making her feel everything she could. When Jo's mouth covered her, though, she felt them beginning to fill her eyes. And when Jo made her come with her mouth, that was it: she was no longer able to hold them back. Then, Jo had kissed them away and used her fingers to make her come again. She'd known then that Jo wasn't going to run away.

"You had me worried for a minute, when I saw the tears." Joanna moved Greene's hair behind her ears. "Lie down next to me, please."

"But I want to touch you." Greene lifted up to check Joanna's face.

"And I want that, too." Joanna kissed her lips gently. "I just also need food." She smiled at her. "I woke you up because I want you to be able to sleep tonight. And it's after eleven; I'm starving. I'm sure you are, too."

"I slept for, like, five hours?" Greene lifted to straddle Joanna's hips.

"You did."

"Did you nap with me?"

"No. I wasn't on a plane all night, babe."

"So, you just stayed here?"

"I watched you sleep," Joanna confessed, and Greene noticed the blush on her cheeks. "And held you."

"You didn't have to do that. You could have gone to work or something."

"Macon, everything about today has been perfect; from the moment you showed up and surprised me, to this moment right now – it's been perfect. I loved watching you sleep and being able to do it, because you're here now, and I can. I loved holding you. You were so cute; you reached for me. I love you. I will happily lie here and watch you sleep any chance I get."

"Yeah?"

"Yes."

"But, now – instead of sex – you want food?"

"I couldn't resist waking you up like that; I just had to touch you."

"And I just have to touch *you* now. Why do you get your way, but I have to wait?" She gave Joanna her famous puppy-dog face.

"Girlfriend guilt-trip?"

"Yes," Greene admitted.

Joanna leaned up on her elbows and looked up and down Greene's body. Her eyes fell to Greene's breasts; her hand lifted to touch just between them before she slid her fingertips over a nipple, and then her other hand joined in on the other breast.

"I can always order a pizza, and then we can continue," Joanna offered, with her eyes seemingly hypnotized by Greene's breasts.

"Alexa?" Greene uttered in the direction of the Amazon AI device that she'd purchased as a gift for Joanna on her last birthday. "Order my pizza," she gave the command.

"I'll order your pizza," Alexa replied.

She heard Joanna's laugh as she was lowered back onto the bed and Greene kissed her neck.

***

"We should go out for dinner," Macon suggested after their most recent round of passionate sex – this time in the kitchen, as they'd been grabbing a late afternoon snack and Macon had come up behind her.

They hadn't had that snack. Instead, they'd climbed into the shower and agreed ahead of time that it was strictly to clean themselves. They'd both managed to behave, but they'd snuck in a few leisurely touches here and there before they climbed out and dressed for comfort, with Macon throwing a load of laundry into the washer to make sure she had clean clothes. She was there to do laundry after all. In the meantime, though, she'd thrown on the jeans she'd arrived in and a shirt of Joanna's. They now stood in the bedroom, apart from one another, with smiles on their faces. The reason they stood apart from one another was that they knew if they touched right now, next to this bed, they wouldn't be going out for dinner.

"If you plan on eating tonight, that's probably a good idea." Macon's eyes raked over her body.

"I had planned on taking you to Italian after I picked you up, but we had pizza for lunch."

"You actually thought I'd want to go out to dinner before I got a chance to get you alone?" Macon asked.

Joanna watched as she gripped the edge of the dresser behind her.

"Don't do that." Joanna pointed to the white knuckles of Macon's hands.

"Why not?"

"Because I know what you're thinking about."

"And?"

"And we have to get out of this apartment."

"We can get delivery."

"Why did we get dressed if we were just going to have food delivered?" she asked.

"I don't know, Jo. This was your idea," Macon answered seriously; her knuckles didn't loosen. "I want you again."

"You just had me ten minutes ago."

"And I want you again." Macon took a step forward, releasing her hands.

"You stay over there." Joanna laughed and took a step away from her.

"Why? Worried you might give in?" Macon teased.

"Yes," she exclaimed in laughter, and then her phone rang.

"Saved by the bell." Macon laughed. "And if that's one of our friends, I'm going to murder them."

Joanna moved to the kitchen where she'd left her phone. Macon followed closely behind but resisted touching her.

"I'm pretty sure they're considering murdering you, given the fact that you abandoned them for close to two months without a word." Joanna reached for the phone. "It's Keira."

"I'm not here," Macon said from behind her.

Joanna turned around to roll her eyes at her girlfriend.

"Macon, stop." She answered the phone. "Hey, Keira."

"Hey. What time is her flight coming in again?"

"Her flight? What time?" Joanna looked at Macon.

"Late. Tell her *very* late," she whispered.

"One sec; let me look it up," Joanna lied and put the phone on mute and on speaker at the same time.

"Look it up?" Keira questioned. "You don't know?"

"They want to see you," Joanna said to Macon, ignoring Keira for the moment.

"I want to see them, too, Jo. But I just got back. I want to see you and *only* you tonight." She placed her hands on Joanna's waist. Then, she grabbed the phone, clicked the buttons to unmute and put it off speaker, and put it to her ear. "Hey, Keira."

***

"Greene?"

"Yeah, I got in a little earlier than expected," she replied.

"Oh. And you're at Jo's already?"

"Yeah, I came straight here."

"Of course, you did," Keira teased.

"I'm sorry I kind of just abandoned you guys. It's a long story, but I had to work through some things, and it was intense on the road."

"I get it. I just wished you would have checked in," Keira said back. "I'm glad you at least had Joanna to talk to, though."

"Me too." She smiled at Jo, who looked at her in confusion. "She's pretty amazing," she added with a wink. "And I would love to see you guys, I would–"

"But you want tonight with your girlfriend; I

understand. Honestly, Emma and I just wanted to do something nice for you guys. We were going to have food delivered for you from *Antonio's*. We figured you'd be exhausted after your trip; and Jo isn't exactly a cook."

"No, she's not." She laughed and placed a hand on the back of Joanna's neck, pulling her toward herself and allowing Jo's arms to wrap around her waist. "We were actually just about to go out, though."

"You're leaving the house? So, not just going to fall into bed together then?"

"We're going out to dinner." Greene avoided the question.

"Wait... She's right there," Keira surmised. "And you don't want to kiss and tell, do you?"

"Keira, I'll call you tomorrow, and we'll figure out when we can meet up."

"You two totally had sex!" she exclaimed. "Em, they did it."

"Keira," Greene said as Joanna pulled back to check what was going on. "I'll call you tomorrow."

"Fine." She laughed, and Greene heard Emma say something.

"They did?"

"Yes, Emma," Greene confirmed more to get them off the phone than anything. "And I'll talk to you both tomorrow." She hung up the phone.

"They guessed it, didn't they?" Joanna asked.

"They know, yeah." Greene placed the phone on the counter behind Joanna. "Now, before we go out for dinner, since I have you here..." She leaned in and brought her mouth to Joanna's.

"Dinner's going to have to wait, isn't it?" Joanna's hands tugged at Macon's shirt.

"Yes, it is."

CHAPTER 23

"OKAY, how many times?" Keira asked Joanna the moment Macon had headed to the bathroom and was out of earshot. "And how good was it?"

"Keira," Joanna objected.

They sat in her apartment the following evening after Keira and Emma had both gotten off work. The two had brought over dinner for the four of them. They'd all enjoyed it in the living room while Macon had regaled them with stories from the road. She'd sat on the floor between Joanna's legs. Joanna sat on the sofa. Emma and Keira were doing the same thing but with the chair.

Joanna felt entirely comfortable in this new pair of couples. She'd run her hands through Macon's hair and massaged her shoulders. Macon had leaned her head against Joanna's thigh as she talked. The four of them had laughed and caught up. It felt strangely normal, despite the fact that it was the first time it had happened. That only confirmed what the two of them had suspected: it had been like this all along. They'd always been on a double-date with these two when they'd hung out before; they just hadn't realized it.

"What? Come on. You guys finally did it after all this time. We're just curious."

"I don't know how many times." Joanna stood and carried her empty wine glass to the kitchen to refill.

"That many, huh?" Emma egged her on.

"You two are perfect for each other," Joanna retorted, grabbing another beer for Macon from the fridge.

"And how good was it?"

Joanna rolled her eyes as she refilled her glass and popped the top on the beer before moving back into the living room and sitting on the sofa.

"I'm kind of hoping you two leave soon so we can get back to what we were doing before you got here. So, what does that tell you?" She joked.

"Damn! That good?" Emma said.

"What's that good?" Macon returned from the bathroom and headed into the living room.

"The wine. I was just saying that I love the wine," Emma lied.

Macon sat next to Joanna on the sofa and took the beer she handed her.

"Thank you."

"We were talking about sex," Joanna told her. "Specifically, our sex."

"Joanna!" Keira exclaimed.

"What? I don't lie to her." She motioned with her thumb in Macon's direction.

"And it was good?" Macon asked her with a smirk. "I was going for way better than good."

"Oh, it was *way* better than good." Joanna winked at her and then rested her head on Macon's shoulder to turn and see the reaction of their friends.

"Should we go?" Emma laughed.

"Yes," Macon said and was probably only half-joking.

"You leave for close to two months without a word to your best friends, and we get like an hour and a half before you're kicking us out? It's Joanna's apartment, right?"

"It's basically her apartment; kind of has been since

we met." Joanna lifted her head and turned to Macon. "It has, hasn't it?"

"I guess. My place has kind of always been your place, too, huh?"

"Lord." Keira stood. Emma joined her. "We'll leave you two alone to figure out who's moving in with whom tomorrow and get home ourselves. But, Greene, Hill wants to see you, too. Kellan's in town this weekend. She's getting in tomorrow and wants to hang out with us."

"Is she bringing Reese?" Macon asked.

"Yeah, we'll all finally get to meet the girlfriend in person."

Emma chuckled at her and said, "Have a good night, guys."

"We will." Macon walked them toward the door.

Joanna stayed back to pick up the empty glasses and waved them off.

"Tomorrow night," Keira pointed at Greene. "You both better be there," she added.

"We will," Joanna said for them.

"Night." Macon smiled at their friends and closed the door behind them.

"Hey, we stayed here last night. Do you want to stay at your place tonight?"

"Why? It's like nine. I'm already here." Macon moved to help Joanna carry the glasses into the kitchen.

"Babe, you haven't even been home yet. You came straight here. We've left once to grab takeout, and we came back here to eat it."

"And?" Macon moved behind her and wrapped her arms around Joanna's waist, kissing her neck.

"You love that apartment."

"I do, yes." Macon kissed her again.

"You don't even want to see it?"

"Not tonight." Macon kissed her just behind her earlobe. "Jo?"

"Yes?"

"Tonight, I want to stay here with you. I missed you so much. Tomorrow, I'll go home, okay?"

When Joanna realized Macon's confusion, she turned around to face her, wrapping her arms around Macon's neck.

"Did you think I was trying to send you away? Macon, I meant that *we* should go to your place tonight. I wasn't trying to send you there alone."

"Oh."

"Yeah, oh." Joanna laughed. "Honey, I just got you back. You're stuck with me now. I want to spend every night with you, if you let me."

"Sorry, I guess I misunderstood." Macon pressed her lips to Joanna's.

"Hey, let's go to your place tonight."

"We don't have to, Jo. We're here. It's late. We can go tomorrow."

"If you're sure, we can stay. But I don't mind, Make."

"I know. I'm tired, though. I think I'd rather stay here. Tomorrow night, after hanging out with everyone, we'll go back to my place."

"Okay." Joanna kissed her girlfriend gently. "Dishes tomorrow?"

"Dishes tomorrow."

"Are you too tired for a movie before bed?" Joanna asked.

"No, I can watch a movie with you." Macon kissed her cheek. "You want to pick it out?"

"No, I trust you. I'll run to the bathroom and be right back."

Macon kissed her cheek again and headed into the living room to find a movie. Joanna went to the bathroom and returned to find her girlfriend lying on the sofa against its back, patting the spot in front of herself for Joanna to lie down. Joanna smiled and moved in front of her, lying down. Macon's arm went around her waist.

"So, romantic comedy, action, horror?"

"That's the movie we watched last time." Joanna stared at the screen where the menu presented some of the most recently viewed movies.

"Yes, it is." Macon chuckled into her neck and pulled her tighter.

"Can we watch it?"

"You want to watch it again?"

"Yeah." Joanna placed her hand on top of Macon's on her stomach. "Is that weird? It's like I watched it before you and I got together; and I kind of want to watch it now that we are together."

"We can watch it again. I will admit to having watched it a couple of times while I was on tour, though." She kissed Joanna's shoulder.

"You did?" Joanna turned her head slightly.

"It reminded me of you. It was the last movie we watched together."

"You are such a sap, Macon Greene. If only all of our friends knew what an adorable sap you are."

"And let's start the movie." Macon pressed play.

"We can watch something else. You've seen it a few times now."

"No, it's good. I'd like to watch it with you again."

Joanna snuggled back into Macon as the movie began. She regretted not grabbing a drink before lying down, because she didn't want to get up. But she took a drink of Macon's beer about twenty minutes in, then passed it to her, and they returned to their position. Joanna found herself continuing to smile at how natural this all felt to her. They'd gone from friends to lovers. She'd worried when Macon was away how it would all come together once she'd returned. And, so far, it had all worked out on its own. Macon was off work until Monday, to give her time to recuperate from the extended trip. She'd report to the orchestra then and would return to her teaching the week after that.

As the movie progressed, Joanna recalled the timing

221

of everything in the relationship of the two female characters. She knew the scene that was about to come up and felt her body tense in response. Macon must have felt the reaction, because once the sex scene started to unfold, she tensed as well. Her hand slid out from under Joanna's and lowered to Joanna's jeans. Macon unbuttoned them as the scene intensified, and once both women were nude, Macon's hand slid inside, cupping her. Joanna had been silent already, but if she'd been speaking, that move would have driven her to silence. Macon slid her leg between Joanna's. One finger dipped inside to slide through her slick folds and gently glide along her clit. Joanna's tension didn't diminish as Macon's mouth met her shoulder and sucked.

"Make," she whispered.

"Revenge for the marks you left on me and that got me teased tonight." She returned to sucking Joanna's flesh while her finger slowly moved up and down. "Keep your eyes on the screen. Keep them open," she whispered into her ear and then nibbled on the lobe.

Joanna refocused on the two women who were now engaged in a similar situation she found herself in, as Macon's one finger turned into two. She forced her eyes to remain open and tried to keep them focused on what was happening on screen, but Macon's teeth were on the collar of her shirt, and they were tugging it down. Joanna moved her own hand to it and held the collar of the shirt down for Macon so that she could continue to lick and suck at her skin. She held it in place with her fingers, pulling it down as far as she could, and used her palm to grasp her own breast and squeeze it. Macon continued to slowly work inside her jeans and underwear.

"Make, faster," Joanna begged as she twisted her own nipple.

"Are you watching the movie?"

"Yes."

"Did it turn you on the last time we watched it

together?" Macon moved her fingers lower.

"Yes."

Macon dipped her fingers inside. Joanna gasped as she applied more pressure to her nipple.

"Lift your shirt up. I want to see what you're doing," Macon ordered in between ever-quickening breaths. Joanna rushed to the hem of her t-shirt. Macon had to lift her arm slightly to allow the shirt to be pulled up over Joanna's breasts. "Put your hand under your bra. Lift it up," she commanded.

Joanna knew she'd just soaked Macon's hand as her girlfriend's fingers dipped further inside. Joanna lifted the cup of her bra and heard Macon nearly growl when she took her own nipple between her finger and thumb to tweak it. Macon's fingers moved further inside Joanna as her reward. They were still side by side, so she tried to roll onto her back to allow Macon more access. Macon held her in place and lifted her head in order to watch both Joanna's hand on her breast and her own fingers inside her girlfriend's jeans.

"Make... God!" Joanna exclaimed as Macon's fingers pulled out and moved back to her clit.

"She's going down on her," Macon said with her eyes moving to the screen again. "Do you want me to do that to you?"

"Yes," Joanna replied as Macon's fingers went to work on her clit, no longer teasing or slow.

"Will you come for me first?" she asked.

"Yes," Joanna repeated, and Macon's fingers moved faster and harder against her.

"Roll over."

As she did, she lifted the other cup of her bra up, freeing both breasts. Macon's hand continued to work against her and went back inside to offer a few well-timed thrusts to the moans of the actresses on the screen while Joanna's hands toyed with her own breasts before one moved behind Macon's neck and pulled her mouth to a nipple. Macon didn't hesitate: she took it and sucked it immediately into her mouth. Joanna's other hand went under Macon's shirt to her perfect breast. She shoved the bra up and away so that she could hold onto it while Macon's mouth, in combination with the fingers alternating between her clit and moving inside, made her come loudly. She was sure she'd squeezed Macon's breast so hard, it likely hurt. But she couldn't stop, because her hips lifted and fell, then lifted and fell again as her entire body trembled.

"Oh, my God! Oh, my God," she said when she was finally able to catch her breath.

"You are so sexy, Jo." Macon leaned over her and kissed her for the first time since this had begun. "I can't believe I get to touch you like this." She restarted her hand movements and lifted enough to watch her wrist bend and flex with each touch. "God!" Her center was now over Joanna's thigh, and she was lowering herself against it.

Joanna wasted no time undoing the button and the zipper on Macon's jeans, shoving her hand inside Macon's underwear and offering her palm to Macon as she ground down against it.

"Jesus!" Joanna exclaimed when Macon's wetness coated her hand as the woman slid against it.

She heard what she assumed was one of the women coming on the screen, but she wasn't about to look away from Macon, who was already about to come on Joanna's hand while she was thrusting her own fingers inside Joanna, trying to bring her to climax again.

They came together, with Macon collapsing on top of her; their hands stilled in their positions because neither of them wanted to move. They remained that way, with both of their chests rising and falling and their clothing in disarray, while the women on the screen finished. Macon's hand pulled out first. Joanna kept hers where it was until Macon began tugging down at Joanna's jeans. Then, Macon was lifting herself up, and Joanna had no choice, but to pull her hand out. Quickly and without a word, Macon had moved to stand, slid Joanna's jeans and underwear off, and knelt in front of her. Joanna stared into greedy green eyes as Macon moved to take her with her mouth. Then, she saw the black from the inside of her eyelids, followed by the blinding white of yet another intense orgasm.

***

Greene couldn't help herself. She wasn't sure how many orgasms she'd had since arriving the day before nor did she know exactly how many she'd supplied, but after the last one she'd given Joanna on her knees and the two right before, she knew she still wanted more of her. She couldn't get enough of Joanna. All the time away from one another still had to be made up for. She wasn't sure she'd ever fully feel like they'd made up for it. She'd keep trying though. Before she could stand, after Joanna released the back of her head from her tight grip, Joanna had slid down to the floor with her.

Greene knew they weren't done yet. She loved that her own insatiable nature seemed to be right in line with Joanna's need for her. Joanna straddled her hips as she joined her on the floor. She reached to the table behind Greene and pushed at it to have more space to work. Then, she met Greene's lips with her own. Greene knew that Joanna could taste herself and that it was driving her on. She could feel Joanna's begging hips crave more as she rocked into her stomach. Jo was still so wet, Greene wanted to slide easily back inside her and fuck her hard over and over.

They'd made love many times already. Each time they touched each other, they'd always been making love, because they loved each other. But they hadn't actually fucked one another until just a few moments ago, when Macon had needed to claim her in that way. Now, she needed to claim her again. She knew Jo wanted to touch her, but she wanted her too much and couldn't wait. She shoved her fingers inside Joanna and felt her mouth stop their kiss as her entire body tensed. It took only an instant before she started moving up and down, allowing Macon's fingers to thrust while Macon held onto her body with her free hand.

Her wrist was killing her. Her back was somewhat pressed to the table behind, but she didn't care. Joanna's breasts were bouncing in front of her eyes, and the expression on Joanna's face told her she was taking her pleasure and loving it. Greene watched her and felt Joanna's arms tighten around her neck as she began moving faster and faster against her. Just as Greene knew she was about to come, she gripped Joanna around the waist and practically flung her to the floor. She added a finger and used her hips to thrust hard and fast, watching the woman come undone beneath her.

"Sit up," Joanna said before Greene had even been able to process that she'd come down all the way. "And stay."

Greene sat up and straddled Joanna's hips. Joanna moved her body down. Greene knew where she was going. Joanna's face was beneath her, and then her mouth was covering her clit. Greene couldn't help the twitch of her body that caused her to start rocking against the contact. She didn't want to hurt her, but she couldn't get her body to slow; she rocked her sex into Joanna's face. Joanna held onto her hips and seemed to be encouraging her to continue. As Greene felt her orgasm begin to build, she fell forward, needing her arms to hold her up as she rocked while Joanna's tongue slid inside. Macon's movements caused the tongue to thrust deeper and pull out, and she came as Joanna's fingernails clung to her hips tightly.

"Fuck," she screamed, falling off Joanna.

Her body was unmoving. Joanna's wasn't moving

either until a few moments later when she'd, apparently, caught her breath, rolled over, and slid on top of Greene; her breasts pressing deliciously into Greene's back.

"Yeah, I think that's what we just did." Joanna leaned back and kissed between her shoulder blades.

Greene laughed and tried to reach for something on Joanna she could touch, but her arms were like jelly.

"I have been completely fucked. I can't believe you just did that to me."

"What?" Joanna leaned back down and pressed into her.

Greene could feel that Joanna was still wet, because her sex was pressing into her ass.

"Are you still turned on?" Greene asked, turning her head slightly, as if that would allow her to see for herself.

"I have been since the moment you walked through that door. What did you mean, though?" Joanna asked against her ear.

"Do you want to go again? I think I need a minute."

"No. Well, yes, but not right now. I do want you to answer the question, though."

"I sat on your face, Jo."

"Yes, I know. I was there." Jo pressed her palms into the spaces of her shoulder blades that still held the tension from the tour.

"That feels good," she said.

"Did I do it wrong or something? Not this part; the other part."

"What? No." Greene wanted to move now. She wanted to see Joanna's face to make sure she understood, but Joanna just went on with her massage. "Jo, that was the best orgasm I've had in my entire life. Every single one with you has been amazing, but that one was the best, and I'm including the times I touched myself." She felt the blush creep onto her cheeks and was happy she'd been prevented from rolling over because of it.

"Really?"

"Yes, beautiful. And I love that you're giving me a back massage and that you're doing it naked; I can feel how wet you still are. But can we move this to the bedroom and turn off the damn movie? I still have a few days of vacation before I need to get back to work. I plan on spending every minute with you."

"Well, one of us isn't on vacation and has a shoot tomorrow afternoon, Saturday morning, and Sunday most of the day." Joanna moved to sit beside her.

Greene rolled over onto her back and placed a hand on Joanna's thigh. The woman had lost her shirt and bra sometime during their activities, and Greene had no recollection of when that had happened. Joanna was completely nude, sitting up next to her.

"Do you need an assistant?"

"You want to come to work with me?" Joanna laughed lightly.

"I have before."

"If you'd like to lug around camera equipment this weekend just to be with me, I am happy to have you."

"There's no one I'd rather lug camera equipment around for."

Joanna stood. Greene stared up at the goddess of a woman above her. Her long blonde hair was mussed and yet, still perfect. Her body was free of clothing. She was long and lean. Greene could now see how turned on the woman still was, and she lifted her body up to hold onto the back of Joanna's legs.

"What are you doing?" Joanna laughed as she placed her hands on Greene's shoulders.

"Kissing you," Greene answered and kissed the inside of Joanna's left thigh.

"Oh, yeah? That's all?" Joanna ran her hands through Greene's already messy hair.

"That's all. Why? Did you want something else?" She teased a finger through wet curls and moved her lips to the other thigh.

"I thought we were going to the bedroom."

"You *can* stop me, you know?" Her lips hovered above Joanna's pubic bone. "You can tell me to stop, or you can push me away." She lowered her lips and pressed into Joanna, smelling her arousal, and finding herself turned on yet again but still not completely recovered from her last orgasm.

"I might pass out if you do that again."

"Sorry, I can't resist." She moved her lips down and kissed the spot over and over until she could feel Joanna's hands grip her shoulders harder. "One last chance."

She kissed Joanna there again, only slightly lower. Joanna's answer came with a hand on the back of Greene's hand as she pressed Greene's mouth into herself. Her leg lifted. Greene moved it to her shoulder before she took Joanna with her mouth again.

CHAPTER 24

JOANNA LAUGHED as Macon knelt down in front of the newborn baby girl in the basket, with a blanket wrapped around her entire tiny body. Macon tried to get her to smile by poking her tiny nose and smiling down at her.

"I'm bad at this." Macon turned to Joanna with the most adorable expression on her face. "You should fire me."

"I would, if I was paying you." Joanna moved toward them. "She's just sleepy. Babies are kind of known for sleeping all day, you know?"

"I do know, yes," Macon answered.

"I'll just get some shots of her sleeping. We'll do the smiling ones later." She turned to the mother, who had shown up for the shoot alone because her husband was out of town for work.

"She's sleeping all the time, which is amazing. It means I get to sleep," the mom joined in. "She's not very fussy at all. That's a miracle, if you ask me. Our son was never this calm."

"Smile!" Macon stood and pointed at the baby. "She's smiling. Go!" She gave Joanna a slight push.

Joanna burst into laughter and took a few steps back to start taking pictures of a now smiling infant. It was a good thing she did, because the smile didn't last long. Before she knew it, the baby's blue eyes were closed again.

"Your job is hard," Macon told her as they played at *7Ups* after wrapping the shoot and dropping the equipment off at Joanna's apartment.

"Says the concert violinist." Joanna aimed the squirt gun at the clown's mouth, trying to beat Macon in the side by side matchup.

"I don't work with infants," Macon replied and then grunted as Joanna won.

"Two hundred points to me, and one hundred to you, dear," she taunted.

"Joke's on you, because that's just three hundred for us both, beautiful." Macon leaned in and kissed her cheek.

"Hey, ladies," Emma greeted from behind. "We're here. And Hill is right behind us; she ran into the bathroom."

"Hey." Macon stood.

Keira approached with a glass of wine for Emma and one for herself, and asked, "Did you guys get drinks?"

"No, not yet. We kind of just started playing." Joanna stood. "But I'll go grab them. Beer?" she checked with Macon.

Macon winked at her and smiled. Joanna smiled back and headed toward the bar, where she spotted Hillary just exiting the bathroom and joining her.

"Did they get me a drink?" she asked Joanna and stood next to her.

"I don't think so. What do you want? I'll grab it."

"I'm here now." Hillary glanced at the bartender, who approached. "Can I get sparkling water?"

"No alcohol tonight?"

"I'm cutting back; have been since I started on this health kick thing a while ago. I allow myself wine here and there, and a gin and tonic once in a blue moon."

"You're really dedicated. That's awesome, Hill."

"Yeah… Better conversation is about you and Greene."

"What?" Joanna asked, and as the bartender dropped

off the sparkling water, she ordered two beers for her and Macon. "Not you, too."

"I don't need any details; I just want to know. And I assume I know already, because you're here together. I just want to know that things are good."

"Things are very good." Joanna smiled. "I love her."

"And she loves you."

"She does."

"And you two have…"

"Yes, we have; many, many times."

Hillary took a sip and laughed after.

"Yeah? That good, huh? No more concerns about you freaking out then?"

"No, I'm more than happy." Joanna glanced over at Macon, who was playing one of those claw games. The woman's back was turned to Joanna, but she could sense Macon's expression as she tried to win whatever prize she'd focused on. "I never thought I'd be brave enough to admit how I felt. I thought about her like this before she left, you know? I thought about her with other women, and how it made me feel. I never thought I'd be able to act on it. And now I'm here, and I'm happy. She makes me happy."

"That's awesome, Joanna." Hillary smiled at her. "I can't believe our little Macon Greene is finally settling down." She watched as two beers were placed in front of Joanna.

They paid and headed back to their group.

"Look what I got." Macon held up a small stuffed bear holding a heart.

"Cute." Joanna handed Macon one of the beers.

"It, like my actual heart, belongs to you." Macon handed the bear to Joanna, who smiled.

"I'll take good care of it." Joanna kissed the little white head.

"And it only cost like fifteen dollars to win," Macon exaggerated and winked before taking a long drink of her beer and pulling Joanna into her by her belt loop. "Hey, Hill."

"Hey, whipped," she teased.

"I am not whipped." She placed a hand on Joanna's waist.

"You are very whipped," Keira agreed with Hillary. "Where is Kellan? I want to meet Reese."

"Me too." Hillary looked around and then at the door.

"She'll be here. Can we play?" Emma asked Keira and then looked toward Hillary. "You too, Hill. I plan on kicking your ass at basketball."

"I'm in the mood to wander right now. You two play." Hillary made her way around the bar, leaving the four of them.

"Is she okay?" Keira asked Emma but really the whole group.

"I think so. She was all smiles before," Joanna said. "You got me this?" She met Macon's eyes.

"I did." Macon pulled her closer. "And now I have to kick your ass at basketball." She pointed to Emma.

"Challenge accepted," Emma replied.

"I'll be back." She kissed Joanna briefly.

Joanna heard Emma doing the same with Keira, and the two ran off to the other side of the room, like children, to play basketball.

"Are our girlfriends acting like children?" Keira asked.

"It appears so. But look what mine won for me." Joanna held out her tiny teddy bear.

"You did manage to tame her, didn't you?" Keira replied.

"I didn't tame her. There was nothing to tame." She laughed. "You two really need to talk."

"About what?"

"About the fact that you think she needed taming by me. She didn't."

"And I need to talk to her about it?"

"I think she lets you guys believe things because it's easier," Joanna said.

"Like what?"

"Just talk to her when you can. It's not a big deal, but I do think it would be nice to get some things straight."

Keira's phone rang. She pulled it from her purse.

"It's Kell." She held it to her ear. "Where are you, guys?" She paused. "We came out to meet you, Kell, and Reese. Mostly Reese, because we haven't met her yet." She paused again. "I get it. I guess we'll do this some other time." She waited another moment and hung up. "They're not coming. She had a vet emergency. They're still stuck in Tahoe."

"Oh, that sucks," Joanna replied and took a drink.

"I wanted to meet this amazing Reese." Keira put her phone back into her purse and looked around for her girlfriend.

"We can still have fun." Joanna clinked their glasses together.

"I know. It's just... you weren't really around for the whole Kellan thing." She then pointed to where Hillary was sitting at the bar, talking to a guy. "Maybe there's something going on there."

"Nice." Joanna followed her gaze and caught Hillary laughing. "And what Kellan thing?"

"Kellan and I kind of dated. We were finally able to get a friendship back, but she still had feelings for me. Then, I met Emma, and Kellan told me about her feelings. She kind of went to Tahoe for a vacation to try to get past it, and she ended up staying."

"Because of Reese?"

"We've only talked a handful of times, which is why I was so excited to see her. I know she's happy now. She and Reese have been together for almost as long as Emma and I. And she's got her own practice there, which was her dream. She's only been back to the city once since she left.

Reese couldn't make it, so none of us have met this woman that our friend fell in love with."

"Maybe we could all plan a trip to Tahoe instead."

"That's not a bad idea. I haven't been to Tahoe in years. We could get cabins up there. That could be romantic." Keira looked over at where Emma and Macon were returning from their basketball competition. "I bet Emma would be interested; she's never been."

"Neither have I," Joanna admitted.

"Neither have you what?" Macon asked.

"I've never been to Tahoe," Joanna told her as Macon's arm made its way to the small of her back.

"You haven't?"

"No."

"Neither have I," Emma added.

"Who won?" Keira asked.

"We played two out of three, because I took the first one and this one wouldn't admit defeat," Macon replied.

"And then she won the second one, too." Emma took a drink of her wine.

"You're all about victories tonight, aren't you?" Joanna kissed the side of Macon's neck and rested her head against the woman's shoulder.

"Where's Hill?" Emma asked.

"Hitting on some guy at the bar." Keira nodded.

"Hillary's doing the hitting?" Macon seemed to be in disbelief; and she went to turn but stopped, because Joanna's head was on her shoulder.

Joanna took her hand and sipped on her beer as they both turned to see that Hillary waved off the guy who was now joining his friends at one of the tables. Then, she turned to walk back to her own group of friends.

"Hillary, who was that fine gentleman, and did you get his number?" Macon asked.

"What? Who?" Hillary asked.

"The man you were talking to."

"Oh, that's a student. He's a Ph. D candidate."

"So, nothing romantic there?" Joanna checked.

"He's married to another student I know."

"We thought you might get a date out of it," Keira said, and then she lit up completely as she saw something no one else seemed to notice. "Oh, my God! Hill, she's here." She pointed and dropped her finger out of fear of being seen, starting to nod instead. "She's here."

"Who's here?" Emma asked and followed her girlfriend's gaze.

"Your mystery woman." Keira nodded emphatically toward the bar.

Joanna followed her nods and saw a woman, who, from afar, looked to be about 5'7" or 5'8". She was attractive, to be sure. She had long auburn hair that was done up intricately in some kind of fancy braid.

"She's not *my* mystery woman." Hillary looked toward that woman. Joanna caught a smile. Then, the smile disappeared when the mystery woman met and hugged a man. "She's *his* mystery woman, apparently."

"They just hugged; no kiss," Emma pointed out.

"And she's always staring at you at the café, Hill," Keira insisted.

"She doesn't stare. She glances, occasionally."

"And you've never talked to her?" Joanna asked.

"No."

"She's scared," Macon said.

"I'm not scared. Just look at her." Hillary motioned palm up in the direction of the woman who was now sitting next to the man she'd just hugged. "She's gorgeous."

"So are you, Hill." Keira finished her wine.

"Do you want another one?" Emma asked, finishing her own.

"No, I'm good. I'll get one for you, though." Keira kissed her cheek.

"Water?" Emma asked.

"Sure. Anyone else?"

"I'm okay," Macon offered, and Joanna shook her head.

"Keira, do not do anything." Hillary pointed at her.

"I'm going to get my girlfriend a bottle of water." She held out her hands in defense. "I'll grab you one, too." She pointed at Hillary. "Lime?"

"Keira…"

"Lime it is," Keira said in response.

"You know she's going to talk to her, right?" Emma said.

"Fuck." Hillary moved away from them and around a corner, where she could hide behind a row of games.

"What is happening right now?" Joanna laughed, and Macon's arms went around her waist from behind. "Where did your beer go?"

"I finished it." Macon kissed her neck. "Come on. I want to play one of those motorcycle games."

"Emma, you joining us?" Joanna asked as Macon kissed her in that spot again.

"No, I'll wait for Key." Emma nodded and smiled toward her girlfriend. "Actually, can I borrow you two before you run off?"

"What's up?" Macon asked.

"I have something I want to run by you." Emma stepped closer. "I want to ask her."

"Ask who what?" Joanna questioned, possibly feeling slightly tipsy from how quickly she'd finished her own beer.

"Shit! Really?" Macon pulled back from her. Joanna turned halfway to check on her. "You're proposing?" she whispered.

"Really?" Joanna moved into Macon and moved her arms back where they were.

"I want to, yes. I still need to pick out a ring and figure out how to do it."

"What can we do?" Joanna asked.

"I don't know yet. I just know I want to marry that

girl. I talked to Hailey about it, and she told me to make some grand romantic gesture. Then, her wife told me to just ask her. So, now, I don't know what to do."

"You know Keira better than anyone. What do you think she'd want?" Joanna asked and ran her fingers along Macon's hands on her waist.

"Her name is Amara." Keira bounded back over. "Oh, I forgot your water," she said to Emma.

Emma laughed, pulled Keira closer to her, and said, "I forgive you. Now, what were you saying?"

"I didn't talk to her, because Hill would be pissed. But I overheard her introducing herself to that guy's girlfriend; her name is Amara. And *he* is just a friend."

"That's good news, I guess, but it doesn't mean she's into Hill," Macon said.

"I know. But, guys, she's at the café nearly every time Hillary is. I've seen her at least fifteen times. She's looking at her whenever she can."

"Okay, but Hillary doesn't want to do anything about it, babe," Emma explained.

"She's just scared."

"I am not scared," Hillary rejected and emerged.

"You're literally hiding right now," Keira pointed out.

"This is stupid: I came out to see Kell, and now this night somehow turned into trying to hook me up with someone. I'm going home." Hillary rolled her eyes at her friends playfully.

"Hill, don't be like that," Emma said. "I'll keep her in check." She nodded toward her girlfriend.

"Of course, you will," Keira replied sarcastically. "I'm bummed about Kellan and Reese, too, though. Maybe we can all grab dinner? We can leave Amara, your mystery girl, here."

"Her name's Amara?" Hillary smiled, and her voice had some levity to it. "It's pretty." She allowed her eyes to drift to the bar, where she watched Amara laughing with her two friends.

"She's pretty, too, Hillary." Joanna nudged her forearm. "Why don't you just go talk to her?"

"Dinner sounds good." Hillary returned her attention to Keira. "What are you guys in the mood for?"

"Another time," Macon whispered into Joanna's ear. "She'll get there, eventually."

"Dinner?" Emma looked in their direction.

"Let's go," Macon replied.

"Make, can I walk with you?" Keira asked.

"I'll walk with Emma and Hillary," Joanna instantly volunteered.

"We're all walking together, aren't we?" Macon checked. "Why are we being weird?"

"Give me five minutes of your time without your girlfriend glued to your hip," Keira teased, pulling Macon along.

"Says the woman that's been glued to her girlfriend's hip forever." Macon laughed.

They all headed toward the door. Joanna noted the blush on Hillary's face as they moved past Amara. Then, she noticed Amara turn and catch Hillary leaving. The expression the woman had on her face told Joanna all she needed to know.

***

Greene watched Joanna, who walked next to Hillary and Emma ahead of them. She noted how shapely her girlfriend's ass was from behind and even tipped her head to the side to check it out from another angle.

"Really, Greene?" Keira laughed.

"What?" Greene bumped shoulders with her. "My girlfriend has a nice ass."

"So does mine." Keira did the same thing and stared at Emma's.

"I can respectfully acknowledge that." Greene winked at Keira. "So, you want to tell me why you wanted to walk with me for some strange reason?"

"I've been talking to Joanna a lot since you disappeared. She was our only way of knowing you were okay."

"Yes, please remind me of that again and again forever."

"Anyway, she's led me to believe that there are some things you allow us to say that may not exactly be true."

"Like what?" Greene asked and glanced over at her.

"She wouldn't tell me, but it sounded like maybe there's something you're not telling us about your little bar escapades."

Greene stared at the ground and shook her head side to side.

"It's not a big deal; that's why I've never said anything about it."

"So, what's the secret, Make? All these women we thought you were dating... you weren't?"

"It's not like that," Greene explained. "I dated them. I just didn't sleep with all of them. You guys think I sleep around a lot. I don't. I never have. I would meet someone, there would be some flirting and maybe a hot make-out session, but that's basically where it ended nine times out of ten. When I did like a woman enough to go out on a date, we'd date. Sometimes, we'd have sex. But I'm not this Lothario you all make me out to be."

"Greene, why didn't you say anything?"

"Because it didn't matter."

"Of course, it mattered." Keira placed a gentle hand on Greene's arm to hold her back.

"We're going to fall behind," Greene deflected.

"Hey, talk to me."

"Keira, sometimes it's just easier to let people think things about me than it is to correct them."

"I'm not people, Macon Greene; I'm your best friend, or at least I was before Joanna entered the–"

"No, you don't get to do that, Keira," she interrupted

a little louder than she'd intended.

"Everything okay?" Joanna turned to check.

"We'll meet you guys there," Greene instructed. "It's fine." She softened her voice toward Joanna.

"Okay." Joanna nodded and gave her a sweet smile.

"Keira, when you met Emma, it was like the rest of us didn't exist for a while after that. I get it: you fell in love. And I'm so happy for you two. I want you to be happy. I love Emma; but it was like you weren't there anymore. Hillary and I were on our own, but that was okay."

"Because you had Joanna?"

"No, not just because of that. I mean, she was a part of it, and yes, she became my best friend. She's amazing, and I love her, but this is about before that. You wonder why I never bothered to correct you?" She let out a deep exhale. "It's because you thought it in the first place."

"What?"

"You saw me flirt with some girl years ago, another one bought me a drink; I remember the night this whole thing started. You made a comment about how the girls were all over me. One of them kissed me. It was a peck more than anything. And, suddenly, I was a player, or at least this habitual dater who slept with women left and right. It caught on with Hill, and somehow it took off from there, but I've slept with fewer women than Jo has slept with men. And neither of us sleeps around, Keira."

"Make, I'm sorry. I didn't know."

"I know. I know. It just sucks when you have this best friend, who's supposed to know you, and she makes an assumption about your character as if she doesn't."

"I never should have said it. I'm sorry. I didn't know, Greene. You always seemed so good at picking up women in bars, and you'd leave with them sometimes."

"We'd talk, kiss, maybe get to second base, but that was it, Keira."

"I'm sorry. What else can I do to make this up to

you? I feel terrible, Greene."

"It's fine. Honestly, it is. This is Jo's work." She turned to see that the threesome was standing on the corner, waiting for them. "I love that woman, but she keeps trying to make me better. It's frustrating sometimes."

"Emma does the same thing to me. It sucks." Keira looked in Emma's direction. "And it's awesome."

"Yeah," Greene agreed.

"It is awesome, you know?" Keira bumped her shoulder.

"What?"

"When you find that person that makes you better. Or, in this case, when you find that person that makes your best friend realize what an asshole she's been for years now because she never bothered to really get to know that part of you."

"Did you just call yourself an asshole?" Greene asked her with a grin.

"Yes, I did. Because I am. I'm sorry, Make."

"I know."

"I'm glad she got me to talk to you."

"Me too."

"But you don't want to admit that to her, do you?" Keira chuckled.

"The only thing I've ever kept from her was how I felt about her. And I couldn't even keep that in for that long and spilled it right after I figured it out." She turned to see Joanna watching them with a concerned expression. "It doesn't do me any good to try to keep things from her. I don't want to, anyway. I like when she's happy; and she'll be happy that we talked."

"You really are a *one-woman* woman, aren't you?" Keira laughed and hooked her arm through Greene's as they walked on to meet the rest of the group.

"Always have been, yeah." She laughed back.

"I'm sorry I never noticed before."

"You notice now, though, don't you?"

"How well you two fit? Yeah, everyone notices that, Greene. Literally, *everyone* noticed. We noticed before you two did."

"And you honestly thought the straight girl would fall for the gay best friend?"

Keira stopped walking, holding Greene back again.

"Make, she fell for you right away." She laughed. "Do you honestly not remember?"

"Remember what?"

"You didn't notice?"

"Notice what, Keira? Speak."

"The day you two met: you guys were at my place, helping me plan that wedding when I needed the staff and the ones I hired flaked on me."

"Yes, that I remember."

"And Emma got you, Hillary, Joanna, Mason, and crew to help."

"Yes… So?"

"You two were sitting next to each other on the couch and wouldn't stop talking."

Greene smiled at the memory and replied, "That part, I remember."

"Make, she would stare at you." Keira laughed. "You grabbed a donut off the table, and she just looked at you with this smile and also kind of this look of confusion on her face; I watched her shake her head. It's pretty funny now."

"How is *that* funny?"

"She was into you and tried to shake herself out of it because, well, probably for a lot of reasons. You were a woman. She was straight. She'd just met you. It probably didn't help that I made a comment about you not hitting on the clients." Keira paused and offered an apologetic smile. "I didn't say anything because I thought you two would figure it out, or that maybe you'd talked about it already and it was a no-go. I didn't want to pry. But once it was pretty obvious that the two of you wanted it, I was happy for you guys, because it works, Greene. You two work."

"We do," Greene agreed. "We should get going though. She's going to start freaking out soon if I don't tell her everything's okay."

"Let's go then."

"Also, you're buying dinner for Jo and I. And you know what? You're buying for Hill, too. We all deserve it."

"No problem." Keira laughed as they met up with the other three women.

CHAPTER 25

AFTER A NIGHT at Macon's apartment, where they'd fallen asleep almost instantly from the exhaustion, Joanna woke on Sunday morning feeling mostly refreshed but still unprepared to spend a full day at a wedding photo shoot. She'd left Macon in bed after kissing her goodbye to return to her own apartment to pick up her equipment and get dressed. Macon was lagging behind, but she promised she'd force herself into the shower and join her as her assistant for the final day of her all too brief vacation. By the time Joanna had gathered everything she'd need for the shoot and had finished her second cup of coffee, Macon had arrived and let herself in.

"Hey. You ready?" Macon greeted after closing the door behind her and moving toward Joanna in the kitchen.

"I made you coffee," she replied and pointed to the other mug she'd already filled and sat on the counter.

"You're the best girlfriend." Macon kissed her and placed a hand on the small of her back. "I almost stopped on the way over, but I was thinking we could grab breakfast burritos at *Eduardo's* before we hit the road." She grinned an adorably wide grin, indicating that she'd very much like to stop for breakfast burritos on their way to the wedding.

"I take it that's something you'd like to do?" Joanna smiled back.

"Yes, it is." Macon turned Joanna around in her arms to pull her in for what was likely supposed to be a sweet kiss but, within a few seconds, had turned into something more.

"We can grab burritos, or we can do something else. We have some time, but not enough time to do more than one thing," Joanna suggested.

"You're saying we can either have morning sex or I can grab breakfast?"

"That's exactly what I'm saying." Joanna wrapped her arms around Macon's neck to pull her in, revealing what she'd prefer her girlfriend to choose.

"I can just eat a big lunch." Macon leaned in and captured Joanna's lips again, before pressing the woman back against the kitchen counter and placing her own thigh between Joanna's.

"Yeah?"

"Well, if you're offering…" Macon pecked at Joanna's neck before returning to her lips.

"Joanna, we're here! Oh!"

"Mom?" Joanna quickly pushed back at Macon as her mother stood in her living room. "What are you doing here? Dad?" she asked of her father, who had entered the apartment.

"What's going on here?" her mother asked as she glared at the woman Joanna had just been making out with.

"What are you doing here?" Joanna avoided the question to repeat her own as she folded her arms over her chest.

"I should go." Macon stuffed her hands into the pocket of her jeans.

"Who are you, and why were you kissing my daughter?" Her mother turned to look at Joanna.

"Mom, this is Macon Greene," Joanna introduced while trying to slow the beat of her anxious heart and dim the deep shade of crimson on her cheeks. "You've heard me talk about Macon."

"You've never mentioned this…" The older woman pointed between the two of them.

"It's new."

"New? Kissing a woman?" Her father was clearly confused as he ran his hand through his light brown hair. "I would have remembered that."

"Why are you guys here?" she repeated, motioning for Macon to move to the sofa and sit with an open palm, but Macon stood still.

"We told you we were coming today," her mom insisted.

"No, you didn't. I would have remembered that." She used her father's words. "I'm working today."

"Did I get the wrong Sunday?" her father asked himself. "I thought you said come in today because you were working next Sunday."

"No, Dad."

"I asked you to check with her," his wife scolded. "I'd say we drove in for nothing, but that's obviously not entirely true." She glared once again at a silent Macon, who appeared to have lost her tongue.

"Mom, I was going to tell you guys." Joanna motioned again with an open hand; this time for her parents to sit.

"When exactly?" They moved to the sofa.

"I didn't have it planned out or anything. Like I said, this is new." She glanced at Macon and tossed her a concerned smile. Macon didn't return it. "Macon and I have been friends for a while. Then, we both discovered we have feelings for one another. And now, we're dating," she explained.

"You're dating a woman?" Her mother remained standing while her father sat and then stood back up immediately after realizing his wife hadn't sat down next to him. "Are you gay, Joanna?"

Joanna gulped at that question, because the truth was that she didn't know what loving Macon made her. She'd thought about it a lot while Macon was away, but she'd never felt settled with any of the labels she tried on. She wasn't gay; she knew that. She'd spoken the words, *"I'm gay"* into her bathroom mirror about a hundred times, and it never resonated with her. She'd shake her head and try it out again. She'd wondered if this is what gay people did in reverse when they were trying to figure themselves out. Did they utter, *"I'm straight"* into a mirror to see if it felt right or if they could force it to feel right? She'd settled on *"bisexual"* because that seemed the closest label, but she wasn't even sure if that was accurate. She'd always loved men and had considered herself heterosexual for her entire life; never thinking of another woman in the way she'd thought of Macon. But once she met Macon, and they started spending time together, there was a definite shift in her thinking. Now, there was a definite shift in her actions and what turned her on. Macon's touch sustained her; that was how good it felt to be with her. At no time in her life had she experienced the need of another in this way. Her desire for Macon was palpable even immediately after Macon's mouth or fingers brought her to orgasm; she needed her again. And while each intimate encounter was completely fulfilling, there was also an insatiable quality to their lovemaking that she'd also never experienced with a man.

"No, I'm not gay," she replied after a long moment of silence.

Macon turned to her and gave her an expression that Joanna couldn't read, which was strange because she could usually read her girlfriend's reactions pretty well.

"So, you're what, then?" her father questioned.

"I don't know," she admitted with a shoulder shrug. "I don't know that I'll ever know."

"Ever?" Macon's voice was shaky, but it was loud enough for Joanna to hear and turn to see that her response had caused confusion in her girlfriend.

"I don't really have time for this conversation right now; I have to get to a shoot. I'm running late now as it is. Can we just talk about it later?" She looked at her parents.

"We can meet up for lunch, or maybe we can talk to

Macon while–" her mother suggested.

"Uh, no you can't," Joanna interrupted. "She's coming with me today."

"We can do dinner," her father said.

"Do you want–" she started in Macon's direction.

"Just the three of us," her mother interrupted. "Family dinner."

"Probably best," her father agreed.

"We should talk alone," her mother reiterated with a glance at Macon and then back to Joanna. "We need to figure out how to explain this. Is this serious? Is this an experiment or a phase?"

"I don't think we should tell anyone until we know it's long-term; no sense in getting all worked up over it if it's just a phase," her father said before Joanna had a chance to respond to her mother's comment.

"What about the girls at the club? When Brittany Weaver dated a woman, her mother told the whole club she was gay. It was a huge scandal because Brittany had been dating Colleen Parker's son. The Weavers stopped coming to the club for months until Brittany ended that relationship and then married a man. She has two kids now. She went through all that for nothing."

"Mom, I–"

"Dinner tonight," her father interjected. "We'll meet at the steakhouse we went to last time. What was it called?"

"*Alexandria*," Joanna answered with all the confidence she'd had in her, drained from just listening to her parents do the back and forth that had been so common during her childhood and throughout her adulthood.

"Yes, that place makes a great old-fashioned," he proclaimed. "We'll pick you up here. You'll need to change first." He pointed at the jeans and a V-neck shirt she'd put on for the shoot.

"Wear that black and white dress your aunt got you

last year," her mother instructed.

"I'll make a reservation for seven, so be ready by six-thirty." He motioned to Joanna.

Joanna wasn't exactly sure what was happening. Macon wasn't saying a word. Joanna appeared to be out of them as well. Instead, she lowered her head in silent acknowledgement of her father's order. As her parents made their way to her front door, pulled it open, and began to exit, she felt herself melt in shame.

"We'll be back at six-thirty. I assume the photography will be done by then," her mother uttered in obvious disappointment in Joanna's career.

"I thought the reception went until ten tonight," Macon spoke up.

"It does," Joanna said. "I'll be done by six-thirty, though," she added for her parents. "I'll take the shots at the beginning of the reception, and then I'm done."

"You said you'd–" Macon began.

"We'll see you later, Joanna. Reservation for three." The woman glared first at Joanna and then at Macon. Her eyes returned to Macon for an instant before they turned away entirely. "We have a lot to talk about, apparently."

Her parents closed the door loudly behind them. Joanna stood completely still. She wasn't sure if she was in actual shock, but it felt like her life had just been tossed into the air and all its elements had landed back on the ground, but completely out of order.

"Um, Jo? You want to tell me what just happened?"

"I don't know," she admitted.

"There's a lot you don't know, apparently," Macon said with obvious frustration.

"What's that mean?" Joanna tossed back.

"It means you just stood there, Jo. They treated you like crap: ordering you around, just dismissing me, and you took it. You just took it." Her voice was slightly louder than Joanna had anticipated. "What the hell was that? I've never seen you shrink like that."

"You've never seen me with my parents," she revealed.

"You're a grown woman in her thirties."

"I know that, Macon. Thanks for reminding me, though. Can we just go? I'm going to be late." She reached for the camera bag on the floor by the coffee table.

"Your parents walk in on us making out, ignore me, assign you to a dinner with the two of them during your work day, and you just want to forget about it?" She reached for Joanna's forearm. "Jo, talk to me."

"Macon, I will talk to you. But I need to do it on the way to my client, who has a wedding going on today and is expecting her professional photographer to arrive on time. I need to focus on that right now so that I don't lose clients because I fucked this up. After that, I will figure out how to react to the fact that my parents just caught me making out with my first girlfriend, and then proceeded to treat me like a teenager they just caught making out in the back seat of the car right in front of my girlfriend. Is that okay with you?" She hadn't meant that last part to come out as loudly, but it had. The moment it had, she recognized that she was in her first fight with Macon. "I'm sorry," she added immediately and took Macon's hand, turning the woman to face her as she did. "I'm sorry, Make."

"It's fine. Whatever."

"No, don't do that. Don't shut down on me."

"What am I supposed to do? You asked to focus on work. Do that. We'll figure the rest out later."

"You're upset."

"Yes, I am," Macon said. "Can I come to dinner with you guys? I'll make the reservation for four instead."

"Make, that's probably a bad idea. My parents haven't been exactly welcoming of the *guys* I've dated, and they're definitely not going to welcome a woman I'm dating. They're old-school and uptight; I don't want to put you through that."

"So, how does this work? We date, but I don't belong in that part of your life?"

"Babe, *I* don't belong in that part of my life." She paused and squeezed Macon's hand. "My parents tolerate me as is. I'm the black sheep of the family, and I have been since long before I met you."

"But I don't help?"

"Make, come on."

"No, you come on, Jo. I defended you to my idiot parents. We went through this already. Why can't you do the same for me?" she asked and let go of Joanna's hand. "I think I should go. I don't feel like being your assistant today." She took a few steps back.

"Macon, I'm sorry. I didn't expect my parents to walk in on us. The last time I talked to them, I told them I was busy and that I'd call when I could to figure out when *I'd* visit *them.*"

"What did you expect? Were you ever going to tell them about me? About us?" Macon ran her hand through her black hair, and her bright green eyes bore into Joanna's. "I need to cool off, and you need to get to work. Let's just talk later."

"Fine." Joanna had no energy left to argue. "I'll call you later, then." She grabbed at the things she needed for the shoot. "I guess, have a good day," she said and then stood up straight again. "You have a key; lock up when you go."

CHAPTER 26

"SHE JUST LEFT you there?" Keira asked.

"In her apartment, yeah," Greene answered. "Her parents basically ignored me, and then Jo just shut down. She turned into someone I didn't even recognize. It was like she wasn't my girlfriend; she was their kid, and had to face her punishment."

"We're all weird around our parents when we're adults. It's like they still have control over us. Remember when mine tried to convince me to move back home when the business started to fail? I had just started dating Emma. I knew she was the one, and I still considered listening to them because they're my parents."

"But she let them," Greene said mostly to herself.

"She let them what?"

"She let them ignore me and be rude to me. I would never let my parents do that to her. In fact, I shut them down in Boston when they tried. I guess, I expected her to do the same."

Greene had made her way over to Keira and Emma's place after Jo left for the wedding. She'd wandered around the city for over an hour, not sure where exactly to go. Since she didn't want to go home to the empty apartment she'd only just shared with Joanna, knowing she'd find several of Joanna's things strewn around to only remind her of their fight, she'd texted Keira and asked if she could come over. Keira had replied almost instantly that Emma was picking up some friends from the airport, so she had a couple of hours before they all got back.

"I'm sorry, Make."

"They're having dinner tonight without me, and I'm worried, Keira," she admitted.

"About what?"

"That they might try to convince her to leave me, and she'll listen." Greene shrugged and fell back against the comfortable sofa, giving over to the emotions of possibly losing the woman she loved.

"She wouldn't do that."

"How do you know? She was straight until she and I got together. She all but admitted today that she doesn't know what she is and might never know."

"You mean if she's gay or bi?" Keira asked. "Some people never know, Greene. And some are perfectly comfortable not defining themselves."

"I know that. I don't care *what* she is, Keira. I love her. She can be any color of the rainbow as long as she's mine. It was just the way she said it; there was this uncertainty."

"I thought you worked out this crap before, Make. You two have slept together. From what I gathered, it was numerous times, and those times were all very good. She seems to enjoy the physical part of being with a woman as much if not more than the other parts. Why are you still worried about this?"

"Because her parents are just like mine," Greene shared. "I know how they operate. They'll try to tell her that this is just a phase or convince her how hard it will be to be out in the open with a woman. They'll set her up with a guy they approve of. He'll probably be someone they met at church or at the country club: rich, good looking, and with a Harvard Business degree. She won't want to go, but she'll do it for them. She'll convince herself and try to convince me that it's just to appease them; that once she goes out with him, and tells them she tried, they'll leave it alone. But they won't. Then, there will be another guy. Jo will have to go to Christmas with them, and they won't want me there. She'll be invited to family dinners that are just for family. I won't be invited. She'll even try to justify it by telling me that I wouldn't want to go anyway, because it'll be boring or that I would hate it because her mom will spend the entire time making her feel like less of a daughter than her sister, who is perfect. She'll do that to try to spare me, but really because she's scared to show up with me. It's already happening. She doesn't see it, but I do."

"Greene, she hardly sees her parents. And Joanna is in love with you; everyone knows that. It's written all over her face. Even if her parents are that bad and try to get her away from you, they won't be able to. I know she's fine with disappointing her mother, because, according to her, she's been doing that most of her life."

"This is different, Keira."

"She may have made some mistakes this morning, Make, but give her the benefit of the doubt. She was caught off guard, and in the act. She may not know how to define her sexuality, but you said you didn't care about that as long as you're together. Her parents are in town for one day, and then they'll leave. Just let her get through today. You two can talk about it. Give her a chance to apologize for whatever she needs to apologize for, and you can apologize for whatever you need to apologize for."

"Why do you assume I need to apologize for something?"

"I'm not. I'm just saying that, sometimes, it helps. I know I do stuff to piss Emma off all the time. I always apologize, then she apologizes, and it just feels better."

"Better?" Greene leaned forward in her seat. "I didn't mess up, Keira."

"I'm not so sure she did either, Greene." Keira offered a shrug. "I get that there were things she could have maybe handled better, but if you were in her shoes, can you honestly say you would have handled it perfectly?"

"I don't know," she admitted.

"I don't know either," Keira added. "If I was straight my whole life – or at least considered myself to be – and then met a woman I fell for but hadn't had the chance yet to figure out how to tell my family, I don't know how I would have dealt with it had said family just burst in the door while I was about to get naked with that woman."

"We weren't naked," she reminded.

"Sounds like you were about to be." Keira lifted an eyebrow and offered a smirk.

"Yeah, well." Greene let out a bit of a laugh, but not one she wanted to let out.

She still wanted to be frustrated. She wanted to be mad at Joanna for not standing up for her, for not insisting that she go to the dinner with the three of them. Was she wrong to expect this from her girlfriend? Was she asking too much when they'd only been together such a short time?

"Be mad if you want, Make. I'm only suggesting you see things from her perspective. It's saved my relationship a few times." Keira revealed.

"Yeah?" Greene turned her head to meet her eye.

"Emma and I are very different people sometimes. We view things differently, or we act differently or want different things. Sometimes, she's right. Sometimes, I am. Sometimes, we're both right or both wrong. Sometimes, I just have to think about how she sees it, though. I know her better than anyone else in the world, and she knows me better than anyone else in the world. We need to remember that, think like the other person for a second, and then, we get it."

"I guess."

"You guess?"

"Yeah, I guess," Greene defended.

"Who knows Joanna better than anyone?"

"Me."

"And it's pretty obvious she knows you better than anyone, including me and the other people in your life you've known for years."

"She does," she agreed. "How does that happen?"

"I have no idea." Keira chuckled lightly.

"One day, I have these best friends – who I think know me better than I know myself – and any woman I'd actually settle down with would have a hard time trying to fit into that," Macon said.

"I know: all the inside jokes, all the drinks and conversations, parties and weekend trips; you start to think that no woman would want to try to fit into the group because it's hard to compete with all that history," Keira added. "Emma and Hailey, for example, have like a century of history. Then, there's that whole group of friends Emma has found herself fitting into. I used to think I was lucky because at least they all live in Chicago; Emma has to deal with you weirdos all the time." She tossed a playful smile in Greene's direction.

Greene returned it and ran both of her hands up and down over her face before standing somewhat resolutely and turning back to Keira, who sat forward expectantly.

"She's always fit into this group, you know that. Emma's amazing. We all love her and the two of you together," she told Keira.

"And it's the same with Joanna, Make. She's amazing. And the two of you together are also amazing." Keira stood and placed her hands on her hips. "Maybe Joanna messed up this morning. I don't know; I wasn't there. Maybe you need to cut her a little slack because she's in a different situation than either of us has ever been in. We don't know what that's like. And maybe you're both right, or you're both wrong."

"Either way, I should apologize." Greene nodded

more at herself than at Keira.

"You have a right to your feelings. Just express them to her and try not to get defensive or make it about you," she advised.

"I don't know how I can do that tonight, since she's on parent patrol."

"And you're really worried she'd leave you because of what her parents might say or do?"

"No." Greene made her way toward the front door with Keira following closely behind. "It's more like I see it happening how I told you before, and tonight is the jumping off point."

"So, if you don't stop it tonight, then what?" Keira questioned.

"They'll start getting more and more involved in our lives because they want me out of their daughter's. Joanna will have a hard time fighting them off. They don't live in Chicago," she reminded. "It's not that long of a drive for them to run interference."

"Talk to her," Keira implored with a gentle hand on Greene's forearm and a softness in her tone that suggested she understood Greene's concerns.

"I will." Greene opened the front door. "See you later."

"Call me if you need me," Keira offered.

"I will. Have fun with Hailey and Charlie. That's one interesting week-long double date." Greene laughed a little.

"Hailey's in town this week for work, and Charlie sometimes tags along with her. I like them both. It was strange, at first, but they're crazy about each other. I know Emma's crazy about me. It's not strange anymore. Plus, I get her wanting to see them whenever she can. I have you guys here; Emma's friends are all in the Midwest."

"Tell Emma I said hi. I'll go figure out the situation with my girlfriend so she and I can end up domesticated like the two of you," Greene said with cynicism in her tone but hope inside her mind for that future with Joanna.

"Hey, you should have dinner with us tonight."

"The four of you?"

"Yes." Keira laughed.

"So, I'd be the fifth wheel? No thanks."

"You wouldn't be a fifth wheel. And you should meet Hailey and Charlie; they're great. Plus, I think Emma would love all of you guys to meet, anyway. I can see if Hill can make it, too, so you'd be one of six. I'll call her now and set it all up. Just come back here. I'll text you the time later."

CHAPTER 27

"MOM, I'M SERIOUS: you need to drop this," Joanna argued with her mother as she raced through the door of the restaurant.

Her father held it open for both women and then moved in after them, closing it behind him. He ambled to the hostess podium to let the staff know they'd arrived for their reservation.

"Joanna, I'm not saying you should break up with Macon. What kind of name is Macon for a woman?" She seemed to be asking herself as she wiped at the bench seat in the restaurant's lobby to remove invisible dirt and dust.

Joanna resisted an eye-roll as she flopped down next to her mother and watched as her father continued to talk to the two women behind the podium.

"It's a family name, Mom. I've asked you at least ten times to leave this alone already. Now, I'm telling you," she retorted.

She'd left Macon in her apartment earlier partly out of necessity; she would have been late for her job had she not left. But, being honest with herself – as she sat and waited impatiently for a table so this dinner could officially begin and then, hopefully, wrap up quickly – she'd also left Macon in her apartment in that moment because she'd been a complete coward and had no idea how to handle a situation like this. When she'd first realized her feelings for Macon, it had been an adjustment in her mind, but it had been a somewhat easy one to make. Macon was already so ingratiated in her life, and they seemed to fit so well together. It was also a simple adjustment, because ever since she'd met Emma at work and begun hanging out with her friends, she'd been surrounded by lesbians. It sounded funny to her, as she watched her father finally lumber over to the bench to sit alongside his wife and child.

A random wedding had led her to an amazing group of friends, who happened to be women that dated other women. She'd never really thought about that before this moment, but spending so much time with them, seeing how normal it is – dating another woman, watching them go through the same things as heterosexual couples go through – helped play a part in her ability to consider Macon in another light. She'd opened herself to Macon and wanted nothing more than to spend her life with that woman. But, this morning, she'd let her overbearing and never approving mother get the best of her. She'd never forgive herself for making Macon feel unworthy or doubt her feelings for her.

Even if they worked through this, she'd always be able to see Macon's fear and disappointment on that expressive face. Joanna lowered her head as the image came to her for the millionth time that day. She'd promised herself, while she'd been snapping photos at yet another wedding, that she'd never make Macon feel that way again. She'd stand up to her parents and get her mother to accept that Macon was the one she wanted. And, if she was lucky, Macon would forgive her. They'd have a photographer take pictures at *their* wedding someday, because she knew that was what she wanted more than anything. Macon Greene was her other half, the one she'd been searching for her entire life; and she would not risk losing her.

"It's a man's name, Joanna." Her mother turned to her.

For the first time, Joanna could see the pronounced crow's feet and wrinkles around her mother's mouth. The woman had pasted a thick coat of red lipstick on, as if to attempt to draw attention away from them, but Joanna saw them clearly, along with the line of foundation her mother had used that morning to cover her entire face before applying layers of powder over it. The foundation was a shade too dark and made the lines close to her ears obvious, along with the fact that her neck was a shade lighter.

"It's my girlfriend's name, Mom. I like it. I love it. I love her." She turned more to her mother. "She's–"

"Here," her father interrupted.

Joanna looked in his direction first, before following his pointed index finger in the direction of the front door of the restaurant. Macon was standing there, looking down at her phone. Joanna stood and was promptly pulled back down by her mother's hand on her wrist.

"Joanna, we said this was a family dinner. Did you invite her after we left?"

"No, Mom," she replied and stood back up, losing her mother's hand in the process.

"The reservation was for three people," her father stated matter-of-factly.

Joanna glared at him before she realized that he wasn't even thinking about Macon. Her father was a very straightforward man. He appeared to be running through how four people could possibly fit into a reservation for three people.

"Dad, I don't think they have tables just for three people here. We'll be fine." She made her way over to Macon, who was still staring down at her phone. Just as she approached Macon, her own phone beeped in her purse, but she left it there and stood in front of her girlfriend. "What are you doing here?" she asked and suddenly felt upset with Macon. "I asked you–"

"I just texted you," Macon replied, and her eyes showed concern that, Joanna guessed, was in place because of her own tone toward the dark-haired beauty.

"Hey, Joanna," Keira greeted as she, too, made her way through the front door, with Emma close behind and two other women behind her that Joanna knew to be Hailey and Charlie, Emma's best friends from Chicago. "Did we know you were going to be here?" she asked Macon.

"I didn't know we were going to be here," Macon answered her and then turned back to Joanna.

"Hey there," Emma greeted Joanna and took Keira's hand.

"I'll check on our reservation; make sure they made the adjustment," Hailey stated and then approached Joanna to give her a hug. "We didn't know you'd be here. It's nice to see you again."

"You too." Joanna hugged her back. "I didn't know you were in town." She glanced at Macon as if it was Macon's fault she didn't know. "Hey, Charlie."

"Hey." Charlie waved.

"We're here for the week." Hailey pulled back and pointed in the direction of the podium where she then walked.

"We changed the reservation to add Greene and Hillary, who's on the way. We should add you, too," Charlie suggested.

"I'm here with my parents." Joanna pointed to the two people sitting behind her, likely trying to listen into the conversation she was currently having.

"I didn't know we were coming here," Macon stated.

"It's true," Keira interjected and separated from Emma's hand. "I told her to meet us at our place. We didn't know Hailey had made reservations here until ten minutes ago. We just drove Make over; she didn't know until we got here."

"I texted you," Macon repeated. "Do you want me to go?" she asked.

Joanna knew she had a decision to make and that it would impact her relationship with both her parents and the woman she loved, who was standing in front of her, giving her the chance to make it.

"Joanna?" her mother interrupted her thoughts.

Joanna turned to see her mother standing behind her, with her father to her right.

"Mom, these are my friends: Keira and Emma; Hailey's over there, and this is her wife, Charlie."

"I'm here. Sorry, had to park." Hillary entered in a rush.

"And this is Hillary," Joanna offered.

"Nice to meet you all," her mother replied in the false politeness Joanna knew all too well.

"Oh, two more?" Hailey returned and noticed the two people standing behind Joanna.

"We have a reservation," her father said.

"We can all sit together, yeah?" Hailey suggested and glanced in the direction of her wife. "They're putting tables together for us. I'm sure they can grab a few more chairs?" she questioned in Joanna's direction now.

"I don't know if that's a good idea, Hailey," Joanna replied.

Macon's face told Joanna she'd said the wrong thing. When the phone dinged again in her purse, indicating at Macon's initial message, Joanna pulled it out merely to silence the incessant sounds. She read Macon's message, and her face dropped. She clicked the button to darken the phone's screen and tossed it back inside before looking up at her girlfriend.

"Keira, I'm going to pass on dinner," Macon stated and turned away from Joanna. "I'm not feeling well all of a sudden."

"Sure," Keira replied with a knowing expression. Joanna wondered what the woman knew of their morning argument, based on how she'd come to Macon's defense earlier. "I'll order you an Uber since we drove you." She pulled out her phone.

"You okay, Make?" Hillary asked.

"I've been better," Macon answered her while still facing away from Joanna.

"Joanna, our table's ready." Her father placed a hand on her shoulder from behind.

"Hailey, can you ask them to add a few more chairs?" Joanna asked.

"No problem." Hailey smiled and headed back to the podium without another word.

Macon turned back with a confused expression on her face.

"Cancel the Uber?" Keira asked Joanna.

"Cancel the Uber," Joanna confirmed. "Stay," she half-whispered to Macon and took her hand by the fingertips, at first, until Macon allowed Joanna's fingers to mingle with her own.

"Should I cancel our table?" her father asked her mother.

"Yes," Joanna replied. She turned away from Macon to face her mother. "This is my life, Mom. These are my friends. If you want to have dinner with me, have dinner with all of us."

"Joanna—"

"Mom, stop," she demanded but kept her tone soft so the others wouldn't hear. "Please."

Her mother pursed her lips, glanced at her husband and then back to Joanna before she nodded reluctantly. Joanna nodded back at her in silent understanding that neither of them was particularly happy at that moment, but that they'd both accepted that now was not the time to bring it up. Joanna turned back to Macon and took her hand.

"We'll catch up," she told Charlie and Emma, who were standing the closest.

"Okay." Emma nodded and took Keira's hand.

The group walked off toward the podium, where they met Hailey. Joanna's parents were still behind her. She couldn't say too much to Macon while they were in earshot, so she pulled Macon aside, with her parents still looking on but unable to hear.

"I'm sorry, Macon," she began.

"It's okay." The woman shook her head.

"It's not, though," Joanna replied. "Your text message nearly broke my heart, Make." She thought back to the message that had told her Macon hadn't known the group was coming to this restaurant and that she'd make herself scarce. It had gone onto say that she'd hide behind someone or something, or leave altogether if Joanna wanted. "Baby, I am sorry."

"I know. Me too," Macon replied. "I shouldn't have pressured you."

"Can we make it through this dinner and then go to your place or mine and talk?"

"*If* we make it through the dinner. Your parents hate me, Jo."

"They don't hate you; they don't know you."

"They hate that I'm a woman." Macon looked behind her, and Joanna didn't need to turn around to know she was staring at her mother. "Your mother is shooting me dagger eyes right now."

"She shoots dagger eyes at everyone; you're not special."

"Jo, I stood up to my parents for you. I told them not to act like pretentious assholes. We left because they couldn't commit to that. I haven't talked to them since then. And this morning, you had the same chance, and you didn't take it. Do you know how that made me feel?"

"It wasn't exactly the same, though, Macon," Joanna explained.

"How was it different?" Macon's eyebrows furrowed in frustration.

"The table's ready," Charlie said to the four members of their party who were still in the lobby, while the rest of them were making their way down a long aisle of patrons dining at their own tables.

"Let's just get this over with." Macon turned away from her to follow Charlie while Joanna stood still.

"Joanna, are all of these women…"

"Lesbians?" Joanna huffed out a laugh. "Most of them, yes. Hillary is bisexual, Mom."

"And you are?" her father asked.

"In a lot of trouble with my girlfriend, Dad," she replied.

CHAPTER 28

GREENE ORDERED a glass of wine, but she wanted something much stronger. Joanna's mother was giving her the side-eye glare, though, so she resisted, not wanting the woman to think her an alcoholic. She thought about abstaining altogether and ordering water or iced tea, like Joanna's mother had done. But knew she needed something to get through the night.

"We have a big convention next week in Chicago," Hailey explained to the large group at the rectangular table. "I'm here to make sure headquarters is ready to roll."

"No Summer or Lena this time?" Keira asked about two of the other friends she knew from Emma's Chicago group.

"No," Hailey returned. "Summer hasn't been involved in the company officially for a while now. She's basically left it to Seth." She paused and looked at Joanna's parents, who were completely lost. "Seth and Summer Taft."

The look of recognition came on their faces. Hailey continued telling the group about why she was here and how Charlie joined her because after Hailey completed her work, they'd go on a short trip to wine country. Emma then spoke about an upcoming event for her department that Keira was planning for them, and that her boss was soon to be promoted to a vice president; Emma was on her way to taking her old position. Hillary then added that the head of the Women's Studies Department was thinking of taking a sabbatical and naming Hillary as the interim department head while she took time off to further her research. Everyone had major updates to provide the group, but as Greene sipped her wine, wanting to gulp it instead, she felt as if she had nothing to offer. Greene felt it more than really noticed it, but there was silence that overtook the group as their entrées were placed on the table in front of them. She brought her mind back into focus and felt a few pairs of eyes on her and a few others on Joanna. It was apparent their friends were waiting for their personal and professional updates. Even Joanna's parents seemed to be waiting.

"Greene just got back from that world tour." It was Keira that finally spoke up for her, not Joanna.

"Which was your favorite city?" Hailey asked curiously as she dove into her food.

"Oh, I don't know." Greene sat down her wine glass. "I guess I wasn't really focused on the cities I was in."

"Oh, of course," Hailey returned. "You were working."

Greene met Joanna's eyes and said, "Sure." She picked up her fork and knife, and started slicing at the pork dish she'd ordered accidentally, because she hadn't been able to focus on the menu, with Joanna and her parents so close.

"You're a musician, correct?" Joanna's mother asked.

It was the first thing the woman had said to her since they'd sat down.

"She's a violinist, mom; you know that," Joanna answered in an irritated tone; she had yet to touch her meal. "One of the best in the world."

"Of course," her mother replied.

"How did you start playing?" her father asked before shoving a bite of near rare steak into his mouth.

"I've always played," Greene replied. "I don't remember not playing."

"And you went to Julliard, then? One would assume..." Joanna's mother looked at her with eyes she recognized as being similar to Joanna's, but not as kind.

"Berklee College," she answered.

"Oh, I didn't realize *Berkeley* had a music program built for the best in the world." The woman's tone suggested she was unimpressed that Greene hadn't gone to a top music school.

"No, she means Berklee, Mom. She's being modest; she went to Berklee Conservatory. It's in Boston. It has *the* best program in the world for someone like Macon: the best in the world." Joanna's eyes were kind, and Greene had a hard time being frustrated with her.

"I see. I only knew of Julliard." Joanna's mother took a small nip at her asparagus.

"So, what do you guys have planned this week?" Hillary asked.

Greene was grateful for Hillary, because she wasn't sure she could make it through this awkward dinner, with Joanna trying to compensate and her parents prodding and thinking she was unworthy of their daughter. It was bad enough that *Greene* often felt unworthy of Jo. She didn't need others doing it for her.

When their meals had been complete, and the plates were taken away, the waiter asked if anyone wanted dessert. Both Emma and Keira said yes at the same time and asked that he bring them the menu. Hailey glanced at Charlie to see if she was interested. Greene looked at her wine glass, only to see that it was empty, and decided she was ready to go. Joanna's parents had asked her several more questions, and with each answer she'd given, she'd felt it less and less likely they'd ever approve of her for their daughter. They'd mentioned a friend of a friend, who had a mayor for a son. He was forty, had been widowed seven years ago, and had an eight-year-old son.

"Well, I don't think we'll stay for dessert. We should be going. We have a bit of a drive ahead of us." Her father stood. "You all should order your dessert and coffee. I'll take care of the check." He nodded in Joanna's direction. "As a thank you for inviting us to your dinner."

"You don't have to do that," Keira replied.

"No, you–"

"Please, allow me." He gave a mock bow and then glanced at Greene.

He offered her a kind smile and a wink. Macon gave an awkward smile in return, not being prepared for his gesture, and watched him button his jacket before heading off to find their waiter to give him his credit card.

"Joanna, walk me to the car." The older woman stood. "Ladies, it was an enjoyable evening. Thank you." She placed her beige linen napkin on the table. "It was a pleasure."

They all said the same in return. Hailey even stood to hug the woman. Charlie gave her a nod but remained seated. Joanna stood reluctantly, from what Greene could tell, and then Greene felt motherly eyes on her. They looked her up and down, and Greene realized she should be standing, too. She did so and nearly tipped over her wine glass in the process.

"Sorry," she said to no one in particular, making sure the glass was safe before she stood up straight.

"I'll walk my parents out and then come back, okay?" Joanna said to her.

"Okay." Greene turned back to Joanna's mother. "It was nice to meet you."

"Yes," The other woman stated without emotion, and Greene knew they at least had that in common.

"Ready, dear?" Her father returned and looked at his wife.

They all said their goodbyes again. Greene watched the three of them walk down the aisle and toward the door before she sat back down and motioned for the waiter. When he arrived, she requested a vodka on the rocks and watched as the others ordered coffee and dessert. Keira stood when her phone rang. She took the call outside, due to the noise of the restaurant, giving Emma plenty of time to take more than her fair share of the lemon tart they'd ordered to split. Greene participated only in parts of conversations here and there while finishing the drink she knew she'd regret later and periodically staring at her phone to check the time. It seemed like Joanna would miss dessert entirely. Keira returned, gave her a smile, and then took the last bite of the tart off Emma's fork for herself. Joanna returned moments later. She appeared to be worse for wear.

Joanna had been driven by her parents, and Greene by Keira and Emma. Hillary offered them a ride instead. Greene gave a goodbye to everyone and then walked with Hillary toward her car while Joanna walked behind them. Greene took the passenger's seat, leaving the back for Joanna.

"Which place am I taking you guys to?" Hillary asked both of them.

"You can drop me first," Greene stated.

"Macon?" Joanna's voice came from behind her, but Greene didn't turn around.

"I'm tired," Greene replied.

Joanna didn't say anything. Hillary glanced between the two of them but said nothing as well. She put the car in drive and took off. A few minutes later, Greene was in front of her building. She climbed out of the car, glanced back at Joanna, and tried to force a smile. She shaped the word, *"goodnight"* with her lips but didn't push the word from her body. Joanna didn't reply and quickly looked away from her before Greene hustled to the door.

She closed the door of her apartment – her sanctuary – behind her, and leaned back against it. She felt the tears form in her eyes and wondered if they were more because of Joanna's actions or her own, as she continued to push the woman away. Then, she fell to the floor to let them out.

It was several hours later that she crawled into her bed, pulled the blanket over her head, and attempted to fall asleep. It was only several minutes later that she threw off the blankets, gave up on sleep, and made her way back out to her living room, where she grabbed her violin case, pulled out her instrument, and grabbed a pencil with blank sheet music, getting to work.

CHAPTER 29

GREENE HEARD the knock through her playing but didn't register the sound to have meaning. The knock came again, and again, before she heard the door open and found Keira standing in her living room. She dropped her violin to her side.

"Keira, what the hell?" she blurted.

"What the hell to you, too, Make," she greeted more than asked. "You try answering a phone now and then?"

"I've been playing. I didn't hear it. Is something wrong?" She placed her instrument back in its case and closed it.

"I got four texts from your girlfriend this morning. When I texted her back, she said she was trying not to be worried, but that you weren't responding. I took it upon myself to get over here and do a welfare check on your ass." She flopped onto the sofa. "Also, I had a meeting with a client about a block away. I came here instead of going to lunch."

"Jo texted you?" She began to move the disorganized pages of sheet music into one stack on the coffee table.

"What's going on here?" Keira asked.

"I was just playing. I honestly didn't hear the phone. It's in the bedroom, I think; maybe the kitchen." She pointed to the kitchen without looking up from her stack.

"Your girlfriend is trying to get in touch with you there, Make," Keira reminded. "She is still your girlfriend, right?"

"Yes." Greene lifted her head and glared at Keira. "I'm just–"

"Delaying the inevitable? Trying to get her to break up with you because you're being an ass, instead of breaking up with you because she wants to be with a parent-approved man?"

"Keira, don't be a bitch. It's my relationship; it's not yours to fix."

"Why is it broken, Make?"

"Were you not at the same dinner I was last night? Did you not witness my girlfriend lead me to the slaughter with her homophobic parents?"

"I was at that dinner. I did witness your girlfriend doing her best while being obviously uncomfortable. Her father politely paid for a very expensive dinner for a bunch of lesbians. I also witnessed you clam up – which is understandable, but so is Joanna's behavior, given how her parents treat her. And, damn, she got them back later, though. I was impressed."

"What are you talking about?" Greene stopped stacking and leaned back to look at Keira.

"Joanna's battle with her mother in the parking lot. Did she not tell you?"

"Tell me what?"

"You really are dense sometimes. I love you, but you're dense." Keira leaned forward and took Greene's hand. "Joanna was awesome, Make. That's why I was so surprised at her texts. I assumed, last night, you had heard her out and made up. And then, this morning, I get these messages that she hadn't heard from you today. I texted you, and I didn't hear back."

"Did you think I ran away or something?"

"No, but I still wanted to check on you. I went by the symphony first, but it didn't look like anything was going on there."

"We're dark today," Greene explained. "Something about the electrical needing to be fixed; I got an email this morning."

"You can check your computer but not your phone?"

Keira lifted an accusatory eyebrow.

"I had my violin plugged into it. I was recording."

"Recording? You do that?"

"Not often," she said. "Back to Joanna."

"She told her mother off."

"She what?"

"I went outside to take that call. I missed the first part of their conversation, but after I hung up, I couldn't help but hear Joanna tell her mother that she loves you; and her mother can try to set her up with guy after guy, but nothing will change that. Her dad basically just stood there and listened to the whole thing. Her mom tried to get a word in, here and there, but Joanna wouldn't let her. She said you were brilliant, funny, and a remarkable musician. She told her mother that she'd never felt this way before, didn't care about what that made her, and had no intention of dating anyone else ever again, Make. Her mom tried to convince her to at least think about it, but Joanna told her that she'd treated you terribly all day because she'd been afraid of confronting her mom, and she wouldn't let anyone treat you like that again; that included her. Joanna, I mean," Keira clarified. "It's hard to talk about all this and be clear with the pronouns, huh?"

"She yelled at her mom?"

"Make, she stood up to them and then came back into that restaurant where you basically ignored her. Apparently, you didn't talk to her after. I think she's probably worried she took that risk for nothing."

"I was afraid," Greene admitted.

"I get it. But you shouldn't be telling me this; tell your girlfriend, Macon."

"What if she's still mad at me?"

"For not talking to her? That's not going to get any better until you actually do. It'll only get worse. Please fix this. And this is going to sound selfish, but please do it before we all go to Tahoe in a few weeks."

"Tahoe?"

"Emma booked this giant cabin for all of us. Hailey and Charlie are going to come back. Hill is coming. And, we're going to finally meet Kellan's girlfriend, Reese. It's a four-day affair. You and Joanna are both required; I already RSVP'd for you."

"You can't RSVP *for* people, Keira."

"I'm an event planner, Make; I know how RSVPs work. And you have no choice. You and Joanna are two of my closest friends, but Emma is my love, and she wants this trip to be amazing. You'll both be there, and everyone else will be there, too. We'll have fun."

"Mandatory fun, huh?"

"Yes, Macon." Keira gritted her teeth at her and then gave her a playful wink. "You going to be okay?"

"I'll be okay. I just need to talk to her."

"Now, you're getting it." Keira stood. "I'm heading back to the office. Text me when it's all clear so I can stop interfering in your relationship."

"Like that will ever happen." Greene laughed.

"For this month, at least." Keira laughed and opened the door. "She really was great last night, Greene. She told her mom – the woman that nothing is ever good enough for – that she was who she was, she loved who she loved; and that person is you."

"I wish I would have seen it."

"You can see it every day, Make. That's how relationships work. I can see how much Emma loves me when she makes the chicken I like for dinner with the mushrooms she hates and then has to scrape off. I can see it when she plans the weekends away for us because she knows I've been working so hard and could use the time off to relax with my friends. She planned one for Tahoe, because she knows I haven't seen Kellan in a while and I miss her. I can see it when she takes my hand when we're walking down the street just because she wants to be touching me. I can see it after we have a fight and she still falls asleep next to me." Keira paused and tried to come back from looking so wistful. "You didn't need to see her argue with her parents to know how much she loves you, and know how she'd choose you again and again, Greene."

***

Joanna stared at her screen for the seventh consecutive minute without looking away from the image. Macon had been an amazing assistant during that infant photo shoot, but she'd made an even better subject. Joanna hadn't had to try hard to capture the woman in the perfect light, with a wide smile on her face and her gorgeous eyes not meeting the camera but looking off to the side of it, where Joanna remembered the baby's mother was standing. They'd been in mid-conversation. Joanna had taken a few photos of her girlfriend because she couldn't resist. Macon's hair was a little all over the place, but something about the imperfection made it an even more perfect image. Joanna smiled before finally closing her eyes and turning away. She closed her computer, and seeing it was after four o'clock in the afternoon, she decided that she wasn't getting anything done in the office; she should head home to drop off her stuff and then hit the grocery store to get the necessities to get her through the rest of the week.

She walked home slowly while listening to songs about breakups on her headphones because it fit her mood. She hadn't had a moment alone with Macon since they'd had their attempt at an apology before dinner. And, even then, they weren't actually alone. The dinner hadn't exactly gone terribly, but it hadn't gone well either. Then, Macon had left her in the backseat of Hillary's car, instead of talking things out, and hadn't responded to any of her messages. Joanna wanted to respect her space, but if she hadn't heard from Macon tonight, tomorrow, she'd make her way over to Macon's place to find out if they were still together.

She arrived home and turned the key in the lock before pushing the door open out of frustration, more than anything, for how the weekend had gone. She tugged the headphones out of her ears, placed her laptop bag on the floor, and then looked up to see Macon standing in her living room.

"Make?"

"Hi," Macon replied.

The dark-haired woman was holding her violin in one hand at her side and the bow in the other. She stood behind Joanna's coffee table on the other side of the sofa, which was facing her as if it was awaiting an audience for her performance.

"What are you doing here?" she asked.

"Last night, I wasn't ready to talk to you because I was afraid you'd end things."

"What?" Joanna took a few steps in her direction. "Why would you–"

"Because your mom clearly hates me, or at least the fact that I'm a woman. And I've seen this before, Jo. I've seen women date other women and then, because of pressure, they end it."

"And you thought I'd do that to you?"

"I didn't think it, but I was worried. It's hard to explain. It's like I didn't *actually* think you would but, at the same time, I had to mentally prepare myself in case you did. I realize, though, that those are *my* insecurities. And you did attempt to apologize last night before I got frustrated."

"I said our situations weren't the same; you didn't agree." Joanna took another step but felt like, given Macon's posture, she shouldn't move any closer to her.

"I'm gay, Jo. I know that about myself like I know my own name, or that I'm a violinist. I know it in my soul, bones, heart, and any other place one can know things about themselves."

"And I don't?"

"I don't care that you don't define yourself as gay; it doesn't bother me. That's up to you to figure out. I can tell you that the question won't go away, and that people will keep asking it, but it's your choice how you answer it. If you tell me one day that you know you're gay – great. If you say you're attracted to men and women, that's great, too. If you're straight outside of loving me, I don't care. If you're undefinable altogether because there's no label that fits how you feel about yourself, it doesn't matter to me as long as you love me."

"But I do love you, Macon." She took another step.

"Will you please sit down for me?" Macon motioned with the hand holding her bow toward the sofa.

"Why?" Joanna asked even as she walked to the sofa and sat in the middle of it.

"Because I want to tell you how I feel."

"Make, I don't–"

"Jo, I love you," she stated, interrupting Joanna's words. "When you said our situations are different, I didn't get it. But I do now: this is all new to you. You haven't had to bring a woman home to your parents, or come out to them in the same way I had. I didn't get that yesterday; I only saw you not standing up for *us*. I failed to grasp that it was more about you having to confront your parents about this new situation you're going through than it was about your feelings for me."

"I did talk to my mom, though, Make. That's why I was so disappointed last night when you just went home instead of talking to me."

"I know. I'm sorry about that; I am. I felt like I needed to just be alone. I knew I'd had too much to drink and that I'd break down and cry – which I never do, but seem to when the idea of losing you hits me like a ton of bricks."

"Honey, you're not losing me. I'm here." Joanna went to stand.

"No. Please, sit."

"Macon, let me tell you what I told my mom, and–"

"I don't need to know."

"But you were worried, Macon."

"I'm not anymore." The woman smiled and brought her instrument to her shoulder. "I stayed up all night writing. And, this morning, I started recording some of it and making revisions. It's why I didn't call you: I didn't hear my phone. I was so into the music, that I thought I needed to finish it before I could focus on anything else."

"You were composing?"

"I rarely write music. I've always felt much better playing the greats than trying to come up with something new. But then I thought about you, and how it felt when we first met: I was so taken aback by you and how amazing you were; how funny you were. Then, I went to this place of misery, because you were straight and not interested, which meant I could never have you. Then, I could. You felt the same way about me, and we did this dance while I was away and had this amazing beginning. Yesterday was a hiccup in an otherwise miraculous situation to me, Jo. I couldn't stop writing the notes and hearing them in my head. I had to start playing them. I had no choice."

"You composed a song about me? About us?"

"About how it feels to love you, yes." Macon smiled at her and looked at her violin before meeting Joanna's eyes again. "I wanted to play it for you. It's not finished; I still have a lot of corrections to make. But I was hoping I could play you the first version at least."

"Yes," Joanna replied without thought and leaned against the back of her sofa, placing her hands in her lap and staring in awe at the woman in front of her.

"Okay. Just remember: it's rough," Macon said.

Joanna knew she wouldn't be able to tell anyway. Macon was the musical genius; Joanna knew only what her girlfriend had taught her.

Macon took a few more moments and deep breaths

before she met the strings with the bow and began her song. Joanna listened to the notes at the beginning – which were light and fast and spoke to the initial feelings of meeting someone new. Those notes lasted for at least a few minutes – which spoke to the length of time Macon had experienced those feelings for her before the notes shifted to a slower and lower pace. Joanna's smile remained but grew smaller as she observed Macon, with closed eyes and tense facial muscles, play through the period in her life where she felt for Joanna but thought those feelings would never be returned. That section didn't seem to last as long as the first one before Macon shifted into the higher note section. The notes were still long, with a few shorter – almost plucks – in between. Joanna wished she knew what the proper terms were to define what Macon was doing. But she was also perfectly content living in the unknown, just watching Macon play.

Macon made her way into the section where Joanna returned her feelings, and Joanna could almost see their relationship playing out in her mind as Macon played with a wider smile on her face. Joanna saw Macon on her tour while they'd spoken on the phone before she could see the woman in Boston and they had a chance to touch one another for the first time in weeks. She saw the dinner with Macon's parents as the notes shifted low just for a moment before returning to the more playful, happy tones. Joanna could see them making love, holding one another, sharing their 'I love you' exchange for the first time, and everything else they'd said and done with one another since reuniting in San Francisco. The piece shifted again. Joanna knew these notes were about yesterday. Her smile dimmed, but she tried to remember that yesterday was just that: *yesterday*. It was gone. They'd work past it together. It was only one day in their relationship. The section didn't last long before Macon's face lit up. She played a quick section with an upbeat melody and a long final note that still resonated in the apartment long after she'd lowered her bow. Joanna could only attempt to hold back her tears for so long until one of them fell down her cheek, and she wiped at it.

"What was that last section?" Joanna asked after at least two minutes of silence between the two.

"The future," Macon replied.

"Our future?"

"I hope so. The last note just fades because I couldn't figure out how to end the piece when I don't want us to ever end." Macon placed the violin on the coffee table.

"Neither do I, Macon."

Macon moved around the table and sat down next to her, placing an arm over the back of the sofa.

"I can't promise I won't get scared again, Joanna. Your mom is a lot." She gave a shy smile.

"I told her that I loved her, but that if she wants to be involved in my life, that includes you now. She has to be okay with that, or it won't work. I don't want that. I do love my parents. But I've always been less than what they wanted in a daughter. I'm used to it now, but it's still not something I'll ever be okay with. I'm happy, though. Parents are supposed to want their children to be happy, and I am. I have my dream job; I'm living in this amazing place..." She took Macon's hand and placed it into her own lap. "And I'm crazy in love with this gorgeous and talented woman, who in one night managed to write the most beautiful piece of music I've ever heard."

"You liked it?" Macon smiled and had nervous eyes.

"Babe, I loved it. You're playing it for me again later."

"I am?" Macon laughed.

"Yes, you are. And probably again tonight; maybe tomorrow, too. Get used to it."

"I'll play it for you every day if you want."

"I want you here every day," Joanna said before she had a chance to think about what it meant."

"You want me to stay over?"

"I want to ask you to move in with me. But your apartment is your favorite place in the world; I can't ask you to give that up."

"I could ask you to move in with me." Macon lifted an eyebrow.

"Are you?"

"Will you?"

"My place has the washer and dryer," Joanna reminded.

"Damn, you're right. I hate the laundromat." Macon ran a hand along Joanna's cheek.

"We'll figure it out later?"

"Later," Macon agreed.

"Don't leave tonight, though," Joanna said a moment before Macon's lips met her own.

"I can't. I have to play for you again."

"That's true." Joanna leaned back ever so slightly, leaving a few inches of space between their parted and waiting lips. "Hey, what's the title of that piece?"

"I don't know. I haven't gotten that far yet."

"Don't all these classical pieces have to end in like something-something Requiem in A minor, or something like that?"

"It's your song. You can call it whatever you want, Jo." Macon kissed Joanna lightly on the forehead before lowering her lips back to hover so closely to Joanna's own. "But can you think of a title later? I haven't kissed you since yesterday morning."

Joanna smiled. She tried to laugh but found herself unable to do so as Macon's mouth covered her own in a slow, deliberate, and perfect kiss.

EPILOGUE

"KELL, I'VE MISSED YOU," Keira told Kellan as she reached to cover the woman's hand from across the picnic table they found themselves at.

"I've missed you guys, too." Kellan glanced in the direction of Reese. "I wish I could get away more to visit, but things are crazy busy here, and–"

"And you love it," Hillary interjected.

"I do love it, yes."

Kellan let go of Keira's and took hold of Reese's hand. Reese smiled back at her girlfriend before giving her a kiss on the cheek. Greene watched this unfold while she waited for her own girlfriend to reemerge from the six-bedroom cabin they'd all rented. Kellan and Reese were staying with the group, since they lived on the south side of the lake and the cabin was on the north.

Hailey and Charlie had arrived last and were currently unpacking for this little four-day adventure. Emma was inside with Joanna, helping to get dinner ready. They'd planned to eat outside, since the weather was so nice and they were only about twenty yards from the crystal blue water of the lake. They had lush trees providing privacy, and the cabin came with a hot tub for twelve people and even a small kidney-shaped pool. Greene couldn't see herself using a chlorinated pool when she had clear water just beyond it, though. She was staring at that water when she felt a familiar hand on her shoulder and then witnessed a steaming cup of coffee placed in front of her. In the foam, Joanna had crafted a heart.

"Thank you," Greene replied and then tugged on Joanna until the woman's other hand joined and wrapped around her own shoulders. Joanna's head rested on the right one, and Greene leaned a little to that side. "How's dinner prep going?"

"Almost done. I just came to bring you that. I know you're exhausted." Joanna kissed her cheek and then pulled herself up. "You had a long week there, professor." She began rubbing Greene's shoulders, and Greene leaned back into the relaxing touch.

"Professor?" Greene laughed.

"Professor?" Kellan repeated as she turned to listen to their conversation.

"I started teaching some students in local music programs."

"I thought you always taught," Kellan replied and took a drink from her water bottle.

"Young kids, yeah. I'm helping colleges now: students in music programs who can't necessarily afford private coaching beyond their school instructors. I just started this week. I have two students so far."

"And that's on top of the orchestra work and the planning for her next tour," Joanna added.

"Another tour?" Hillary asked.

"We're in the planning phase," Greene explained. "They're thinking about me going on another tour next summer. It would be longer this time; maybe six months. I'd go more places but stay in them longer, too."

"You'd be gone for six months?" Emma's voice came from behind her as she emerged from the cabin.

"Yeah, probably leave in April, at the earliest, and be back in September." Greene met Emma's eyes as she came around to the other side of the table and placed a bowl of some kind of pasta salad on it.

"But... Back by September for sure?" Emma questioned her.

"Yes, Emma." Greene laughed.

"I'm going to go with her," Joanna revealed. "If it happens, I mean."

"My own personal photographer," Greene shared. "It's a part of the contract I'll sign. Makes me seem like a diva, but it means Jo gets to come with me, so I don't care."

"That's awesome, Make," Keira told her.

"Just as long as you're back by September," Emma repeated.

"Why are you so concerned about September, Em?" Keira laughed a little at her girlfriend.

"I'm not. I just know how busy things are for both of us during the summer, and that fall typically gets slow enough that we can plan something; a trip or something."

"We all get pretty busy during the summer. I get what she's saying," Greene tried to help Emma out.

"Fall is when I get busy, actually," Hillary added and then took a glare from Greene. "But I'm sure I can do something on a weekend with no problem."

"You're all acting strange. It's not like we won't see each other until next fall," Keira said.

"I'm going to go back inside to grab the plates and stuff." Joanna changed the subject. "Emma?"

"Yeah, I'm coming," Emma returned.

"I love you. I'll be right back. Drink that coffee I made with love." Joanna kissed the top of Greene's head and moved back toward the cabin, which was up a slight hill.

***

"I can't believe I almost screwed up," Emma said to Joanna once they were alone in the kitchen. "Did I screw up? Do you think she knows?"

"That you invited us here to propose? No, I don't think she knows, Emma."

"Why didn't you and Greene tell me about this tour? You know how busy Keira's schedule gets during spring and summer. We pretty much have no choice but to have our wedding in the fall or winter. And she hates winter. She told me when we first started dating that she wanted a fall wedding and that she wanted to plan it herself."

"Emma, calm down." Joanna took Emma's shoulders and lightly shook them. "She doesn't know; you didn't screw it up. And the tour came up this week; it's only in the early stages. If you two set a date for this time next year, we'll make sure we're there. No tour will keep us from your wedding, okay?"

"Okay. I just know the two of you will be in it; she'll want you both as bridesmaids. And we'll need your help planning because you know she wants to, but she won't be able to plan the whole thing herself. And here I am, worrying about planning a wedding when she hasn't even agreed to it yet."

"Em, stop it." Hailey's voice came from just beyond the kitchen before they saw her enter, with Charlie close behind. "You know she'll say yes. She loves you."

"But—"

"Let's go for a walk before dinner, okay?" Hailey asked Emma and slid an arm through hers.

"Okay. But not too long because Keira will get suspicious."

"Sure." Hailey laughed at her best friend. "Charlie, will you help Joanna here with the rest of the food?"

"Emma, if it makes you feel any better, I was crazy nervous about asking Hailey to marry me."

"You were?" Emma asked.

"Yeah, I was." Charlie laughed. "I knew she loved me; I knew she'd say yes. But then, I didn't. It's weird, isn't it?"

"Yes," Emma agreed. "What the hell is that about?"

The entire group laughed.

Hailey tugged on Emma's arm slightly and said, "I've known you forever. I don't think I've ever seen you this nervous. That's how I know this is right, and that she'll say yes. It matters enough for you to be freaking out, and you never freak out."

"What about you, Joanna?" Charlie helped change the focus on the conversation, since Emma looked as if she was about to hyperventilate.

"What about me?"

"Think it will be you or Greene that proposes one day?"

"Oh, I don't know. I haven't really thought about it. We're still in the process of figuring out our living situation."

"What about our living situation?" Macon entered the kitchen from the back door.

Suddenly, the room felt very small to Joanna.

"I was just requesting an update," Charlie lied as she recognized the situation. "Also, Emma and Hailey are going for a walk."

"Yeah, we'll be right back," Hailey said, pulling Emma along.

As they both left the room, Charlie moved further into the kitchen to grab a stack of paper plates and plastic cutlery. She also lifted a few bags of potato chips and headed back outside without saying another word.

"So, she wanted an update about our living situation?" Macon grabbed at an almond that was in a dish someone had set out earlier.

"No, they were talking about Emma proposing and asked me if I thought you'd propose or if I'd be the one doing it."

"Oh… That came out of nowhere." Macon nearly choked on her second almond.

"*They* asked the question; it's not coming from me. You can stop choking now," Joanna replied.

"And you said that we're still figuring out our living situation?"

"Yeah." Joanna moved the condiments for the hot dogs and hamburgers onto a tray before moving to the stove where she'd placed another tray with those items on it. "Can you grab that for me? I think we have everything else."

"Jo, can you hold on a sec?"

"Macon, I'm not expecting a proposal, okay?" She laughed again. "I know it feels like we've been together since we met, but–"

"I'm not worried about that," Macon interrupted and moved in front of Joanna, placing her hands on Joanna's hips to still her frantic movements. "I'll ask, or you'll ask, or we'll ask each other. I don't care, honestly. We'll get married when we want to get married, but I think I've figured out our living situation."

"You have, have you?" Joanna quirked an eyebrow at Macon and placed her arms around Macon's neck.

"I love my place. I've lived there forever. I don't want to move."

"I know that, babe."

"But it's smaller than your place and doesn't have everything your place has."

"Also something I know, Macon." Joanna leaned in and pecked her lips. "What's the new information I need?"

"There's a unit behind mine that isn't for rent but is actually for sale. Long story: I reached out to my landlord, and she confessed that she'd been trying to sell the whole building but hadn't had any luck. She's decided to sell the individual units instead. Long story short: she told me she'd sell me the unit next to mine, if I was interested and I can buy my unit, too." Macon paused. "We can buy both units, break down the wall, have two bedrooms, and put in a washer and dryer."

"Oh," Joanna replied.

"Just listen to me for a sec, okay? With the tour

money and the orchestra, I can afford it on my own. I'd be doing it without you, but I'd rather do it with you and make it our first home. It'll take a while before you could officially move in. I'd actually probably like to live at your place once the loud renovations start. Then, we could move in there together. It could be our starter home. We could both use the extra bedroom as an office or music room for me. One day, we'll take the time to find a house we both love and can afford, and we'll move in there and maybe add some bedrooms."

"Add some bedrooms? You need a private recording studio or something?" Joanna smiled.

"I'd like one of those one day, but no," she answered and leaned forward to press their foreheads together. "Extra bedrooms, Jo."

"Oh!" Joanna finally understood Macon's meaning and pulled back a bit. "Extra bedrooms? Is that a requirement?"

"No, not a requirement." Macon laughed. "I know where we both stand on it today. If we have a recording studio or a photography studio instead of a nursery and a swing set out back, I am more than fine with that option. I just wanted us to have the option in case we change our minds later."

"After we propose to each other?" Joanna laughed.

"You knew what I meant."

"I did. I think this whole buying your apartment thing and us making it our own is a good idea, but I want to explore the fine print before we go signing anything."

"Skeptical?"

"Not about you, but if we're going to own a place together, I want to make sure it works. For example, it might be nice to see this other unit."

Macon laughed and pulled her back into her body, pressing her hips into Joanna's.

"You want to see my *other* unit, huh?"

"I was not making a strap-on joke. Yes, I know you

packed it. And no, we are not doing that here, with our best friends in the room next door." She kissed Macon chastely on the lips and pulled away. "Carry the food, Macon."

Macon's laughter followed her outside to where Joanna met their friends and set down their dinner before Macon placed her tray next to Joanna's.

"Where's my girlfriend?" Keira asked after noticing Emma wasn't among the group.

"She ran off with Hailey," Macon stated and then realized how that sounded, remembering that Hailey and Emma were once very much in love. "That came out wrong."

"It's okay. I know she loves me." Keira winked at Macon.

"I do," Emma stated.

Joanna turned to see that Emma and Hailey were close behind them. Emma had that look on her face that said she was about to do something she'd been planning for a long time, but not quite in the way she'd planned it. Joanna took Macon's hand and moved them both off to the side as Hailey met Joanna's eye and moved to join them.

"Where'd you two go?" Keira asked her and stood up, freeing herself from the confines of the picnic table bench seat.

"What's happening?" Macon whispered to Hailey.

"I have no idea. We talked, but we didn't talk about this."

"She's doing it now?" Macon asked her.

"Apparently." Hailey smiled at her best friend and former girlfriend as Emma got down on one knee in front of her girlfriend.

"Key, when we met, I wasn't exactly your number one fan," Emma began.

"Oh, my God!" Keira's hands both went to cover her mouth in shock.

"I'd begun to wonder if I'd ever find someone to love and share my life with after so many failed attempts. I definitely hadn't expected to find someone right after I moved from Chicago. I hadn't planned for you at all." She smiled a huge smile, paused, and removed a small black box from the inside pocket of her jacket. "But I've been carrying this around for a while now. I had this plan of proposing to you on our last night here. I've rented a boat, and I was going to take you out on the lake and ask you to marry me under the stars. But when I got back from my walk with Hailey, where she tried to convince me not to be so nervous, I saw you sitting there, surrounded by our friends, and realized that my plans never seem to work where you are concerned. Maybe that's a good thing, because our friends wouldn't see this if we were on the lake." She opened the box and revealed the ring, which Joanna couldn't see much of due to the distance and the low light of the sunset. "I love you. I want to share the rest of my life with you. Will you marry me?"

"Yes," Keira shouted and knelt down in front of Emma because, apparently, she couldn't wait for Emma to stand.

She wrapped her arms around Emma's neck; not allowing the other woman to even put the ring on her finger while the rest of the group applauded and cheered their friends' happiness.

"You want to try it on?" Emma managed through Keira's haphazard kisses.

"Yes." Keira finally pulled back and held out her hand for Emma.

Joanna felt Macon's arms wrap around her stomach from behind. She knew they'd be doing this someday. She smiled as she placed her hands on top of Macon's and leaned back against her.

"I love you," Macon whispered into her ear.

"I love you," Joanna replied.

Charlie moved over to her wife and took her hand

while Kellan had her arm around Reese. Joanna watched a little sadly as Hillary took in all four couples and smiled, but there was also sadness in those eyes, because while they were all coupled off, Hillary was still on her own.

"She's next," Macon whispered and kissed Joanna's neck. "We've got to find her someone."

"I think Hillary is capable of finding the right person for herself, babe," Joanna replied.

"You guys know I'm an ordained minister, right?" Hillary spoke up after Emma and Keira had stood; Keira still couldn't take her eyes off her new ring.

"You are?" Kellan asked.

"I got ordained a few years ago to marry Anthony and Andrew, remember?" She stood up from the table.

"Who are–"

"Two professors in her department," Macon told Joanna.

"I'm just saying... I could marry you two next September," she offered.

"Wait." Keira turned back to face Emma. "Is that why you were so concerned about everyone being free in September?"

"Maybe," Emma admitted.

"Did you already plan the wedding I only just agreed to?"

"I didn't plan it. I'll leave that to you. But, like I said earlier, September is kind of perfect because your work would have just died down. We can pick a date later, but that was my idea, since you won't be a winter bride and I don't want to wait forever to marry you."

"You're cute. I think I'll keep you," Keira replied and leaned in to kiss Emma.

"Why not do it now?" Reese questioned. "Sorry, that's probably a terrible idea."

Kellan kissed her girlfriend and pulled her in closer on the bench.

"I think it's a great idea," Hailey added.

teaching college students, really enjoyed it, and had begun composing. She was also about to play her most private composition to a group of people she knew she wanted the approval of. She put the violin to her shoulder, gave Joanna a reluctant nod, and turned to face the rest of the group.

Joanna moved to sit at the second picnic table, which was to the left of the first, while Hillary joined her. Keira and Emma moved to the first table and sat there while Kellan and Reese sat on the other side. Hailey and Charlie were standing off to the side, holding onto one another. As Greene turned to look at Joanna to play this song, Joanna took a quick photo and dropped the camera in her lap to focus her attention on Greene.

"What's the song called?" Hillary asked.

"Something-something Requiem in A minor, right, Jo?" Greene smiled at her. Joanna laughed. Then, Greene knew the title. It came to her in an instant of pure clarity. "*Macon's Heart.*" She lifted her bow, took in Joanna with that beautiful smile, and began to play the truest thing she'd ever played.